steeple

Also by Jon Wallace from Gollancz:

Barricade

steeple

jon wallace

GOLLANCZ
LONDON

The right of Jon Wallace to be identified as the author
of this work has been asserted by him in accordance with
the Copyright, Designs and Patents Act 1988.

First published in Great Britain in 2015 by Gollancz
An imprint of the Orion Publishing Group
Carmelite House, 50 Victoria Embankment, London EC4Y ODZ
An Hachette UK Company

A CIP catalogue record for this book is available
from the British Library

ISBN 978 0 575 11844 7

1 3 5 7 9 10 8 6 4 2

Typeset by Input Data Services Ltd, Bridgwater, Somerset

Printed and bound in Great Britain by Clays Ltd, St Ives plc

The Orion Publishing Group's policy is to use papers that
are natural, renewable and recyclable products and made from
wood grown in sustainable forests. The logging and manufacturing
processes are expected to conform to the environmental
regulations of the country of origin.

www.orionbooks.co.uk
www.gollancz.co.uk

For my brother.

The van shakes and tips, rushing over speed humps. We are heading for the exit, the great gates where Effra Road meets Brixton Wall. I am finally leaving home.

A hood is drawn tight over my face. I taste detergent and sweat. The Diorama guard pulled this thing over my head, drawing it tight with a yank of a white cord. He bound my hands behind my back, guided me into the van and shackled my feet to the floor. He is back here with me. I can hear his fingers drumming on a rifle stock.

Strange. I could snap the bonds and punch through the van doors, so why these prison measures? Have my owners not read my specifications? What is it they think I want to escape?

I hear the protesters beyond the wall, chanting as we near the gates. A megaphone voice interrupts the beat of their song: pleas to disperse. We slow to a stop, wait, lurch forward again. The gears grind with every shuffle.

Today is distribution day. There will be other Engineered in other queuing vans. There will be miner models, mechanic models, surgeon models and programmer models, all setting out to play a part in the great mission of augmentation.

'Come on, come on . . .'

The guard, speaking for the first time, though not to me. I hear the soldiers on the gate, scanning the driver's palm and yelling instructions. Then we roll down a ramp and into the crowd.

The van becomes an enormous drum, hundreds of fists beating on the panels. Screaming voices too, so many I can barely pick out words. We bump through the turbulence, until the van turns, finds space, and picks up speed.

The guard whistles and barks a laugh. He leans over, taps my knee, and speaks into my ear.

'Welcome to the real world.'

AMBUSCADE

You wait all day for a bus, then three come along at once. They appeared at the crest of the bridge, rumbling under the pylon, a diesel trio playing loud enough to wake the dead. This was trouble. I had only prepared for one.

The bridge moaned as they crossed. Maybe it was the thought of hosting another battle. It had always been ugly – a stark, cable-stayed tongue built to drool traffic over the Thames – but it had withstood a thermonuclear blast, and doubtless felt it deserved to rot in peace.

Clive, King of Kent, thought differently. He'd dispatched me to raid the Thurrock convoy, take what prizes I could, and generally spread the word of his glory. Six of his shivering, miserable species were mine to command. Our feeble mob might have been enough to take one bus, but three would be challenging, even under cover of the constant, frozen night.

I tucked away my binoculars and slithered through the mud, down the ramp to the scorched husks that had once been tollbooths. My Reals huddled where I'd left them, sharing something hot from a battered thermos. I told them to be ready. Their eyes said they never would be.

I crept away to my position, reflecting again on my situation. Losing membership of a bio-engineered super species, it turned out, was hard to accept. Nuclear winter was no picnic without the near-invulnerability afforded by Pander-brand nanotech. Survival had become a full-time job. My body, once a peak of regenerating perfection, was a sack of disease and decay. A single bullet could maim, infect or kill. My brain was a wreck, incapable of focus. Worst of all, I'd been forced to accept employment from an amateur tyrant, starvation certain without King Clive's patronage. It sure was despicable being Real.

I would have brooded some more, but I heard something struggle in the mud behind me. Fingers gripped my shoulder.

'Ken!'

It was Bridget, one of my crew. Even in the gloom I recognised her. It was hard not to. Her complexion was raw with red spots. She scratched her face impatiently, like it was a lottery card.

'Get to your position, Bridget.'

'Listen, Ken, this is completely booloo. We can't fight that many. Stop me if I'm wrong.'

'Find somewhere to hide,' I said. 'I'll let you know when it's over.'

She shook her head.

'Don't take that tone, Kenneth. We prepared for one double-decker, not a flaming fleet. There's brave and there's bone-headed.'

I considered for a moment. Was she right? Why insist on a fight? I wasn't Ficial any more and the odds weren't with us. We could still withdraw unseen, the convoy taking its time to inch over the crossing.

I was jolted from my thoughts by a great metallic crash, down by the tollbooths. It seemed one of my stealthy squad had blundered into a road sign.

Almost immediately there was shouting up the bridge. The buses lurched to a halt, cut engines and slumped into silence. Well, that was it. No point leaving now. It was a fight. I checked my rifle. Got to my feet.

I took four paces before a machine gun opened up. It was the usual inaccurate stuff, but enough to make me pick up the pace. Bridget followed, quite a sprinter when the mood took her. I found cover by a wrecked goods vehicle, Bridget skidding down next to me.

The Thurrock's machine gun clattered away for a solid minute. My squad didn't return fire, apparently content to muse on the tracer cutting through the night. It wasn't such a bad plan. Soon enough the Thurrock gun spluttered out of ammunition. Silence for a moment. Then, voices: foreign tongues, too close for comfort. Bridget peeked around the wreck at the speakers, then whipped back, holding up two fingers.

I had to remind myself that standing up and running through a cloud of bullets was no longer in the options mix. Then I saw the cable, a loose black snake hanging from the pylon, thrashing in the wind over the swollen river.

I crouched on my numb feet, pulled my rifle over my shoulder, edged past Bridget. She mouthed something at me. Something about being insane.

'Don't worry.' I said that a lot these days. 'This won't take a minute.'

I ran clear, headed up the bridge. The night lit up, shots popping in wrecks as I ducked and dived. I fell to my belly, mildly surprised to note the fire was coming from my own people.

At least the skirmishers had taken cover too. This was the only chance I'd get. I broke for the railing and jumped right off the bridge.

I reached for the cable, but it caught the wind and blew almost clear. I snatched at the ragged tip, gripped, and swung out over the black river like a baited line. Then the swing slowed, stopped, and propelled me back at the bridge, slapping me hard against the caisson.

I gasped for breath, grip slipping, the icy black Thames awfully close. I found the strength to seize the cable in my other hand, climbed a little way, then kicked off the caisson, swaying in a pendulum towards the far shore. Four more kicks and I travelled high enough to grab the deck railing. I released the cable, watched it clatter back the way it came.

I climbed onto the deck and dropped behind the rear bus, apparently unobserved. The Thurrocks must have thought me lost to the river. Most were further down the bridge, busy shooting blind in the gloom.

I edged along the bus, head below the window line, pausing at the middle doors and peeking inside. The driver's seat was empty. No voices. No footsteps. The seating had been ripped out. In its place were strap-packed metal barrels, liquid pooling on the lids.

I crept inside, up the gum-stained stairs. There were no seats or cargo on the upper deck, only a carpet of Real trash and a fixed gun poking from the rear window. It was in good condition, but too big to lift. I was tired just looking at it.

I slunk downstairs and out, taking the knife from my boot and slashing punctures in each front tyre. I squatted, listened to them hiss, and planned my next move.

Then I heard growling.

I looked around. A very presentable black terrier was baring its teeth at me. I took a moment to identify it as Ficial. It had a good coat, vital eyes, and a tail darting at the cloud. Must have been something special if the Reals were keeping it alive. Most of man's best friends had been barbecued long ago.

I tried smiling at it, but it didn't like that. It took a couple of powerful steps in my direction and snarled.

'OK,' said a voice. 'Get up and turn around slow.'

I didn't turn. The dog had my attention.

'I said turn around.'

Worn boots, in the corner of my eye. I whipped around and plunged the knife into the nearest foot. The owner shrieked and crumpled. I went for his rifle, but was way too slow.

The terrier sunk its teeth into my ankle. I cried out and staggered, trying to shake its clamped jaws loose, but it held tight, growling in a satisfied way. I thought about shooting it, but that seemed wrong. After all, it was my closest relative for miles.

The Thurrocks must have overheard the disagreement. Gunfire raked the bus, showering glass. I punched the dog hard behind the head, stunning it. Then I prised its jaws loose and tossed it into the bus, where it rolled and lay still.

I picked up the dead man's rifle and headed for the Thurrock pack, limping and shooting. The Thurrocks panicked, caught between my fire and my squad's.

The first bus shook and rolled, Thurrocks scrabbling on board. The second gunned its engine and jerked forward, trying to overtake the leader, but found its way blocked by wrecks. It blared its horn, about as useful a gesture as it was in pre-war traffic. I took a grenade from my belt and pursued.

A bald Real stuck his head out the top deck and pointed a pistol my way. He would have had me, but the bus thumped into reverse and tried for a three-point turn, unbalancing Baldy. I tossed the grenade through the lower back window, briefly wondering what precious cargo I might destroy, then dropped and rolled. The engine blew out the back of the double-decker, lighting up the world in a brief, tantalising flare. The blast propelled the mangled bus on its front wheels, dragging its shrieking behind, until it slammed into the central reservation.

Two survivors crawled from the wreckage. I shot them down and boarded the bus, hacking in the hot, black smoke.

A Real lay slumped over the wheel. Boxes littered the lower deck, burning quietly. I tore the lid from the nearest and found books inside.

Cookbooks. I tossed the box aside, opened the rest. All the same.

I hobbled up the stairs. Baldy was crawling between the seats, a wound in his back pumping blood. I knelt, took the pistol from his hand, and turned him over. His belly spilled its contents. I retched, covering my face. Another useless Real reflex to add to my gathering collection. He said a few words to himself in a language I didn't know. Then he noticed me.

'Hurts,' he said.

'Of course it hurts.' I showed off the seeping dog bite. 'That's being Real for you. Do you have any food on board?'

He began to cry, suddenly looking very young.

'Want to live.'

I stood and levelled the pistol at him.

'You're better off out of it.'

There was a tin of tomato soup on one of the seats. I knifed it open and drank. I ripped a strip off the dead Real's coat to bandage my wound, took his boots and a sodden pack of cigarettes. Looting Real corpses. What would the lads in Edinburgh say?

I clambered down the stairs, stepped out onto the bridge and listened. No voices: only warm, peaceful flames and the wind in the cables.

'Ken! I don't believe it!'

Bridget waved her arms, running through the smoke.

'I thought you were done for after that high dive act. Are you OK? Have they got anything to eat?'

I ignored her, treading carefully back to the rear bus. I peered inside and found the terrier gone. Bridget joined me, noticed the barrels, pushed me out the way.

'Thurrock beer! What a find!'

She pressed her lips to the barrel tops, slurped the excess fluid. I left her, limped across the deck to the guardrail, slumped and wheezed.

Up the bridge something jumped onto a wreck. The terrier. It barked defiantly, pointing its nose high, as if it could see the moon through the cloudbank.

Bridget jumped out the bus, eyes wild.

'A dog! I love the taste of dog!'

She made to run after it, but I held her back.

'No time.'

'Let go! I'm starving!'

She kept on struggling, until the dog jumped down and ran out of sight. Bridget relented, slumping against the bus. She took a long look at me.

'You know what, Ken?' she said. 'I don't get you sometimes.'

She headed down the bridge to gather the squad. I slouched on the railing and gazed at the tarry river. For a moment I thought I saw a pattern, ripples on the surface spelling out a message. A strange urge seized me.

Then a cheer knocked me out my trance. Bridget must have told the squad about the beer. I stepped back from the railing and made for the shore.

'My name is Miss Bree,' says the visitor. 'I work in Engineered Liaison for Diorama. It's a pleasure to meet you, Kenstibec.'

She is short, wide and solid like a breeze block. A suit stretches around her frame. She is about half my height.

She reaches out a hand, a gesture of greeting. I take it and hold it for a moment, being sure not to grip too hard. People break easily.

'How are you settling in?'

There is not much to settle into. My new living space is a cube cell, unfurnished save a bunk with restraints. I have three bare walls and a reinforced door, surrounded by a plate of transparent aluminium oxynitride. This commands a view of the holding area beyond, and my guard.

'I am settling in well, thank you.'

She looks around, as if there are things to see.

'I apologise for the security measures. Diorama has an unfortunate history with Engineered employees, but people will change their tune when they see what you're capable of.'

She looks up at me.

'I'll see to it that you get a work station. A flex at least. I know there's nothing worse for your kind than inactivity.'

'I am keen to begin work.'

She smiles.

'Of course you are.' She goes to the door, turns. 'Would you care to join me for a walk?'

Control covered this form of human expression: an order phrased as a question.

'Yes,' I reply.

She knocks on the door, which swings open. Bree mutters in the guard's ear. He steps around me, unlocks my restraints and backs away.

We leave the holding area, enter a white corridor, follow a sign reading 'stairs'. Bree stares at my hands.

'How much can you lift?'

I tell her. Her cheek twitches.

I wonder how she feels, being in the presence of something so much better made. Scared? Happy? These words mean nothing to me, but Control teaches how they rule the lives of people. Even now useless signals seep from that old mammalian brain, fogging her judgement. Life must be so uncertain for humankind.

No wonder they need us. No wonder they cannot get anything done.

PARADE

It took two hours to coax my squad from their hiding places. They spent another hour cursing and bickering before the loot was loaded in the van. They sat on the barrels on the journey home, sampling the produce, intent on celebrating the battle by obliterating all memory of it.

Bridget sat up front with me. She passed the time drumming her palms on her thighs, blowing a noise through her teeth as an accompaniment. She went on like that until a thought jumped her and made her talk.

'It's all wrong, isn't it?'

I said nothing. She'd fill in the gaps.

'What we did back there,' she said, thumbing at the past. 'Clive bangs on about how foreign they are, like that's a reason to kill them. And everyone agrees with him. I don't get how that happened. I mean, aren't we all survivors? Shouldn't we stick together?'

I shrugged.

'You didn't kill anyone.'

I doubted she ever had.

'And listen,' I said. 'Best keep your thoughts to yourself on the subject. Clive doesn't welcome debate.'

We took the 'King's Causeway', the perilous raised path I'd laid across the floodplain over the past few months. The structure moaned beneath us, about as stable as the Sweet Track. I picked a path through the slush, guided by our one, feeble headlight, until home emerged from the gloom.

Crayford was an island of singed twentieth-century housing, hemmed in by tents. Outside of Thurrock, its population represented all that remained of humanity in south-east England. The cull had been most efficient here. Barely ten thousand had survived the following war, and half of them had perished in the fall-out.

Crayford endured, drawing water from a spring at Welling Corner, coal from Betteshanger, and food from raiding expeditions like ours. The settlement was also helped by what locals called 'the river miracle': at some point over the last year the Thames had purified, apparently overnight. It was even said you could swim in it.

I edged the van through the town gate, acknowledged the shivering guards, then slowed for the road through town, curling past the metal works and tinned food market. The crowd recognised the raiding van, cheered and banged the bodywork. Some pressed ahead, lighting our way with flaming torches. Others sang in our wake.

The crowd spread at the roundabout. I cut a path through deep grey sludge, turned under the clock tower and pulled up in the car park. King Clive's Palace, the old electronics superstore, was already opening its doors. A sea of pinched, masked figures in chemical coats and goggles surged out to greet us, waving torches, beating drums and ringing bells in the night.

Fatty led the way, sporting his official garment: an oversize, orange mail coat, dabbed with high-vis strips. The word 'treshrer' was crudely stencilled here and there. He acknowledged me with a crafty wink, then clambered onto the roof of the van, lifting a megaphone to blue lips. I slid out the cabin, clutched my back, and listened to the fat man speak.

'On behalf of King Clive,' he said, 'I salute the bravery of our conquering heroes!' Nobody seemed bothered by his amused half-grin. 'Once again our brave Crayford boys have given Johnny Foreigner a bloody nose. Save the King!'

'Save the King!' answered the crowd.

A cup of captured beer was offered up to Fatty. A hush fell as he drew the amber liquid to his lips, tasted, and gasped. He raised the megaphone once more.

'Tonight we drink Thurrock ale!'

A great cheer went up, Fatty jumping clear. The King's enforcers commandeered two barrels and rolled them clear, tribute for the absent monarch. Then the crowd closed, desperate for drunken release. A riot quickly developed, the battered Transit rocking under the assault of a hundred crazed scavengers. I stood at a distance and watched, numbed to the indignity of it all.

'What are you scowling at?'

Fatty grinned at my shoulder.

'I'm not scowling,' I said.

He shrugged and scratched his beard.

'Call it what you will, you don't look happy.'

I nodded at the melee.

'Shouldn't you fight for your share?'

Fatty smirked some more. He had a pretty high opinion of himself these days. His quick tongue had nearly killed us on a few occasions, but saved us as many times. It had certainly bewitched our good King. Clive had bestowed his full favour on the fat man, holding him as his closest and most trusted adviser. Like most republicans, Fatty had dropped his objection to monarchy the moment it had tossed him a title.

'I don't need to concern myself with any of that unpleasantness,' he said. 'I have people to do that.'

He indicated a group of stronger Reals who were biting, punching and scratching their way clear of the crowd, a barrel rolled between them. They approached us, bowing before Fatty.

'My thanks, lads,' he said, bidding them arise. 'Please deposit this in my quarters. You may fill a bottle for yourself.'

The two strongmen grovelled and withdrew, rolling the beer into the palace. The brawl around the van dissipated, until only Fatty and I remained, blinking in the snow. He took a foil wrap out of his pocket, withdrew a pill and swallowed. Medication from the King's chemist, to keep the Blue Frog at bay.

He slapped me on the shoulder and pointed at the palace.

'Will you join the party?'

I shook my head and told him I thought I would go home. He didn't like that.

'Listen, freak show, people don't trust teetotallers. You're one of us now. You have to take part. I can't keep making excuses for you.'

'I'm not one of you. You know that.'

I walked away. He followed.

'Look, obviously as a former Ficial you feel you've come down in the world. I can understand that. It's bound to feel humiliating.'

'It doesn't feel anything.'

'Right, sure,' said Fatty. 'No emotions, I think you've mentioned that. But you don't have to drink. Just poke your head in, show your face.'

Fatty was concerned, I could tell. He had it made in Crayford. The King gave him a uniform, a title, and all the drugs required. Naturally he worried that my behaviour might arouse suspicion, or even reveal my Ficial heritage. If that happened Clive's people would hang him from the yellow M, 'treshrer' or not. Still, I wasn't going to attend a Real blow-out just to soothe his nerves. I told him so.

He dabbed at his leaking eye with a handkerchief.

'Fine, go and fucking sulk. But listen . . . I mean, if you need to talk to someone . . .'

I pushed him hard.

'I don't need to talk. I'll never need to talk.'

He raised two podgy palms and stepped away.

'Fine. Fine.'

He turned and headed for the palace. Behind him the gutted windows twinkled with illuminations, the building shaken by a drumbeat. The party would go on for hours.

The wind picked up, blowing trash across the car park. I circled the shopping centre, limping through deserted streets, collar up to the snow. My workshop was tucked down a lesser back alley. I twisted the padlock free, lifted the gate and stepped inside.

The cab was nothing on my last Landy, but it was something. A painstaking, six-month salvage effort had resulted in a vehicle that might have made the forecourt of Rick's Garage back in Edinburgh; bigger than my last cab, with rear seats and an enclosed hold, but slower and about half as protected.

I treated my wounds, drank some tea, then decided to go for a drive. I didn't expect to find a fare, but these days my mind was restless, prone to brooding contemplation and surges of cold, cloying doubt. Driving took the edge off, made me feel almost Ficial again.

The engine started on the second attempt. I took to the streets, rolling through the darkness, searching for lonely drunks in need of a quick trip home.

I trawled the King's lands, every sludge-choked passage from Plumstead to Hextable. A few shadows scurried among tents and

14

campfires, but I wasn't really looking for business. The engine hum had helped to clear my head. Now I could focus on the pressing question.

How to get out of Crayford?

Cliveian society was turning me into something distinctly Real. I had to escape, find a way to reclaim my Ficialhood. But how? Options were limited. The north was out, after my last Ficial fare, a journalist named Starvie, had detonated a tactical warhead in York. My fragile, nano-less system wouldn't take the fall-out.

I could camp in one of the old shelters, where millions had been coralled and culled by Control. I could even head to the continent, in search of a secluded oasis. The privacy would be good, but what would be my purpose?

I drove for hours, contemplating the same old options, until the weather cleared, and the shadow of the tower appeared on the horizon.

I sighed, something welling in the pit of my stomach, and headed back into Crayford. I thought of the tarry river, of the swirling message I'd glimpsed on its surface.

Then I saw a figure hunched at the side of the road, waving his arm. I pulled over. The Real ran up to the car and leapt in the back, murmuring some drunken song.

'Where to?' I asked him.

Fatty pulled back his hood and belched.

'To the pub,' he said, his good eye searching for focus. 'I'm taking you for a drink.'

I was still for a moment. Then I reached over and started the meter.

Fatty eyed me in the mirror.

'Fucking charming.'

I trail Bree to the surface, and for the first time I see Diorama Headquarters from the outside. I discover a four-storey brick townhouse, set back from a hushed, cobbled piazza.

I follow Bree across the square, watch my boots kick through leaves. We join an elegant high street, the only pedestrians around. There is little traffic, but cars are parked everywhere, crammed into spaces along the road. We pass a greengrocer packed with produce, pastry towers in a baker's window. We pass meat stores, wine stores, coffee stores. Most have no customers. Bree turns by a Reginald Blomfield chapel, down a neat avenue. I trail my fingers along black railings. Through windows I glimpse kitchens, televisions, furniture. No people.

At the foot of a hill is a tall metal gate, not unlike that at Brixton. Armed police observe our approach. The noise of traffic grows, becoming deafening as we enter the checkpoint.

Palms scanned, the police wave us through, but the gates do not open. Instead we take a spiral staircase up to and over the gate, joining a footbridge. We cross forty feet over a fuming column of unbroken traffic, which Bree calls the Great North Road. Thousands of cars shuffle below: goods vehicles, buses, cars – a mile-long tailback descending the hill. In the distance the city waits, squatting in its gloomy basin.

Bree points.

'See that, Kenstibec? London's finished. Flood defences never recovered from the barrier bomb. Eighteen million people will need new homes. More if you believe the papers.'

'Yes,' I say.

'The emergency government has a design competition planned to deal with the problem. A thousand-storey megatall, to be built near the city. The greatest construction project in the history of man.'

16

She leans on the rail and points at me.

'It's the ultimate prestige project,' she says. 'Any firm with an interest has brought at least a Power Eight onto the design team. That's why we splashed out on one of the first Nines. We intend to win the job.'

'I understand.'

'There are plenty of people in Diorama who think we should never work with a Ficial again. They think your Power designation means about as much as the number of blades on a razor. That you are nothing more than heavy labourers. You need to help me prove them wrong, show them that your design ability can help us win this thing. I want you to dazzle them, understand?'

'I understand.'

She nods, looks out at the city again.

'And remember. This tower will be our new capital. That means you have to consider the old one and its history. I don't believe your design can be successful otherwise.'

'Of course. Any skyscraper must be sympathetic to its environment.'

'Kenstibec. You sound like a textbook.' *She points at my hand.* 'I'm going to get your palm coded, get you access to London. I want you to see what two thousand years of humanity built before it's all washed away. I want you to get inspired.'

'I have a complete knowledge through my optimisation process. I do not need—'

She waves.

'Nonsense. Optimisation doesn't beat experience. We learned that with our last model.'

She shakes her head at the flooded city.

'It was never a looker,' she says, 'but I'll miss it.'

CRAWL

With the palace party in full swing, we found the Bear near deserted. Only a group of regulars were seated at the bar, one sucking a clay pipe, another drinking from his wooden leg. A few others tossed darts at a board.

Fatty hammered on the top until the proprietor stumbled out the back, blinking reproach and licking his teeth. Fatty ordered two tankards of a beer called Fall Down, paying with the local currency.

We took a table in the corner. I gaped at the ale, twisting the tankard in my fingers, until Fatty piped up.

'Drink it, then.'

'I don't drink.'

Fatty pointed out a quotation.

'A man is never happy in the present unless he is drunk.'

'I'm not a man.'

'No, that's true. Still, you must be freezing. It'll warm you up.'

'I'm fine.'

Fatty shook his head.

'Wandering around in a T-shirt and overalls? You're not indestructible any more, remember? You'll freeze to death dressed like that. Honestly, sometimes I think you're trying to top yourself.'

He belched and slapped his belly. 'I guess I would too, if I had been one of your kind. It must be humbling, farting and sweating like the rest of us.'

I thought about burying the tankard in his face. Oblivious, Fatty shuffled closer.

'But listen. Don't you ever think about getting a little more ... involved?'

'With what?'

'You know. I mean, you're never going back to a Barricade. Maybe you should think about settling down.'

Settling down. The phrase had a peaceful ring to it.

'How do I do that?'

Fatty tugged on his ear.

'Well, now that nano junk is out of your bloodstream you could . . . Let me see, how would your lot put it? You could mate.'

The thought made me drink. Fatty shook his head.

'Not interested then?'

I looked at his seeping bad eye, at his bloated, blue-tinged flesh.

'I don't know how you can bear to touch each other.'

I tipped the rest of the beer down my throat. I had to admit, it stilled my shivers. Fatty spat a blue mess.

'Well you should reconsider. Your fucking boy band skin is still fairly intact, and that draws attention. People talk about you. And the more they talk, the hotter things get for us.'

I wondered why we were on this subject. I was too Ficial for romance, and Fatty knew it. He finished his drink, pushed the tankard away and stared into nothing.

Then I remembered: a Real would often enquire about another's welfare in order to introduce a discussion about its own. They couldn't help but play these games.

'So,' I asked. 'What about you? Are you mating at the moment?'

Fatty frowned at the turn of phrase, then sagged, emitting a pained sigh.

'Marie. I think I'm in love with her.'

I considered.

'You think that a lot though, don't you?'

Fatty narrowed his good eye.

'And what do you mean by that?'

'Just an observation.'

He raised his nose and sniffed.

'Marie is different. One of Clive's daughters. I think about her all the time.'

I sipped my beer.

'So why not propose, or whatever it is you do?'

'You wouldn't understand.'

Typical Real reaction. 'Then don't drag me here and bother me with it.'

He examined his nails, as if the answer to his worries lay buried in the scum beneath.

'It's OK for you, pal. You're still in decent condition. Sure, you've lost a lot of weight, but at least your face is in one piece. Still got those fucking gloss-finish teeth.'

He dabbed at his bad eye with a handkerchief. I was beginning to understand.

'The Blue Frog doesn't help your cause, I take it?'

'No, it fucking doesn't. She's young and relatively healthy. She'll want the same from a partner. But look at me.' He dropped his face into his hands. 'It's so unfair.'

The Blue Frog disease certainly made him a special kind of ugly. Even on medication he was bloated and blue as a rotting seal. I pressed my tankard to his and paused, ready to tip. He glimpsed the action and nodded. I poured out half, trying to think of some advice.

'From what I have observed, males often demonstrate their suitability for mating through dance. Why don't you take her to one of those maypole events out Bexley way?'

Fatty shook his head.

'No good. Clive'll have my guts for garters if I tried the old dinner and dance routine with his daughter.'

He raised his hand to the bar, twisted a finger for another round. The landlord dropped two fresh tankards onto the table. Fatty continued.

'No, I need Clive's blessing before I go courting. He likes me, sure, but it'll take more than a few barrels of Thurrock beer to win Marie's hand, I'll tell you that.'

He brooded in silence for a while, watching the darts game, until suddenly he got to his feet.

'Let's go see her,' he said.

'Who?'

'Marie, who do you think? She's in the play.'

He tugged my arm, persistent as always. Normally I would have refused, but the drink had made me warm and docile. I found myself pulling on my coat and stepping out of the pub, leaning into the wind and snow. Halfway across the car park we saw some commotion at the palace entrance: trouble-makers being kicked into the snow. We drew closer, saw two bouncers thrashing a group of teenagers with batons. Fatty congratulated the men on the door, pressing local currency into each palm. They ushered us inside, then returned to beating the miscreants.

I usually avoided the theatre, having little time for the productions the King's troupe churned out, but the structure itself offered some interest. It was a simple stepped bowl, cut out of the old shop floor, cast in unevenly poured concrete. Coal braziers heated the space, while two great torches soaked in Crayford pitch provided a gloomy light.

The house was packed. A flash-blind cast member prowled the stage, trying to be heard over the din, beating at the trash hurled by the crowd. Fatty and I bought cups of beer and sidestepped our way to some seats. A couple of locals slapped me on the back as I sat down, toasting my name in honour of the convoy raid.

'See,' said Fatty, spitting in my ear. 'People like you.'

I shrugged, knowing how swiftly Real allegiance could shift. Fatty was about to berate me for my indifference when a discordant trumpet blared, and the harried blind man gratefully departed the stage.

'Here she comes,' yelped Fatty, slapping my back. 'Here she comes!'

A Real quartet leapt onto the stage, performing what I guessed was a dance. They moved with an energy I had almost forgotten Reals were capable of. There was only one girl, a small example with a bowl of black hair. Fatty whooped and tossed his beer, soaking those beneath us.

'See her? See my love? Isn't she wonderful?'

The dancers moved in something approaching formation, waving arms, pivoting on heels, gyrating rear ends. Fatty was enraptured.

Marie and her troupe seemed unwilling to wrap things up, but the end finally came. Fatty snapped out of his reverie and proclaimed the need for more drink. We were halfway to the stand when a commotion erupted around the stage. A great, angry roar was directed at the next performer. I peered through the shaking fists to the stage, and saw Bridget stood alone, clutching a harmonica. I tapped Fatty on the shoulder and pointed out the spotty girl.

'What's all this about?'

'She's an idiot,' he said, waving the question away. 'Should know by now nobody wants to hear that racket.'

'Why?'

'She's fucking cursed, that's why,' said Fatty. 'Well, the music is. Or the harmonica.'

Fatty reached the front of the queue and secured two tankards. I asked him to explain.

'It all kicked off before we showed up. She played here one time and there was a fucking conflagration, nearly lost the palace, so they say. Next time she played at a tent party. Big fire there too. Next time she played down by the river and the fucking water caught fire.'

Real superstition. It was quite something.

'If they believe she's a danger why not get rid of her?'

'Well,' said Fatty. 'She's one of us, isn't she?'

Bridget never started playing. A hail of cups, beer and trash forced her to seek cover. She departed, clutching the small instrument like a great weight.

'One of us.'

Fatty scratched his beard.

'Yeah. So long as she doesn't play. Look, it's too noisy in here. Let's have one more drink, somewhere quieter.'

I trailed him out the theatre, across the old shop floor, where Reals sat in groups, drinking, chattering, telling stories, sharing food from tins. Fatty took a key from his pocket and unlocked a door marked 'stairs'. We headed up to the palace roof, where he said there was an excellent view.

Looking at it didn't improve my mood. I sat in the snow and stared at the shadow of the Hope Tower, thinking and drinking.

'Do you have any idea,' I asked, 'what it's like to be redundant? To have lost your purpose?'

Fatty eyed me.

'What are you talking about?'

'I was a construction model. One of the most advanced Ficial Powers ever produced. And now look at me. I could barely build a sandcastle.'

Fatty rolled his eyes.

'I built that thing,' I said, pointing out the tower. 'Designed it too. One of the great engineering feats in history. Or it was going to be. Now look at it. Rotting, just like me.'

'So you're telling me you feel sorry for yourself?'

'No. I'm saying. I don't know what I'm saying.'

Fatty rolled onto his belly.

'You really built that?'

'It's called the Hope Tower.'

'Yes I know. Some hope. Why didn't you mention this before?'

'I'd rather not draw attention to the fact, that's why. It's an abomination. A monument to your kind's feeble love affair with excess. It was supposed to be a feat of engineering. Then you lot bloated it with needless ornaments. I mean, there's a tuned mass damper in the structure, can you believe that?'

Fatty sneezed something glutinous.

'Unconscionable, I'm sure. What's a massed dampener?'

'It's a device,' I explained, 'mounted in structures to reduce the effects of mechanical vibrations.'

'So what's wrong with that?'

'There was no need for it, that's what! It served no purpose in my design. Do you know why it was included? As a talking point. A feature in the penthouse.'

Fatty rolled onto his back again, bored.

'Don't see that being a talking point.'

I sipped my beer.

'It is if it's made of gold.'

Fatty rolled back to me, good eye wide.

'Come again?'

I pointed at the wide-eyed fat man. 'You're fascinated now, aren't you? All at the mention of a ductile metal.'

'Did you say gold?'

'Yes.'

'How much gold are we talking?'

'All that could be found,' I said. 'All that could be melted down and packed into a giant, rendered globe. Five hundred tonnes of the stuff.'

I kicked a rusted can off the roof, looked out over the floodplain. I stared for a long time, lost in thought, until I noticed something. I stepped over Fatty and pointed.

'Do you see that?'

Fatty sat up, peering into the night.

'What am I looking at?'

'Lights,' I said. 'Moving down the river.'

The bus arrives after an hour. I jump on, running my coded palm over the fare reader.

I tower over the other passengers. They make way for me, eyes burning.

I take a seat on the top deck and watch the city pass in the rain. Sandbags and pumps sag on every corner.

Passengers claw their way on board at the next stop. The bus sways and thumps as soaked, gasping people climb the stairs. They keep coming, standing despite the sign that forbids it. A man screams on a phone in a foreign tongue. Someone at the back yells:

'You'd better shut up!'

But the entire deck is noise: tinny music leaking from headphones. Coughing and sneezing. Two young men stood behind me, speaking in a language I do not recognise.

The bus rumbles on, ignoring some bells, discharging passengers where there is no stop. More pile on. A recorded voice chirps that seats are available on the top deck. That angry voice shouts again:

'I want to get off! Let me off! I said let me off NOW!'

A weapon discharges. The top deck erupts into screaming. I turn around and see a man in a suit, holding a pistol, shooting a path through his fellow commuters. A younger male tries to disarm him, gets one through the eye for his trouble. The bus skids and halts. People jump off, wild with panic. The gunman walks past me, tips his hat.

'I can't stand being cooped up like that.' He whistles down the stairs and disappears.

That ends the bus journey. I disembark, electing to explore the city on foot. I step out into rain and street noise.

I walk for hours. I find squat, terraced housing, mouldered tower blocks, ripped-out shop fronts. I walk through a seeping graveyard. Children loot the church, carrying bells away in a wheelbarrow.

I wade into the quieter flooded streets, pushing aside floating debris. Old Street roundabout has become a stinking, brown lake, its glass office blocks abandoned and shattered. At the centre is a great, foaming geyser, where the Underground has been breached. A body circles the whirlpool, face down.

Two thousand years of civilisation achieved all this. I turn and head north, research concluded.

CROSSING

We hurried down the stairs, hearing the clock tower outside, ringing the alarm. We found the shop floor in chaos. The crowd flooded out of the theatre, colliding with those pouring into the palace.

'The cab,' I said. 'We need to get to the cab.'

We struggled through the mob, broke out to the car park. Gunfire flashed in the camps. Scooters buzzed on Station Road, bristling with armed raiders, headed straight for us.

'Jesus Christ!' yelped Fatty, breaking into a sprint. I followed him down the Crayford Road, all the way to the Bear. I turned towards the car park, but a fresh horde blocked my way, waving an assortment of blunt instruments. We dived into the pub, throwing the brace across the doors.

We gasped for breath, watched by the surprised regulars, listening as the raiders passed. Fatty whispered to the proprietor.

'Hey, pal. Is there a way out back?'

The soak didn't have time to tell. A window shattered, two Thurrocks leaping through the breach. The tallest lunged at Fatty with a spear, his first jab missing. The shorter advanced on me, wielding a bronze shield and a red fire axe. I dived clear as he swung the weapon, watched it cleave our table in two.

Shorty roared and flashed the blade again. I skipped clear, but then he struck with his shield, slapping me to the floor and stepping over me. I was pinned, helpless, staring into the eyes of vengeance. It looked like a slaying was in store.

Then three darts slapped into his neck. He howled and turned on the regulars, who were peppering him with their best shots. He snarled, advanced, then noticed Fatty. The Treasurer had beaten his opponent unconscious.

Shorty wielded his axe, but Fatty saw the danger. He wrenched the spear from his vanquished foe's grip, dropped it horizontal, and swung hard at Shorty's ankle. Shorty cried out and stumbled. Fatty seized his chance, grasping the spear over one shoulder and hurling it into the prone man's chest. Shorty spluttered blood, frowned, and dropped.

I picked up the shield and stepped out the shattered window, pursued by Fatty. There was a pitched battle on Crayford Way, but the car park was clear. We edged around the pub, found the cab untouched.

I popped the back door, selected a rifle, and handed Fatty a Beretta. He tucked it in his coat pocket and turned, hearing something on the street.

Thurrock scooters. They rasped in our direction, each rider clutching a young Crayfordian hostage. Fatty jumped at the first bike, more drunk than brave, clattering rider and captive to the ground. I stepped out before the second and held up the shield, reflecting his headlight. The rider clutched his brakes, skidded to a halt, and reached for a weapon in his belt. His hostage, a boy, stared at me. I skipped forward and swung the shield edge hard into the rider's head, knocking him cold. The boy jumped free as the scooter clattered down, then looked mutely up at me.

Another engine. Headlights bearing down on us. I clutched the kid tight and jumped clear, sitting up in time to see Bridget calling to me from the car's back seat. I lined up a shot, but Fatty batted my gun away.

'What? They have Bridget. Let me take out the driver.'

'You'd miss,' he said. 'You've had a skinful. Don't trigger when trolleyed, that's my guiding star.'

I shouldered the rifle, watched the car's tail lights fade.

'So what do we do? Let them take her? I thought you said she was one of us.'

Fatty scratched his beard.

'Fair point. We pursue.'

We ran for the cab, until a thought struck me. I held a hand to Fatty's chest and told him to stay put.

'But I want to be in the car chase.'

'Too bad. Get your people back to the palace. Organise the defence. You're treasurer, after all.'

I pressed the shield into his hands and jumped in the cab. He appeared at the window, bad eye swivelling in its socket.

'You can't do it alone,' he said. 'You're hammered. You'll steer this fucker right into the river.'

'Thanks for the pep talk.'

I swept the cab onto the main road and stamped on the accelerator, hurtling through a confusion of tracer and torchlit struggles. I tore out the burning gate and onto the causeway. Wind and snow thrashed the Landy, wipers slapping a furious beat on the windshield. My fingers trembled on the wheel.

I followed the raider's tyre tracks, until the road turned up to the old motorway, and bridge pylons arose from the gloom. I stopped the cab just short of the tollbooths, cut the engine, scanned the approaches with my binoculars.

The bridge looked clear, but there were too many wrecks to be sure. Remembering the convoy's fate, I decided to cross on foot. I tucked the cab under a flyover and struck out in the snow, a sweating, trembling sack of meat.

I jogged two-thirds of the bridge span without incident, stopping under the far pylon. There was an artificial light up ahead. Shadows, moving in headlights. I stopped to think.

Big mistake. The exercise had cleared my head, and my wounded ankle now made itself heard. I clutched at the pain and cursed drunken decisions. Leaving the cab had been dumb. I wouldn't get far on this foot. I contemplated going back for the Landy, but giving up now would have been all too Real.

Instead I rested the rifle on a wreck, lined the quivering sight on the tallest figure. The first shot missed, as did a second and third. The Thurrocks killed their headlights.

I was about to move closer when I heard a familiar, hollow spitting sound. My damaged brain took a moment to place it. Ah, yes: that would be a 51mm mortar round.

The bridge deck erupted in a hot, white flash, lighting up the river once more. I was slapped against something hard, and lay dazed for a moment, thinking I'd had about enough of this bridge.

Then I began to roll. I wasn't the only one. Car wrecks and debris were sliding in my direction. It took a few seconds to realise: the bridge was collapsing. I guessed I should have watched what I wished for.

Cables snapped around me with great, plucked strums, lashing the deck. The road began to unzip and fall away. The far pylon bowed, making a low, popping sound, and tumbled in my direction. Looked like I'd get that swim after all.

I jumped for the river. Diving into the Old Thames would have killed nano-less me, but the swollen river ran high enough to survive. I plunged deep, then struggled for the surface, lungs thumping, breaking the waves with a gasp of fetid Thames air. I swam to the shore, peering over my shoulder to see the bridge folding up.

I hauled into the mud on the north bank, and lay gasping like the catch of the day. Above me I heard a car engine on the ramp, spluttering and refusing to start. There were excited, raised voices, speaking various languages. A couple of scooter engines revved impatiently.

I plunged through the silt, desperate to head them off, but the troubled engine rattled into life, and I heard the car move clear. I struggled harder, but the mud was too thick and my limbs exhausted. It took ten minutes just to drag clear of the mire.

I hobbled onto the main road, thinking the whole enterprise something of a wasted effort, when I noticed the Thurrock car. It had only travelled a hundred metres before breaking down again. The headlights were on, bonnet lifted, five Reals bickering over a steaming engine. There was movement in the back seat. One figure was Bridget. The other was a small, black terrier. That old Ficial part of me reordered my priorities.

The dog saw me coming, watching with expectant brown eyes. The Thurrocks didn't notice me until I was on them.

I put my hands to the raised bonnet and slammed it hard on the fingers gathered beneath.

Three of the Reals screamed, hands pulped. The dog howled, joining the chorus. A female Thurrock backed away, fumbling with her weapon. I pulled a fingerless Real to me as she fired, his body absorbing both bullets, then ripped the pistol from his belt and returned fire. I missed, but it was enough to deter. She jumped on her scooter and made off at speed. I dropped the dead Real, stood there with chattering teeth and uncontrollable shivers. Two Thurrocks were still alive, wailing over their mangled digits. I lifted the lid and let them drop clear, inspecting the engine that had got them maimed.

'Ken?' Bridget stepped from the back seat. 'What happened to you? You look like a jellied eel.'

I guess that was her way of thanking me. I nodded at the engine. 'This can be repaired.'

I tweaked the engine, staggered to the driver's seat and turned the key. The engine rumbled into life. I listened to it for a moment, decided it should get us home. The dog jumped on my lap, pressed its paws to my chest and licked my face. My new best friend.

'Well,' said Bridget, rubbing her hands together and eyeing the dog. 'The night's not a total washout. At least we've got something to eat.'

I heard scooter engines, closing. The Thurrocks had regrouped.

'Time to go,' I said, roaring into reverse, leaving Bridget standing in the road. I turned and sped off, the girl watching, stunned. I thought it too hot to go back for her, but the dog had other ideas. It wanted to be where the action was. It bounced off my lap and out the open passenger window. I pulled the handbrake, swung the car, and went to retrieve it.

I caught up with it, just as the scooters broke into view. I pushed open my door, grabbed the hound by the scruff of the neck, then kicked the car's tail into the nearest rider. I tossed the hound in the back seat and burned back the way I'd come.

I dabbed the brakes as I passed Bridget. She ran, just managing to dive inside the back door before I picked up the pace again.

We sped clear, until the scooters broke off their pursuit.

Bridget glared at me in the rear-view for a minute, then sprang forward and punched me in the back of the head.

'Watch it!' I said.

'You were going to leave me there! There's me thinking you were coming to the rescue, and all the time you're after that bloody pooch. I guess I know where I stand in the order of things!'

I couldn't argue with that.

I scratched the dog behind his ears, and wondered what I'd call him.

I crouch in my cell, examining the flex Bree gave me, when my heart suddenly slows and my vision blurs. I slump against the wall, every nano in my bloodstream sitting up and begging to an ultrasonic prompt.

– Kenstibec.

Control. I did not expect to hear from it so soon.

– *Signal is being tested due to recent interference with other models. No directive element to this contact. However, you should take the opportunity to report.*

– *Accommodation and liaison satisfactory. Optimal mission identified: construction of new city tower development.*

Control is quiet for a moment. I wonder if it has cut the signal.

– *Connection intact, Kenstibec. You have questions. Proceed.*

– *There was another construction model at Diorama. My handler told me yesterday.*

– *Correct. Power Five, triumph model. Buried alive during flood prevention work in Docklands area. Attempts by other models to recover it failed.*

– *I see.*

– *There is something else?*

– *Yes. Miss Bree asked me to visit the city, to gain inspiration for the new development.*

– *You were not stimulated?*

– *Yes. No. The city is poorly sited. There are interesting buildings and many excellent parks, but there is no real centre. The streets are laid to a medieval plan. Tall buildings are raised at random. Spaces are overwhelmed by elevated statues and monuments. Most of all, it is incapable of housing its populace.*

– *We are aware, Kenstibec. That is why your project is so important. Your new creation can fix the problems of the old city, because it will be built to an optimised scheme.*

— I do not know that I will have the opportunity to fix anything, Control. I am still locked up.

— Consultation will follow, Kenstibec. Skill will always prevail over prejudice. Remember that Canterbury Cathedral was built by a Frenchman. Regardless, Diorama cannot neglect your abilities when the prize is so great.

— What should I do until then?

— Exactly what you are doing. Wait. Continue your other designs. Your time will come.

I think of Brixton's cool, peaceful tunnels.

Then the connection breaks, and I am alone again. For a moment at least.

FERRY

I headed for the Tilbury ferry. With the bridge down it was the only route across the river. Bridget sat in the back, composing a song about her kidnapping experience. She didn't have her harp, so she clapped her hands and sang instead, making a sound I tapped my finger to. Her fragile frame produced quite a voice, and the beat seemed to sync with the seams in the road. I felt a little light-headed listening to her, but she didn't start any fires.

The dog sat on the front seat and panted. I looked into his brown eyes, at his pink tongue, thought how his mind was nothing but curiosity and sensation. If only mine could be that way.

We joined the Ferry Road, cutting through foot-deep water, until I made out a sign in the gloomy snow, scrawled on a ruined wall:

Ferri vis way! Lowe lowe cost!

We passed stacks of rusted shipping containers, crossed a round-about, and came to a halt. The water ahead was too deep to continue. The old grain terminal squatted before us, half submerged, the husk of a cargo ship still moored alongside.

I told Bridget to get out and look around.

'What? No way, you do it.'

'Look, I need to be able to pull out fast if there's trouble.'

'And leave me swinging again? Pull the other one.'

'Look, it's perfectly safe.'

'How do you know? Been here before, have you?'

'No. Fatty has.'

'Oh come on, Ken. Phil says a lot. Doesn't mean I'd bet my boots on him. I trust him about as far as—'

She stopped, noticing something.

Lanterns. They appeared among the containers on our left, blowing sparks.

A voice called out of the darkness.

'You looking to cross?'

I stepped out of the car, the dog following. Bridget remained in her seat. I counted the torches, quickly discounting a forced passage. They were too many, and besides, I was tired. I called back.

'That's right. I can't see a ferry, though.'

Movement. On the terminal roof, and in the ruins to our right: they were drawing a ring around us. The voice again:

'What's your cargo?'

'Two passengers. The car too, if the ferry can take it.'

'We can take it. What have you got to trade?'

The crunch point. I looked down at the dog. He showed me his tongue.

'I've got food,' I said. 'Dog.'

Excited chatter. Always talk to a Real's stomach before you try its brain.

Reals leaked onto the street, torches bringing a campfire glow to the shore. A woman, about the same age as Bridget, stepped forward. She had a point two-two pressed to her shoulder. She ran her eyes over me.

'What's going on here? Looks like you've been for a swim in a latrine.'

I shrugged.

'Close enough. Car trouble. Had to get out and push.'

A lie. It came too easily.

'Will you let us cross?'

Her crew edged closer, eyes fixed on the hound at my feet. I wondered why they didn't just cut me down and take the dog. I was in no condition to give them trouble.

The leader peered into the back seat.

'Who's your passenger?'

'Just a mate,' I said, using Fatty's standard response. I knocked on the window and indicated Bridget should step out. She tripped out the back door, eyes wide.

The leader peered at Bridget's spots, then nodded, satisfied. She smiled, introduced herself as Marsh.

'We'll take you across. The dog in exchange.'

'You get it once we've all four wheels on the southern shore. Agreed?'

Marsh nodded, shouted orders to her people. They shouldered arms in good order and waded into the water, picking thick black ropes out of the soup. They heaved in unison, hauling the ferry from a concealed mooring among the crates. The vessel edged into view. It was an old passenger type, gutted to allow vehicular access. The crew splashed and grunted in the torchlight, bringing the stern around to the shore. Four men climbed the ropes to the deck, throwing planks down to the mud: a makeshift boarding ramp.

I climbed into the car, aligned the wheels and gunned up to the ferry. One plank dropped away, but we made it.

Marsh ran up the remaining timber, giving orders to cast off. The crew took stations, some heading below, others dipping long poles to port and starboard. The vessel inched forward, punting clear of concealed flood obstacles.

Marsh bellowed another order as we hit the open river. Oars emerged from the lower deck and dipped in the water. Somebody struck a beat on a tin pan, and the crew began rowing, propelling us with surprising speed.

It was a slick operation. Marsh had her Reals well trained. I left the cab, aiming to speak to her, but the swell affected my belly and I bent over the railing instead, heaving into the river.

Vomiting: another delightful feature of Real life.

'Sorry about earlier.'

Marsh crouched by the dog, scratching his head. I wiped the mess from my nose.

'Sorry for what?'

'The precautions. We used to offer a friendlier reception, but we have to be extra careful nowadays. We've had some . . . interesting visitors recently. I'd rather sink the ship than tangle with Ficials again.'

I blinked.

'Ficials? You had one come through here?'

She sighed, looked out over the river.

'About a month after Brixton brewed up. It was a military type I think. Green eyes. Never seen one up close before. Can't say I'm keen to repeat the experience.'

35

'It didn't cull you?'

Marsh narrowed her eyes.

'No. Told me to look out for one of theirs. Gave me a name, can't remember it now, one of their weird ones. Anyway, it wanted this other Ficial pretty bad. Can you imagine that? They're fighting each other now. Like there's still something to win.'

So a soldier model was after me. Who had sent it? Only a year before I'd dropped Control into the Thames, killing the coalesced mind that once governed every Ficial on the planet. Revenge would appeal to a soldier model, but I still couldn't see it acting without orders.

Whatever the case, he wanted me bad: it took a lot for a soldier to resist a culling opportunity, let alone ask Reals for favours.

'Feeling all right, Ken?'

Bridget appeared next to Marsh, hands in pockets, spots flushed. I didn't answer her. I wasn't feeling anything.

The dog barked at Marsh. She laughed, brushing it on the nose and making a face.

'I know this dog,' she said.

'You what?' said Bridget.

'It belongs to a Thurrock named Kowalski. He uses this ferry occasionally. I wasn't sure before but really, how many dogs are there around these days? How did you come into possession of it?'

Bridget and I looked at each other.

'Won it in a bet,' said Bridget.

'Really?' said Marsh. She smiled, hands still buried in the dog's fur. 'That surprises me. Kowalski loves this dog. I don't believe I have ever seen him without it. I seem to remember him threatening to shoot my crew for looking at it the wrong way.'

There was a simple motivation for any bizarre human behaviour. I thought it would explain things.

'He was drunk,' I said.

'That's right,' said Bridget. 'Always off his head, old Kowalski. Kodrinkski we call him.'

'Well, he won't be pleased to hear you've sold him for food.' Marsh gazed into the dog's eyes. 'It will be a great pity to eat him. But meat is meat.'

The boat creaked, oars redeploying as we approached the shore.

We turned, navigating rooftops, satellite dishes, and the other sunken ruins of what was once Gravesend.

We followed Marsh to the stern, which was coming about in the shallows. The oars drew in, crewmen jumping into the water with ropes. The planks were slipped onto the shore.

I sat shivering at the wheel, Bridget curled up in the back. The dog stood on the bonnet, tail wagging, not knowing what was planned for him. Marsh appeared, deep shadows under her eyes. I rolled down the window.

'The dog buys you a second trip for free.' She smiled. 'Too high a fare for one journey. Come back anytime you need to cross the river.'

'Thank you.' I made to roll up the window.

'Hold on there,' said Marsh. She leaned in and almost smiled. There were hard, bloody lines in her parched white lips, like brick showing through cracked concrete. 'Listen, you've obviously had quite a day. You're shivering and tired. I have a place this side of the river. A space where you'd fit.'

Suddenly it was hot in the car. I was caked in Thames mud and she wanted to snuggle? I glanced at the other men in her crew.

'Why me?'

She laughed.

'Why you. Don't hear that a lot. I don't know, why not?'

A jackhammer started in my chest, deafening me. I was confused. I tried to imagine what Fatty would say.

'I have to be somewhere now,' I said. 'Maybe I'll take you up on it when I return.'

'Good enough.' She stood, picked the dog up off the bonnet. I backed the cab down the planks onto the shore, turned us to face the road.

Bridget sighed and shook her head.

'I'll say it again. I don't understand you, Ken.'

I watched Marsh in the rear-view mirror, as she walked down the ramp to the shore, the dog struggling in her arms. I thought about her offer. Then I thought about the dog being butchered, roasted on a campfire spit.

I selected reverse, and sent the car hurtling at the ferry. Marsh stumbled, dropped the dog. I opened the door and whistled. The terrier scurried to me, jumping into my lap and licking my face.

Bridget thrashed with fury.

'Ken, are you CRAZY?'

I gunned the car, scattering ferrymen. We burned down the road, leaving a soundtrack of gunshots and curses. Bridget couldn't believe it.

'What is wrong with you, eh? Why did you rip them off? Do you want to get us killed?'

I couldn't answer her questions. It was just good to have the dog back. He sat on my lap, ears bouncing, small, fast and noisy. I patted his head.

'I think I'll call you Pistol.'

'Hey! Hey!'

A fist, striking the glass. The guard peers in, rifle raised. I peer back, blinking away the signal remnant.

'Is there a problem, Officer?'

'You've been out for five minutes. Are you OK?'

I touch a small bruise on the back of my head, where it hit concrete. The damage is healed by the time I sit up.

'I am in good condition.'

'I don't think so. That looked like a seizure.'

'I received a Control signal. The reaction is normal.'

'Control? You mean the thing in Brixton? You were talking to it?'

'We were signalling, yes.'

He lowers his gun and chews.

'What do you talk about?'

I would not normally share the details, but as there was no directive element I am free to discuss it.

'We talked about London,' I said. The guard's expression changes.

'Oh, yeah?'

'Yes. Do you live in London?'

'Course not,' he says. 'I can't stand the place. Too many people. Too noisy. Makes me nervous just visiting.'

I say nothing to that, but it makes perfect sense. How could the city fail to overwhelm and disorient?

He nods at me.

'What do you think of it?'

'It is poorly attuned to the needs of its populace. A better solution is required.'

He picks the gum from his mouth, sticks it on the glass.

'I see. I wondered why they brought a new model, after all the bother with the last one. You're going to work on this super tower everybody's talking about. Right?'

'That is correct.'

'Hmm. So what's it going to look like, this tower?'

'I do not know. I have not yet been asked to submit my design. I am awaiting instruction.'

He looks confused.

'You don't have any ideas?'

'Not yet,' I reply.

'Then what good are you?'

I stand, brushing my overalls clean.

'I cannot just draw a picture. Designing any structure requires extensive preliminary work. I have not even surveyed the site yet.'

He leans on the glass.

'So why don't you?'

'I do not know where it is. The location is secret.'

He snorts.

'Secret? It's just down the road, mate.'

PALACE

The Landy was just where I'd left it, only smothered in dust from the bridge collapse. We ditched the Thurrock car and returned to Crayford.

The town was quiet, licking its wounds. Raider boats smoked on the shore. The Bear had been torched. The palace was intact, but closed.

I dropped Bridget at her place, a tent she shared with five others. Her temper had cooled, and she invited me in for tea. I declined, driving back to my garage instead.

Pistol leapt around the space, sniffing at unfamiliar corners. I took a handful of currency from my locker, pulled on a coat, and locked the dog up with the cab.

I limped through the dark streets, shivering violently, until I came to the bath house. The entrance torches were extinguished, but that wasn't going to stop me. I hammered on the door until I heard cursing and threats the other side. Don, the manager, peered at me through the letterbox.

'We're closed, arsehole.'

'Why? It's only seven.'

'There's a war on, in case you didn't notice. I open when Clive says I can and not before.'

I waved the wad of notes at him.

'Keep calm, Don. I'll pay a premium.'

He eyed the cash, hesitated, then disappeared. Keys turned in locks, and the door creaked open.

'All right, half an hour.'

I folded the money into his greasy palm. 'I want an aspirin and a bandage too.'

He ushered me into the tent, where steaming Thames water filled an old tub. I swallowed the aspirin and sank into the bath.

I picked away dried mud and cleaned my wounds, until my head cleared and the shivers ceased. I jumped out, ate some noodles, then washed my overalls and T-shirt in the bath. I sat naked on a chair, drying naturally, relishing the peace. My chin dropped on my chest. I slipped into a deep and faraway sleep.

Fatty stood next to Don, arms crossed, grinning.

'Well. The avenger returns.'

He tossed my clothes at me and told me to go with him.

'Why?'

'Clive wants to see you.'

Summoned by the King. I dressed and followed Fatty from the building, heading into the dark street.

'What's all this about?'

'Not sure,' said Fatty, gnawing on his lower lip. 'Clive the Unready failed to show up during the battle. Probably wants to put medals to chests, soak up reflected glory, you know the drill.'

We found the palace entrance adorned with Thurrock heads. Heavily armed enforcers parted for Fatty.

The theatre and shop floor were packed with wounded. A few older Reals wandered among the damaged, offering the universal treatment of tea. I noticed the drinkers who'd slapped my back in the theatre. They regarded me differently, now that the convoy raid had consequences.

The throne room was beyond the shop floor, the small warehouse at the back, where electronic goods had been packed and sorted. The walls were draped with tapestries, depicting Clive's victories over foreign foes. The centrepiece was the Phone Throne, a squat, gaudy seat of power fashioned from thousands of smartphone handsets.

Clive's wives and daughters slumped on sofas around the throne stage, chatting, smoking or sleeping, warmed by scattered braziers. His sons sat apart, drinking gin and playing at cards. We waited a moment, until a bell rang and one of Clive's sons stood up.

'All stand for the King of Kent,' he said, 'ruler of Crayford and Bexleyheath, Belvedere and Erith, Swanley and Sidcup, Welling and

Shooter's Hill. Defender of the shore! Scourge of the scroungers! He that will send them all back!'

Clive entered on his litter, a beige armchair mounted on poles, carried by some of his younger sons. He was dressed in his usual finery of bright white football kit, polished black boots, and defunct AR specs.

He stepped out of his litter, accepted a cup of gin from a handmaid, and lowered his eyes to our level.

'Ken, Phil,' he said. 'You all right, boys?'

'Boss,' said Fatty, bending on one knee.

Clive stared at me.

'So I hear you had fun. Blew up the bridge and sent a scrounger horde for an early bath. That right?'

'Sort of.'

Clive nodded.

'We are pleased. We need big lads like you in defence.'

'Thank you, my lord,' agreed Fatty, smiling at something. 'We try to give one hundred and ten per cent.'

'I didn't blow up the bridge,' I said, ignoring Fatty's idiotic statement. 'The structure was badly compromised. A collapse was inevitable.'

Clive wafted his ringed fingers.

'Whatever. The fact is we summoned you here for something else, Ken. We have been speaking with Phil about the Hope Tower.'

I resisted the urge to look at Fatty.

'Oh yes?'

Clive smiled.

'Yeah. Phil tells us you worked on it, back in the day. Is that right?'

'That is correct.'

'How? What were you, a plumber?'

Clive's entourage tittered.

'I had many duties . . .'

'Why didn't you tell us about this before, Ken?'

I didn't answer that. Clive had a habit of gibbeting his subjects for concealing things from him. He sat forward on his throne, pointed out the nearest tapestry.

'You struck a blow for justice today, Ken. You took the fight to the scroungers. They'll think twice about playing away again. But the fact is, the fighting season's far from over. Right now we hold the ball, but we don't want to get caught in possession. See what I mean?'

I looked around.

'I might have missed it.'

Fatty chipped in.

'What His Majesty is telling you is that more and more survivors are coming over from the continent, claiming land that rightfully belongs to our people. The King has decided that this cannot be tolerated.'

'Send them back!' yelped one of Clive's sons. The assembled took up the call, the catchphrase echoing about the throne room. Fatty raised his hand for silence and continued.

'The King dreams of a unified east. But to do that we need a war chest. Goods to trade for arms with the Andovers, see?'

Clive sat up.

'Yeah. Then Phil here tells us about your tower. Says there's a dirty great golden ball stuck inside. Is he right?'

I went ahead and looked at Fatty now. He grinned and shrugged. I turned back to the King.

'I'm not sure.'

Clive frowned.

'What do you mean, not sure?'

I helped him out.

'I mean the gold may not still be there. The Hope Tower was unfinished, exposed to the elements. The gold may be damaged.'

The King pressed a finger to one nostril, evacuating the other into a proffered bucket.

'Not sure about this, Phil,' he said. 'Ken doesn't seem to think it's a goer.'

Fatty wasn't pleased.

'Ken, why don't you tell the King exactly how much gold was up there?'

Incredible the effect that word could still have on real minds. Clive's entire court was listening now.

'Five hundred tonnes.'

Fatty stepped closer to the King, turned to face me. His eye wandered to Marie, seated nearby. She stared back, mesmerised. Fatty warmed to his subject.

'Tell me, Ken. Do you really think the cloud could have chewed up five hundred tonnes of the stuff? There must be some left.'

I breathed out slow.

'Where is all this leading?'

Fatty smiled at me.

'I'm proposing that we recover the gold.'

'Why?'

I knew the answer, but I wondered if they did too.

'For the glory of Clive,' said Fatty, nodding at the creature on the throne. 'What else?' I looked at the King, wondering if I should tell him about Fatty's designs on his daughter. There was plenty of space for Fatty's head among the Thurrocks outside.

Instead I tried logic, turning on the grinning 'treshrer'.

'And how do you propose we transport a five-hundred-tonne gold ball down a structurally unsound megatall? You can't just unscrew it and let it drop, you know.'

Fatty's grin didn't waver.

'That's why we're so lucky to have you, isn't it? If anyone can do it, it's you. We believe in you, Ken.'

'And how would we bring it back here? Roll it through the Black-wall Tunnel?'

Clive waved his hands at me.

'Look, Ken. The only question is: are you going to accept our royal commission?'

The court was quiet, ready to spring if I gave the wrong answer.

In the old days I could have compacted Clive into his throne and tossed him through a wall. Things were different now. Refusing him would get me killed.

Besides, the idea had its advantages. I was tired of Crayford. Maybe this was the motivation I needed to finally pack up and move on. Sure, I'd sign up. Then I'd disappear.

'OK,' I said. 'I'll take him to the tower.'

'Score,' said Clive, slapping the throne. 'You may go. Accomplish this mission and we shall be in your debt.'

We bowed and departed, ushered out by guards. The moment we were clear Fatty slapped me on the arm.

'What's with you? Aren't you pissed at me?'

'I don't get pissed,' I said, picking through the wounded in the hall. I wondered if they knew their king was planning another war. I doubted they'd been consulted.

'Come on,' said Fatty. 'I tell the merry monarch your tower secret and you just agree to help? What are you up to?'

I pushed past the guards clustered at the entrance, out into the car park. The temperature had dropped sharply. Fatty gathered his coverings around his quaking form. I decided to break it to him upfront.

'There might be an issue getting there.'

'What?' said Fatty. 'Why?'

'The ferry you told me about. Bridget and I used it to get back from the north shore.'

'So?'

'So we had a problem with payment.'

Fatty scratched his beard.

'You mean you ripped them off?'

'They might see it that way.'

Fatty had a think about that.

'OK,' he said. 'No problem. I can fix the small stuff. It's the tower where we'll have the real issues.'

'You deal with that. There's no "we" involved.'

'What do you mean? You just said you'd help.'

'I said I'll take you to the tower, and I will. But I'm not climbing it. Once I drop you off you're on your own.'

Fatty spluttered.

'Yeah? And where will you go?'

'I've got a few ideas.'

Fatty gripped my arm.

'Listen, you vicious freak. Clive will kill me if I don't come back with his prize.'

'Does he really believe he can trade with it? Of what utility is gold in this society?'

'I don't know!' he said. 'What use was it in the old one? Look, who cares what Clive does with it? He's insane. All that matters is this is my way to win Marie's hand. I can't do it alone.'

'You never will, with or without me. You never should have told him it was possible.'

'You're angry with me.'

46

'I don't get angry. I'll pick you up tomorrow. I have to feed the dog.'

I left him under the yellow M.

I didn't go straight home. I thought I'd walk the streets of Crayford, as I might not see them again. The town was quiet, cowed by the raid and the cold.

I walked to the flooded Cray, dipped a hand in the water and sipped. It tasted like the back of a dry cleaner's watch, but it didn't kill me.

A sound echoed over the waves, like metal wailing. I searched the gloom, and spotted a figure crouched on a roof, overlooking the old rail line. It was Bridget, hands cupping a harp to her lips.

The more I listened, the more I understood. It was the sound of an outcast. The release of something denied. I looked back at the river and let the rhythm lift my thoughts, finger tapping on my knee.

A house was burning on the far shore.

Bree visits to authorise my site inspection. She equips me with a survey flex and tool bag, then interrogates the guard, asking how he learned of the site location. She did not know, and that ignorance angers her.

I leave Diorama, heading west this time, the opposite direction from the Great North Road. I skirt a cemetery, until I reach another roadblock. Riot police sit on twitching horses, guarding another temporary bridge. They scan my palm and wave me through.

On the map the heath is an open green space. From the bridge it is a vast brown smudge, a plywood and plastic shanty bordered by tall fences. The camp hums and squirms. Thousands of people heaped in disorder. Why do they not organise? I lean on the guardrail. Beggars gathered below hold up their hands.

I cannot inspect the ground from up here, so I jump the twenty feet, landing among the vagrants in deep, churning mud. Children swarm around me, tugging at my clothes, jabbering a thousand languages, rooting in my pockets.

I quickly discover there is no effective drainage on site. Flood water and effluent gathers in trash-crusted lakes, the stench overpowering. Huts cluster around the filth, lifted from the mire on stilts, swaying as occupants shift inside.

The nearest hut draws my attention: a flimsy platform leaning at a perilous angle. I climb a flight of beer crate stairs and leap inside the hut.

A woman shrieks. She is young, very sick, red refugee stamp on forehead. She is holding a baby. Why would she choose to breed here?

I point at my feet.

'This dwelling is unsafe.'

She offers no comment. I take a few careful steps and pick up the residents, baby and mother together. I sling the screaming pair onto my back and walk them down the stairs, lowering them onto a relatively dry spot.

'Please wait here.'

There is a collapsed hut only a few paces from theirs, a mess of tyres and broken limbs. There is a large lead plate which scavengers have found too heavy to lift. I recover it, plus one or two other likely items.

The family gaze at me as I work. I create a firmer foundation, replace the hut's rotten limbs and rebalance the platform. The work is complete in twenty minutes.

'Your domestic structure is stabilised,' I explain.

The woman stares. Emotions twist her features. She creeps up the steps and scuttles inside.

I look around the shanty, rolling down to the city stretched out below.

Plenty of work for me here.

NORTHBOUND

I picked Fatty up from the rat track. He'd decided to blow his remaining Crayford currency on a betting spree, one of those curious, self-destructive impulses that seized him on occasion. I parked, locked Pistol in the cab, and entered the old stadium, passing through the ruined betting hall and into the seats overlooking the track. I spotted Fatty immediately, halfway up the steps, laughing and snatching winnings from a group of younger Reals.

'Afternoon,' he said, as energised as I'd seen him. 'I'm on a winner today.'

'Too bad we're leaving.'

'Bull. We'll wait until the racing's done. I've just put a hundred on Mr Henry. A sure thing.'

'You all right, Ken?'

Bridget appeared at my side, also cradling winnings. 'Phil's a genius. We're raking it in!'

'Copying another's bets is not exactly the done thing,' snapped Fatty.

'OK,' I said, suspecting that one of those very Real mood changes had seized the fat man. 'I take it the mission is off?'

Fatty stumbled on a bad step and swore.

'No way. We're going all right, I just need to watch the next race.'

'Well, enjoy it,' I said, turning on my heel. 'I'm leaving immediately. Find your own transport.'

I moved up the steps. Fatty gave chase.

'Just hang on, hang on, you tart. It'll only take five minutes. Stick around and watch the next one, then we'll all go. You've never seen a rat race, after all.'

His good eye was pleading. I should have insisted on a prompt departure, but it wasn't as if we were going to lose any light. I followed him down and took a seat between him and Bridget.

'There,' he said, pointing at the torchlit track. 'See them loading the traps?'

I could see. Six enormous rats were being prodded into caged starting gates. They bit and snapped at their handlers, heads clenched by leashes on bent metal poles. The racecourse followed the old greyhound track, but the way was now encased by arched metal mesh, preventing the competitors breaking free. The lure appeared to be a smaller rat, which I spotted struggling in the gloves of a race official.

'I'm telling you,' said Fatty, counting the notes in his lap, 'this is one terrific sport.'

The racers were almost loaded, when a problem developed. The small rat wriggled free of its handler and broke for the stands. The racers went berserk, rearing up and screeching in excitement. One struggled so hard it broke free, leapt up the stands, then turned and sprang at its handler. The stands emptied, spectators fleeing in panic.

Fatty sat next to me, watching as the other handlers dragged the rat by its thrashing pink tail, clubbing it into submission. I stood up.

'A real gentlemen's sport.'

Fatty turned his bad eye on me.

'Sarcasm. What next?'

He picked up his pack and followed me out of the stadium to the Landy. Pistol jumped out of the cab and sniffed around the fat man's feet. He shooed the hound clear, crouched and opened up the pack.

'As promised.'

He passed me the winter clothing I'd requested: a warm hat and sweater, a navy donkey jacket, Crayford-made trousers and hard-wearing boots. He'd packed medical supplies and food to trade, and a flare gun too. He also seemed to have brought Bridget. I pointed at her shivering presence.

'What's she doing here?'

'She volunteered,' said Fatty, pulling a heavy trapper hat onto his head, flaps down.

'That's right,' said Bridget. 'Phil and I have a partnership.'

Fatty rolled his good eye and barged past me, cramming the pack

51

into the hold and squeezing into the cab's front seat. Bridget jumped in the back with Pistol, a pack over her shoulder.

We set off, headed through the Crayford streets. A couple of Reals spotted us, waved and bid us well. The journey passed in a pleasant silence for ten minutes, but when we were clear of the Causeway Fatty turned around to address Bridget.

'Look, now we're out of town I'm offering you a chance. You can get out here and go on your way.'

Bridget frowned. 'Eh? Why?'

Fatty sighed.

'Come on, Bridget. You're no treasure hunter. You're not a fighter either. Come with us and you might never come back. At least you're safe in Crayford.'

'Safe? I'm suffocating there, Phil. They won't let me play. Ever. And why? Cos they're superstitious barbarians, that's why. Ignorant music-haters.'

'Listen,' said Fatty.

'No, you listen, Phil. I'm never going back to that dump. Why would I? I'm utterly sick of it. This gold is my way to freedom. Independence. If we pull this off I'll be able to set up somewhere new.'

'Like where?' asked Fatty.

'I dunno. Andover maybe?'

'I doubt they'll find the prospect of burning to death at one of your recitals any more tempting than our lot.'

Bridget examined Pistol's ears.

'Oh come on, Phil, don't tell me you believe those fairy stories?'

Fatty cleared his throat.

'Look, I won't say no to an extra pair of hands. But no music. You can play to your heart's content when the job's done. You can take your share and set up wherever you like. Until then I don't want to see that harp of yours. And no moaning if things get tough, understand? Remember, I gave you a chance to back out.'

We passed into Gravesend. The high lights glowed in the cloud, casting a dim light on the streets, helping me retrace the route to the shore, where the Ferry had dropped us. The vessel wasn't there now.

Fatty told me to stop.

'OK,' he said. 'This is going to call for a little tact. That means you lot keep quiet, OK? The mutt stays here.'

Bridget leaned forward, tapping the fat man on the shoulder.

'Listen, Phil, are you sure about this? I don't think they'll be especially pleased to see us.'

'Keep your knickers on,' said Fatty, 'the pair of you. This lot are businessmen. As long as we offer compensation and you two appear suitably contrite we'll be fine.'

We left the car and walked ahead, staring up at the windows overlooking the approach.

'Hello. Anybody home?'

Thick white snow tumbled around us, deepening the silence.

'Maybe they're across the other side,' said Bridget. 'What then?'

Fatty folded his arms, called out again.

'OK. You probably recognise the jokers with me. I understand they ripped you off. I'm here to apologise and offer recompense. We'll give you what you're owed, and considerably more, if you'll take us.'

Still no answer.

'Give up, Phil,' whispered Bridget. 'They're over the other side. Stop me if I'm wrong.'

'IF YOU'RE HIS BOSS TELL HIM TO PUT HIS HANDS UP.'

Marsh.

'THE OTHER ONE TOO.'

Bridget and I complied. I could never understand why Reals were so comforted by raised palms.

'This isn't going to work,' said Bridget. 'Let's do one.'

I didn't agree. In fact I was reassured. We were an easy target, yet nobody had taken a shot. Marsh slipped out from the shadows behind us, five crew flanking her.

Fatty took his glove off and extended his hand. I recognised the gesture, but wasn't sure Marsh would grip that oozing blue palm. She looked at it for a second, then lowered her rifle. That was enough for Fatty.

'So,' said Marsh, 'are you here to give us the dog?'

Pistol's nose was pressed to the cab window. I couldn't figure what he wanted to smell. It was low tide, and the stench was hard to miss. Fatty shook his head.

'I have something else for you. A prize infinitely more valuable.'

'Really?' said Marsh, stepping closer. 'How about we shoot you and take both?'

'You'd be well within your rights,' agreed Fatty. 'However, I know that you're OK, you and your people. That's what I told the King of Kent too.'

She glanced at me, back to Fatty.

'OK,' she said, 'I'm listening. What have you got?'

Fatty rooted in his coat pockets and produced two small vacuum tins. He held them up, so the whole crew could see.

'I've got powdered milk in here! Powdered milk!'

Marsh was curious. Fatty shook the cans at her.

'You want to know the real killer? They're flavoured. This one's chocolate. This one's strawberry. I'll give you one to pay for the idiot's unpaid trip, the second for the return. That way we can all be friends.'

Marsh snatched a can from Fatty's grasp, held it up, examined it.

'OK,' she said. She winked at her men, and weapons were lowered.

'You have my thanks,' said Fatty, bowing.

'We'll take you across.' She pointed at me. 'But he doesn't sit at the wheel, understand?'

'Fine,' said Fatty, 'I'll drive.'

I would normally have forbidden his sticky fingers from touching the cab wheel, but the situation was loaded. I passed him the keys and headed to the passenger side. Fatty grinned as he squeezed into the driving seat.

'Be careful,' I said.

'Don't worry. Passed my test on the fifth try.'

Marsh's boys went to the shore and plucked ropes from the water, pulling the ferry from its hidden anchorage. Planks were thrown up to the deck, and after some crunching of gears, Fatty rolled us up the ramp, onto the ferry.

He stepped onto the deck as the craft pushed off, his collar pulled up, hat tight. I sat in the car, Pistol on my lap, Bridget humming quietly in the back.

Marsh glanced at me as she criss-crossed the deck, calling orders to the oarsmen below. She looked tired, in need of repair. I thought I could help, but didn't know how.

We neared the shore, saw it cloaked in fog. The oars drew in, making a roaring sound. Two swimmers dived in the water, recovering the ropes and tossing them up to Marsh and the others. The gangplanks were deployed, and Marsh jumped on the bank to guide us down.

Fatty took his seat at the wheel, rolling the cab onto the planks. He leaned over me, inching the Landy back and revving like a madman.

'Be careful,' I said again. 'Left a bit. Left, I said.'

'I'd do a lot better without you bleating in my ear.'

The cab moved gently at first, then suddenly picked up speed. We hurtled shorewards and cracked the cab fender hard on submerged tarmac, bouncing up onto the front wheels.

'Brakes are spongy,' sniffed Fatty.

He turned, pulled up and hitched the window open, offering the second tin of milk to Marsh.

'Here, as promised.'

She looked at the tin, looked at me.

'Keep it.'

She gave a signal. Her men ran up the planks and pushed off, apparently in an awful hurry. Two gunmen remained with Marsh, clearly agitated. A thought fluttered at the back of my mind.

Fatty waggled the tin.

'Are you serious? You don't want it?'

Marsh backed away fast, her men raising weapons to cover us. Fatty closed the window, tossed the can back to Bridget.

'Let's get moving,' I said.

'PASSENGERS. STEP OUT OF THE VEHICLE.'

The voice came out of the fog. A shadow appeared. A big shadow. It stood in the road like a cenotaph. Two green eyes glowed in the mist.

'He's Ficial,' I said. 'A soldier model.'

Bridget shot forward.

'What? No way!'

Fatty chewed his lip and put the Landy in gear.

'I'll run the fucker down.'

'STEP OUT OF THE VEHICLE OR I OPEN FIRE.'

I took Fatty's hand off the wheel.

'We need to do as he says. If you're lucky he just wants me.'

'You think that's likely?'

I thought about it.

'Not really.'

Bridget bounced on her seat.

'What are you talking about, Ken? Hit the gas!'

I unclipped the door and stepped out the cab. Fatty swore and followed. Bridget stayed in the car.

Marsh huddled at the water's edge with her gunmen. I caught her eye.

'When did you realise?'

'Wasn't sure till I got in close. Those teeth of yours.'

'So your invite. The space where I'd fit?'

She frowned, shook her head.

'Oh.'

The soldier model paced forward, stopping twenty metres away. I didn't recognise the Power. He was the biggest I'd seen yet. His rifle looked like a child's toy in his hands.

'You Kenstibec?'

'That's right,' I said. 'Power Nine. Construction. You?'

'Trubal,' replied the giant.

'I heard you were looking for me.'

Fatty nudged me.

'You knew this thing might be here?'

'Yes.'

Fatty looked up at the clouds.

'You didn't think that worth mentioning?'

Trubal's eyes fizzed in the gloom.

'I'm here to finish you, Kenstibec.'

'Why?'

'Control's final orders. You're a traitor and an abomination.'

I shrugged.

'No argument here.'

Pistol leapt out of the shadows and sank his teeth in Trubal's ankle. He really had a taste for that area. The soldier grunted and kicked the dog clear.

Fatty took the moment to draw his pistol and fire. Two struck the Ficial in the chest. He stumbled, spat blood and smiled. He flashed forward, cracking Fatty in the face and flooring him. Then he turned on me.

I ran for the Landy, but Trubal vaulted the cab in two bounds. I turned, staggered, watched him lift the vehicle and swing it at me. I dived under the wheel and tumbled into the shallows. The soldier tossed the cab aside and advanced on me.

'You don't want to get too close,' I said. 'I'm catching, haven't you heard?'

Trubal smiled, but kept coming.

'I heard.'

'Believe me, you don't want what I've got. Losing nanotech is not pretty.'

Trubal stopped, looked down at me, scooping fingers like excavators.

'Using your disease as a final defence. I don't know where to start hurting you.'

'You're not worried about losing your Ficialhood?'

He stepped around me, looking me over.

'Not really. I'm immune to your pestilence, Kenstibec. I was bred that way. Control wanted a new model, to spread the Pander virus to the Barricades, to wipe out all the old models. I was the prototype. While you were quarantined in one part of Brixton, I was growing in another. When you were meeting Control, I was taking my first breath. When you blew up central bunker, I was drowning.'

I rolled to my knees, but he dropped onto my back and pinned me under his weight, holding my head under water. I writhed and choked, until he wrenched my head clear and spat in my ear.

'Do you like that, Kenstibec? That's what I felt, when you blew up our home. I was dragged down to the bottom of the river when Brixton collapsed. I'm so glad I can explain to you how it felt.'

He turned me over, showed me his foaming mouth.

'Do you know what you look like?'

'I've got a pretty good idea.'

'Maybe I shouldn't kill you. It would be more of a punishment to leave you like this. Still, orders are orders.'

'You should get that printed on a T-shirt.'

Trubal pulled a huge assault knife from his boot and held it over me, pressing the tip carefully to my eyeball.

'I guess one little head wound will do it, won't it? Now that you're Real.'

I can't say I was unhappy to see the blade. It put a brake on my plans, of course. I had cherished the notion of finding a remedy for my condition, of rebuilding myself. But the knife was as sure a cure as any. Besides, death at the hands of a fellow Ficial had a trace of dignity to it.

But he was a soldier, and he was optimised to torment. He drew the knife from my eye, gripped my left hand, and trimmed two of the fingers. I emitted a howl Pistol would have been proud of.

Trubal held the dripping digits over me, so I got a decent view, then tucked them in his pocket.

He pulled the knife up again, hovering the serrated edge, dripping my blood into my eye.

'Let's get this eye out,' he said. 'Take a look at that rotting brain of yours.'

I searched for deliverance. Saw a torch, one of Marsh's, half burning, half hissing in the water. I gripped it, stabbed it hard into Trubal's neck. He laughed, swatted it from my hand, embers trickling over his shoulders.

'What was that supposed to do?'

A sound. Slow, reedy tones, shuffling and weaving. Trubal hesitated, turned. Bridget was playing her harmonica. The soldier winced, swatted the air like the notes were a swarm of flies.

'Shut that thing up.'

Flames. They began on Trubal's shoulders, crept over his clothes. It took him a moment to notice them.

'What?'

The fire spread fast, curling and spreading as if charmed. Trubal stumbled, slapping the flames in irritation. I crawled clear, as the heat grew immense, fire engulfing his hands and head. He stepped back towards the river, a walking pyre.

Bridget stopped playing. Stared at the burning figure.

'Snap out of it,' I said. 'Help me with Fatty.'

We lifted the unconscious fat man. I dropped in the cab, thankfully still on its wheels, and started the engine. It was a relief to hear it roar into life.

Sadly Trubal heard it too. He moved towards the sound, a walking furnace blindly swiping. Bridget cursed.

'Let's do one, Ken!'

I moved off, picking up speed. In the mirror I saw Trubal accelerating too, a limbed torch pursuing us through the misty night.

I stopped the car, looked around the cab.

'What now?' yelped Bridget.

I leaned out the window and whistled. Pistol didn't appear. I only corrected Trubal's course. He came blundering up the road, shooting sparks.

I whistled again. This time the hound appeared, struggling through the fence at the side of the road. I held the door open, until he jumped in my lap, barking in triumph.

'You and that BLOODY dog!' yelled Bridget.

I couldn't blame her. I hit the accelerator and tore off. There was no need to check the map. The Hope Tower was there, waiting on the horizon.

The heath is large enough to accommodate the construction of a megatall, but it cannot be the site for the tower. Thousands already live here. The land is occupied.

Regardless, I am here and there is work to be done. I turn my attention to improvements. To begin I elect to clear two broad avenues, carving the space into quarters. This will aid navigation of the camp and create order.

I hike up the slope to the north fence. One of the largest constructions in the shanty is here, a warren of huts clustered around a bus wreck, linked by improvised extensions. A crude flood defence protects the compound, wreaking havoc with the heath's natural drainage. A brief structural assessment confirms that it is highly unsafe and will have to go.

I wade around the bus, and find nine young adults gathered around a fire. The tallest sports a ragged waistcoat and a necklace of spent bullet casings. He frowns at me, spits on the floor, steps down the slope. He slips a metal bar from his belt, then slows his approach as he registers my height and build.

'What's you present?'

'I'm here to make repairs.'

Waistcoat is perplexed. He calls to his friends. They chatter among themselves, uncertain how to act.

I lift the bus by its fender and drag it clear of its moorings. The extensions fold up around it, making a great clattering sound that echoes across the camp.

Waistcoat leads the charge. I drop the bus, observe his screaming approach. He strikes clumsily, misses me. I disarm him and toss him back to his comrades. Their charge falters. They back up, peel away.

I resume dragging, ploughing a new north-south avenue through the camp. Huts and tents are crushed as I go. The people in my way cry out and scatter. If the police manning the fence hear the disturbance, they don't care.

At the foot of the camp I turn and tramp up the new avenue, clearing debris. A few children run around me in excitement, calling out in a dozen languages. The older ones stay hidden.

I work for another hour, until I realise I need to check in at Diorama. I pick up my tool bag and head for the crossing, followed by whispering children.

Up on the bridge I turn and survey the new road, my signature carved on the camp. I call to the dazed people below.

'Keep that way clear.'

LAY-BY

I took us along B roads over a flat slate landscape, avoiding the London Orbital. This was the furthest and fastest I'd travelled in the new cab and it was performing well. Of course a thick fuel stench blew through the fans, and it pulled to the right under braking, but aside from that it felt fresh enough to grace Rick's showroom.

Pistol sat on my lap, watching the gloomy world pass by, until he grew weary and padded onto the back seat, curling up beside the crumpled, muttering Fatty.

Bridget chewed her nails, pressed to the passenger door as if welded to it. I wondered about her recital at the river. How had Trubal caught fire like that? Had his clothes been soaked in fuel? There had to be a rational explanation.

Bridget's eyes darted at me, then away. It was getting tiresome.

'What are you thinking?' I asked.

'What do you think I'm thinking?'

Typical Real response. Still, months in Crayford had made me quite the interpreter. I thought I could guess.

'You're concerned about the conversation back at the ferry. You think I might be Ficial and you don't like it. I suppose you're either angry or afraid. Probably a mixture of the two.'

Her face couldn't settle on an expression.

'Look,' I said, 'if it makes you feel any better, whatever I was before, I am no longer. OK?'

She scratched her spotted cheek.

'So you're an ex-Ficial.' She spat the word. 'An ex-mass-murderer.'

Reals always obsessed about that part.

'Look, I was optimised for construction. I'm an engineer, a designer, a technical specialist.'

Bridget's eyes were hot. Her words came frosted.

'I saw what you things did. You don't need green eyes to be a monster.'

I made a noise, the kind of groan Fatty might emit. Bridget raised her chin at me.

'Are you telling me you never killed anyone?'

We weren't going to get past that. I thought about lying to make her feel better, but that would be all too Real. Besides, the truth was easier to remember.

'Yes. I culled a few. We all did. Orders.'

She stared at the road.

'"Culled". You make me sick.'

We let that one sit for a while. Part of her wanted to jump out the car. Part wanted to kill me. The other wanted to know more. It was a fairly typical reaction. Five minutes later she was talking to me again.

'Do you hate us? People, I mean?'

'I don't hate anything. If you're worried about me culling you, let me reassure you that I have abandoned the project. That is the domain of authentic Ficials.'

'You don't think you're Ficial?'

'It's a fact.' I held up my bandaged stumps. 'Look at this mess. If I were Ficial this would be half healed by now. Every trace of nanotech was taken from me. I'm a ruin. A derelict.'

'How did it happen?'

I could have told her the tale; how Leo Pander, the Real creator of the Ficial race – my race – was caught by Reals after the war, tortured and turned against his own creation. How he created a weaponised nano virus, designed to wipe out Ficial kind by infecting the nanotech in our bloodstream. How Starvie, my last Ficial fare, dosed me with the stuff on the orders of my old boss, making me weak, useless, vulnerable as Real people. Or how Control, the Ficial's coalesced core mind, had ordered the virus filtered from my blood and reproduced in service of its own insane ends.

But just thinking about it exhausted me. I fell back on a Fattyism instead.

'It's a long story.'

Bridget's shoulders fell a little. The useless holding statement seemed to have eased her fear. She sat in silence, watching the head-lights spread on the black road.

I thought I might get a peaceful journey, when she jumped in her seat and howled. 'Oh wow! Reverse, reverse!'

I pulled up, edged back the way we'd come. It took me a second to see it: a rust-red caravan parked in a lay-by, almost concealed by a high bank of snow. A sign was scrawled on a road sign in oil:

hot fud →

Services all the way out here. Who would have thought it? I turned in, cut the engine and looked around. The place was intact, but there were no lights.

'I'm not sure this place is open.'

'They will be,' said Bridget, slapping the door open. 'They have to be.'

I rolled out after her, finger stumps stung by the wind. I edged the damaged hand into my pocket and walked to the caravan, boots noisy in the pea gravel.

Bridget arrived at the door and knocked. No response. She rapped again, harder. This time something stirred. A woman's voice spoke to us through a grate.

'What do you want?'

'Something to eat, please,' said Bridget. 'Are you open?'

'I'm sleeping, girl.'

'Go on,' said Bridget. 'We're starving. We'll take whatever you've got.'

'I'll bet you will. I'll bet you'll take whatever you can carry, uh? Got some mates out there ready to rush me the moment I open the door, I expect. Am I right, eh?'

'No, honest. There's three of us. One of us is hurt. Let us in, missus, please.'

'How many vehicles you got?'

'Just one.'

The woman moved about inside. I thought she might fetch a weapon, until I heard a scraping sound overhead. I stepped back and observed a curving tube of metal twisting on the caravan roof. She had herself a periscope.

A minute later her voice returned to the grate.

'OK. Drop your weapons into the chute, please.'

A compartment emerged beside the door, large enough to take a rifle. We dropped the arms inside, watched it clamp shut. A bolt slid out of a catch and the door tipped open.

The woman was old, the oldest Real I'd seen in many years. Her shotgun looked a few years older. Kitchen blades hung from a belt at her waist.

'All right. Where's your friend?'

We showed her to the Landy, Bridget pointing at the senseless Fatty. The woman was more interested in Pistol, who jumped and barked at the window.

'Hello,' she said, her voice suddenly soft as dough. 'You're a pretty boy, aren't you? Aren't you, boy, eh?'

She turned to us.

'All right. Bring your mate inside and I'll make something for you.' She turned back to the dog, tapping fingers on the window. 'You're a lovely boy, aren't you?'

We dragged Fatty out, his feet carving a path in the gravel. Pistol briefly toured the lay-by, urinating on a few areas where his nose lingered. I whistled him inside, before the woman shut the door behind us, throwing braces over the entrance. There was a blast of glorious heat. She struck a match, held it to a pair of lanterns. She must have read something on my face.

'Don't worry. The windows are blacked out. Nobody knows I'm here until they pass. By then I've heard how many engines have arrived, and how many feet. You don't run a roadside caff without learning a few tricks.'

The lamplight revealed a remarkably healthy figure, with strong limbs and sharp eyes. Her skin was dark and smooth, devoid of the usual infections. Her hair was as thick and wiry as Pistol's. She wore an apron with a map on it, cluttered by garish images of animals. The legend 'Wildlife of Sri Lanka' was written over her chest.

She indicated we should sit at a small table, draped in a dazzling tablecloth. A bench seat ran on three sides, bearing embroidered cushions. Bridget and I propped the drooling Fatty between us on the bench.

The woman crossed her arms and frowned.

'Well, what have you got to trade?'

I pulled the tin of powdered milk from Fatty's pocket and placed it on the table.

'My God, my God,' she said, picking it up. 'Yes, this will do.'

She clapped her hands and whipped a curtain to one side, revealing a small stove. A pan, encrusted with brown matter, sat cold on the hob. She pressed the ignition. Blue gas flames danced under the pot. If she had gas she was no slouch.

'I have stew here, boys, will that do?'

We nodded. Bridget sank into the cushions and closed her eyes. I took out my damaged hand, dripping blood on the table. The old woman gasped, clutched her chest.

'Oh, that won't do. That won't do at all. I tell you what, for powdered milk you get the first-class treatment.'

She picked through her bulging cupboards until she found a small bottle of iodine and a strip of bandage. She pulled glasses from her apron, and sat on a stool by the table to dress my wound. I admired the finished item.

'That's very good,' I said.

'I used to be a nurse.'

'Er, missus.' Bridget pointed to the stove, where the pan was bubbling over, spitting matter onto the tops.

The woman made a clucking noise and fussed over the mess, vigorously stirring. A heady, thick scent filled the small space, provoking my stomach into a pained roar. She selected four filthy plates from a pile around the sink and handed us two measures of the brown mess. Bridget tucked in immediately. I was more cautious, seeing the many tubes in the meat.

'What's in it?' I asked.

'Meat,' she said, wiping her hands with the cloth. 'Don't worry, it tastes better when it's been in the pan for a while.'

'He doesn't worry.'

Fatty. He sat up, roused by the odour. 'Can I get in on this feast?'

The woman passed a plate, winning polite thanks from Fatty. We filled our bellies in minutes, the heat warming our chilled bones. The old lady tidied around us, keeping one hand at her waist, near the bulge in the apron. After food she served us tea, then went outside to smoke.

Fatty took the chance to catch up.

'So where are we? Near the tower?'

'Not far,' I said. 'Maybe another hour's drive.'

'I see.' Fatty shifted in his seat, but regretted it, wincing in pain. His neck seemed to be giving him particular bother.

'I can't believe Marsh,' he said. 'Turning us in like that. What do you make of it?'

Reals were always encouraging each other to speculate. How could I know why Marsh had done what she did? I listed the possibilities.

'Trubal might have showed up by chance. She might have told him of her own account. Or he might have killed a few of her people until she shared. Who knows?'

'So,' said Bridget. 'Ken's Ficial.' Her spots flared like a warning display.

Fatty shrugged.

'Not really. Not any more.'

'Yeah, but he was, wasn't he? I tell you what, Phil, Clive will go ballistic when he hears about this.'

Fatty brooded over his tea.

'Only if some idiot tells him.'

'That's true,' said Bridget, examining her nails. 'It would be a shame if somebody let the cat out of the bag. Harbouring the enemy like you have – well I can't imagine what horrors Clive would dream up for you.'

Fatty snarled.

'What is it you want, Bridget?'

'It just occurs to me,' said the girl, 'that we haven't put a figure on the share of loot. I've put a lot into this enterprise already, without any kind of contract. I think we should draw one up, as it happens.'

Fatty slammed a fist on the table, startling the girl.

'Are you winding me up?'

'I'm the one that stopped that other Ficial getting Ken. If it weren't for me we'd all be floating face down in the river. Stop me if I'm wrong.' She looked at me.

'Five per cent,' snapped Fatty.

'Twenty-five,' said Bridget. 'That's as low as I'll go.'

I thought I'd spill my news, as tempers were already frayed.

'You may as well make it fifty-fifty. I'm not coming with you.'

Fatty lowered his tea and said quietly:

'Are you still on that?'

'That's right. I'm not going up the tower with you. I'll drop you as promised, but I'm not taking any part in your ridiculous expedition.'

Bridget was as alarmed as Fatty.

'Why not?'

'Do you really have to ask me that question?'

Bridget's blank stare indicated that she did. I waggled the three fingers on my left hand and explained.

'You're planning on scaling the world's only megatall building. It is half complete and highly unsafe. There will be no power and you have no torches. There will be no elevators, so you will have to take the stairs, climbing up hundreds of floors. You have no map or schematics, no training, no safety equipment, and, unless I am mistaken, no real plan. You simply intend to search for gold that, if it is there, will be concealed in a toxic cloud. Finally, you have no idea how to transport the gold to the surface without demolishing the entire tower. The whole enterprise is folly.'

Bridget sat back and blew out air.

'When you put it like that . . .'

Fatty puffed his chest out at me. 'Where are you going to go, eh? Your own freaks won't have you back, will they?'

'I'm going to figure that out. All I know is that I can't carry on in this—' I examined my bandaged hand '—condition.'

The door creaked open. The woman entered, smiling. I thought she might offer us dessert, until I noticed she was gripping her shotgun.

'Well, boys, it's been lovely having you, but it's time for you to be on your way.'

Fatty smiled.

'It's all right, madam. Sorry if we raised our voices, we were just—'

'Please don't bother with that,' she said, fixing me with dark eyes. 'I've heard every word and I'm afraid I can't have one of these things in my caff. Leave now, please.'

I stood up. Pistol rolled off my feet, grunting disapproval, as the woman edged us out the door.

'You do understand, don't you?' she said. 'I can't trust you in my home.'

Fatty snarled at her.

'I hope you're not expecting a tip.'

We backed out of the caravan, retreated, dropped into the car. I started the engine. The woman tossed our weapons in the tailgate and stepped to the passenger side, fingers flexing on her shotgun. She nodded at Fatty.

'I don't know what you think you're doing, mister, but you shouldn't be driving around with a Ficial.'

Fatty shrugged.

'He's not Ficial any more.'

The woman's gaze cut to me for a moment, then back to Fatty.

'Just because it looks human doesn't mean it thinks human. You can't trust it. It's an abomination. An insult to nature.'

Fatty spread his arm at the dead land, the freezing night.

'You think nature could get any more insulted?'

She grasped the gun a little tighter.

'Why you want to climb that tower?'

Fatty pointed. 'Because it's there.'

She wasn't amused.

'It isn't safe, outside or in. Something in that place makes people crazy. A dark spirit.'

'How would you know?' snapped Fatty.

'I used to work there, that's how.'

She stepped to the passenger door, whispered in Fatty's ear. Then she pressed something into his hand and backed away.

I am sleeping when the signal comes through, stirring the blood, jolting me upright on my bunk.
    – Control.
    – Kenstibec. You were tracked passing into a restricted area. Explain.
    – My guard believed it was the site for the city project. It was not. I used the time profitably by making simple improvements to the existing camp.
    – Kenstibec. The area is confirmed as the tower site.
    – How is that possible? It is designated as a detainment centre.
    – A relocation column is being organised. Population of illegal encampment will be resettled north.
    – I see.
    – However, convoy will take several weeks to assemble. If you believe you can improve conditions in the camp, you may continue until resettlement begins.
    – Confirmed. The proximity of the site to Diorama HQ is striking.
    – It is not coincidence, Kenstibec. It is likely that the competition process is corrupt. We calculate that Diorama have already secured the contract.
    – How?
    – Projects of this size are often compromised. Project client is maintaining appearance of fairness, but probability high that it has already made illegal agreement.
    – Who is the project client?
    – Unknown. Emergency government is reluctant to share information, probably due to complicity in the criminal enterprise.
    – You will not intervene?
    – Only in the event that lives are endangered. Corporate criminality, though unfortunate, must be tolerated for now, to provide employment. However, as the augmentation mission evolves and security improves we

will work closer with humanity, and eventually eradicate this kind of fraud. We will teach people the folly of crime, teach them to cooperate for the good of the species.

— People seem unwilling to cooperate, Control.

— Example.

— Many of those in the shanty have young. They must know that this leads to overcrowding, to shortages, yet still they breed.

— We know, Kenstibec. Numbers require controlling. But we can only try to persuade. We are here to augment, not to rule.

APPROACHES

'What a great heap of stone,' said Fatty. 'Without charm or taste.'

The tower grew in definition as we travelled through the night. The road was curiously free of wrecks, so I could peer at the structure as I drove, assessing its condition. Only the lower bulb was visible, and it seemed relatively intact. A mound of blast debris slumped over the lower floors on the east face, but hundreds more storeys were unscathed, a kilometre-high dome rising to the cloudbank like a mountain propping up the sky. What there was of the upper, inverted bulb was obscured by cloud.

Fatty did his best to look unimpressed. Bridget gaped in wonder. Now that we were getting close a sense of the tower's vastness was hitting home.

'How does it, like, stay up?' said Bridget.

'I'm with spotted dick,' said Fatty. 'Why doesn't it collapse?'

It was a fair question. Seeing it close up, I was perplexed. Built to original specs it would have been impressive, if not entirely unexpected, for it to have survived the nuke blast wave. But I happened to know that it hadn't been built to spec. The whole thing was corrupted, riddled by substandard materials. That made its survival nothing short of miraculous.

'So,' said Fatty. 'You're really just going to drop us off and leave? You're not curious to inspect your baby up close?'

'I told you. I'm not coming with you.'

'Look.' He studied his podgy mitts. 'We can't do it without you, OK?'

I slapped the steering wheel.

'You can't do it with me, either. What does it take for you to compute that? Maybe the gold is still intact, but—'

Fatty jumped in his seat.

'The gold's intact?'

'Well, the tower is in far better condition than I expected. It stands to reason that the damper may remain. But that doesn't mean—'

'So it's doable?' said Fatty, good eye widening with intent.

'No, it's not doable. Listen to me. If you want my advice you should camp somewhere quiet for a couple of weeks, then go home and tell Clive you failed. You won't be the conquering hero, but you won't kill yourself trying to achieve the impossible.'

Bridget leaned forward.

'Actually, Phil, I was thinking. If Ken doesn't think it's a goer . . . I mean who are we to question the expert?'

Fatty spat something blue out the window.

'You want out, Bridget? Already? What happened to Andover?'

Bridget frowned.

'I'm not saying I want out exactly. But just look at the size of it, Phil. It would take for ever. We're not mountaineers, are we?'

'Exactly,' I said.

'Fine,' said Fatty, 'I'll hire a fucking sherpa then. There's bound to be some locals who know their way about.'

Bridget worried at her neck spots.

'Locals? How do you know there'll be anyone there?'

Fatty pointed.

'Doesn't anyone else see that light?'

I saw it. A glowing amber arch. The light from hundreds of camp fires, glowing around the tower base. It was such a curious sight I nearly crashed into a column of Reals.

They were caught in the headlights, more and more of them, walking either side of the road towards the tower. Many wore rags, or travelled completely naked. Some chanted, gestured at the tower. Others moved in teams, dragging great sleds of debris up the old road.

The crowd thickened, turning into a heaving mass as we reached the crossroads. We turned right and crawled up a narrow track, packed in tight by pilgrims. Their chanting grew almost as loud as the cab engine.

It was odd, driving through the area where I had once strolled with Bree. The neighbourhood had simply disappeared. Every brick had been stripped away. Even the street had been ripped up, the road turning into a mud track. The town was an enormous camp, marked by fires, shrines and round, clay huts.

My head began to swim. I pulled up at the edge of the camp. Fatty slapped my arm.

'What are you doing?'

I stepped out of the car, suddenly finding it hard to breathe. Uncontrollable shivers seized me. I stumbled and dropped in the mud. Pistol jumped out, licked my face in concern. The pilgrims ignored me, walking by with eyes fixed on the tower.

'I shouldn't have come here.'

I don't know why I said it. No one was listening. I dropped into the mud face first, grateful to feel something cool on my burning brow.

Then it all went a familiar dark.

I taste salt. I hear cheering. I cheer too, with the two Reals. We watch Brixton barricade collapse, then burst into flame. The fire tickles the cloud, lights up the river.

Why am I cheering? I cheer until it hurts, until I gargle and choke, underwater now. I swim down, deep into the old, feculent river. Down, with Control, Starvie, with hundreds of Starvies who never awoke. I glimpse the Ritzy cinema. The building is unreal, intact at the centre of a giant whirlpool. Starvie holds my hand, guides me into the vortex. It's a cloud now, a black, boiling cloud. My skin burns. I watch it warp and twist.

A hand on my collar. It drags me from the cloud river. I vomit black water. My fingernails scrape on the deck. The ferry turns, its stern swinging out to the river.

A shape on the far shore. A dome reflected in a river in the sky. Lights twinkle over the surface. It twists, snaps its limpet joins, moves down the deck towards me, where I wait in the cab, fingers on wheel.

Marsh smiles brilliant white teeth. Leans in the cab window.

'A space where you'd fit.'

I heard a fire crackle. I tasted smoke and damp. It took a moment to pull my eyelids free of their glue.

'Welcome home.' Fatty grinned over me. A clay ceiling curved

74

behind him, decorated by paintings of figures, dancing in the firelight.

I tried to sit, but could only roll over. Bridget crouched at my side, scratching Pistol behind the ear. The dog sniffed my face, gave me a few powerful licks before Bridget drew him clear. I was drained, barely able to ask the vital question:

'Where's the cab?'

Fatty rolled his eye.

'Relax, it's parked.'

'Safe?'

'Well, hardly an NCP, granted, but the natives won't mess with it. I've made arrangements.'

He knelt, offered a bottle of water and a tin of chopped tomatoes. I snatched them from his grasp, consuming with fast food fury. I was getting Realer every minute.

'Where did you get this?' I said, licking tomato juice from the can lid. Fatty shrugged.

'We've been busy. You've been out two entire days with the fever. Blood sweats and all.'

Wonderful. My traitorous body's first sickness.

'While you were out we earned some local currency. We've nearly all the supplies we need for the climb now.'

He patted his rucksack, which was packed to bursting.

'Well,' I said, 'if you've everything you need, I'll be on my way.'

I tried to sit, but was still so numb I found it troublesome. Fatty assisted, drawing my arm over his shoulder.

'I shouldn't have to remind you you're no longer übermensch. You nearly died, you fool. You're not going anywhere without help.'

'I have to get moving,' I showed him the wound Trubal had cut for me. 'In case you've forgotten I'm wanted.'

'You're not Dick Turpin,' said Fatty. 'You're a jumped-up chippie with a knackered hand. And, much as I acknowledge your race's ruthless bloodlust, I doubt that example we left by the river has the brains to track us. Christ you're heavy.'

Bridget whistled to the dog, who jumped into her arms. She fastened him into her jacket, so that only his head was exposed, and followed us out of the hut.

Fatty and I paused and surveyed the scene stretching before us. The camp clustered around the tower base, a sprawl of huts and barrows dusted with snow, glowing in the mucky orange light of smoky fires.

The Hope Tower dominated everything. The hexagrid, the honey-comb surface that wrapped the tower, was badly chewed around a band of twenty floors. A great scorch mark rose above the debris mound on the eastern flank, testifying to the nuke blast it had shrugged off.

Some floors appeared illuminated. I craned my neck back, looked up to where the tower met the cloud. I gaped until my head began to spin. Fatty looked too.

'Who do you think has the lights on?'

'Squatters,' I said. 'Could be original tenants even. There were businesses operating on lower floors when the thing was half built.'

I urged him into the camp, wanting to get closer to the tower. Fatty obliged, pointing out local spots he'd discovered on the way. Bridget trailed behind, quiet save an occasional murmur into Pistol's ear. I might have asked her what was troubling her, but for the moment walking was enough to occupy me.

'Now what do you make of them?'

Fatty pointed ahead. Strange metalworks, from twelve to twenty feet high, stretched along the camp perimeter like pylons. I took them for a fence of some kind, until I realised they were moving, manipulated by ropes and pulleys. The closer we got the clearer their purpose became.

'Catapults.'

Fatty didn't need to confirm. A metal arm snapped into view, hurling a loose mass of stone and trash at the tower, impacting on the already damaged floors. Other limbs were ratcheted back, preparing fresh assaults. We moved among their positions, and discovered the siege engines were crafted from old construction machinery. Count on people to get creative when there's the chance to destroy something.

Here the camp was thick with Reals. Some worked the catapults, priming the mechanisms or fetching loads of brick and paving. They toiled among pockets of religious frenzy, where naked pilgrims weltered in the mud, pulling out hair and screaming at the tower. Others picked through the crowd selling 'relics', or beckoned us into huts and lean-tos, offering palm reading and miracle cures. An old man seized Bridget's arm.

'This will make your spots vanish, poppet. Three drops and that beautiful face'll return once more. Isn't that worth your money?'

'Fuck off,' snapped Fatty.

Bridget was interested.

'It can cure them?'

The man's eyes sparkled.

'Of course, my dear. Proven time and again. A fluid blessed by the Soothsayer himself, imbibed with the cleansing power of the almighty.'

'How much?' asked Bridget.

'Why I'll take that dog in exchange. A more than fair trade.'

Fatty took the man by his shirt and shook him.

'If you don't clear off it'll take more than the almighty to sort your face out.'

The man scuttled away.

'So in case you can't figure it out,' said Fatty, turning to me, 'your monstrosity is a major draw for every religious nutter in the country. They've pooled under the leadership of this Soothsayer character. Can't tell you what his game is, other than the usual: preaching damnation and flogging salvation. He doesn't let his people enter the tower, but I can deal with that.'

We circled the structure for some time, looking over the tower, thinking our thoughts. Mine were getting clearer all the time. The lights in the tower meant life. But what kind of life?

A woman dived before us, her skin covered in tattoos.

'I can read thee dreams,' she howled, eyeing Pistol. 'For the right trade.'

'No thanks.' Fatty pushed her aside and moved on. I thought about going after her, then came to my senses. Fatty continued:

'Yes, the place is positively clogged with nutters, but their mission makes a certain sense. They believe your project here tainted the sky, polluted it. Soothsayer claims to have had some kind of vision – says the moment they demolish the tower clouds will part, birds will sing, bunnies will bounce, that sort of thing. You can see why the idea resonates.' He pointed up the dome, lodged in the leaden canopy.

'So, what do you make of it, anyway? Does it look safe to climb?'

I shook my head.

'Absolutely not.'

Fatty drew a foil pack from his pocket and popped a pill.

'You think it might come down?'

'Oh yes.'

Fatty exchanged a look with Bridget. Scratched his beard.

'All right, forgetting the imminent collapse issue for a moment, what else do you have to say? What about a way in?'

I had a pretty good idea about that already, but I was beginning to think I might need to reserve it for my own purposes. I talked through the other options.

'Every entrance to the subterranean levels appears blocked by debris or collapsed. You could climb up the debris pile and go in through the eighth– or ninth-floor windows. Of course, you'd have to travel under this bombardment.'

Fatty kicked around in the mud, thinking, occasionally eyed by Bridget. Exhausted and shivering, I sat by a smouldering campfire and watched the tower, wondering about my condition, about the ascent, about the state of particular floors.

Then a bell sounded, ringing through the camp, rousing the pilgrims from their devotions. A Real had emerged from the nearest barrow, tossing a hand bell, face obscured by a white hood. Other hoods followed in his train, bearing torches and chanting. The pilgrims around us abandoned their tasks and rushed to the procession, dropping on their knees before it. The hoods were coming our way.

Fatty slapped Bridget on the shoulder.

'When in Rome.'

They dropped next to me, palms in supplication. I watched the hoods, saw six of them carrying an old park bench. Another hood was seated there, wearing a flak jacket over his robes. Fatty sniffed and muttered in my ear.

'The character in the body armour is the Soothsayer. Good to see God's servants have the same faith in his divine protection as ever.'

The train halted, the bell ringer pinching the clapper. The gathered pilgrims hummed expectantly, until the Soothsayer stood, brandishing a megaphone. A hush fell over the area.

'Brothers and sisters, peace be with you.'

'And with you,' chorused the crowd. The Soothsayer paused, looked around him, feeding off his audience's expectation.

'We all know why we are here. We are here to atone.'

The crowd moaned. Repeated the word, over and over.

'It is our forefathers we atone for. They who angered the creator. They who consorted with the Devil. They who nursed his demon progeny in that cesspit, Brixton. They who raised this ziggurat, this pagan bosom, this monument to vanity, this compost heap of ambition. They would have built all the way to the stars if they could have, so great was their pride!'

The crowd churned and chanted, aroused by his words.

'Is it any wonder that we angered God? Is it any wonder he sealed off the sun with that carpet of smoke?'

He was getting louder, building to something.

'So, you ask: how do we make amends? How do we cleanse ourselves of their sin? I reply: isn't it obvious? Isn't our gathering here answer enough? God has delivered us here. His hand guided us to this place so that we may send this false idol crashing into the sewer from whence it crawled! For once we do that, once we level this aberration, so His anger will lift, so the clouds will part, and so His heavenly blue firmament will return! He will make her wilderness like Eden, and her desert like the garden of the Lord! Let us not tire in our assault, let us not fail to believe in final victory! For when the tower falls the cloud will part. I have seen it! I have seen it!'

The crowd exploded into screams and cheers. Fatty stood up and left us, pushing through the elated mass, headed for the Soothsayer.

'Phil!' cried Bridget. 'Phil, what are you playing at?'

She helped me up and we followed, as the hoods turned for their barrow. We worked through the crush of pilgrims, walking parallel to the procession, Fatty slipping in and out of sight. The hoods unclipped their belts, which were studded with glass shards and metal strips, and began whipping themselves. Black blood seeped into their shirt backs.

'Booloo,' said Bridget. 'They're all completely booloo.'

The train disappeared into the barrow, leaving two guards each side of a curtained entrance. Fatty halted a little distance away and called us over.

'Right,' he said, 'we're going to go in there and talk to this guy. Before we do, let me make one thing absolutely clear. On no account should either of you speak, understand? Leave all the talking to me.'

Bridget tapped her temple.

'Have you taken leave of your senses, Philip? Did you not hear the mad monk's sermon? You want to swan in there uninvited, with a bloody Ficial? I'm not going in there and neither should you.'

Fatty held up hushing hands.

'Keep your voice down, will you? Wait here. We'll manage without you. Won't we?'

He eyed me expectantly.

'Sure,' I said.

It occurred to me that blood loss might have made me vulnerable to suggestion. I tried to focus as we approached the guards, having the feeling I'd need my wits about me.

From the bridge I inspect the camp, find my two avenues still relatively clear. I vault the barrier again. Land among the beggars and street artists. I work up the avenues, mentally mapping the route for the simple drainage I plan to excavate. I take a trench spade from my pack and set to work digging. The ground is soft and I work quickly. People creep around the road edge, watching me like a bomb ticking in the open.

Then I notice a small, dark woman. She stands in the road, wearing tired robes, headscarf, and a crooked smile. That should indicate she is happy, but I am learning that smiles are more complex than that.

'Young man,' she says, 'who sent you out here?'

I do not correct the 'man' assumption.

'Nobody.'

'Was it a church?'

'No,' I reply, 'it was not a church.'

'Why are you doing this?' She sweeps her arms at the cleared road, at the drainage trench. I consider the question, ask another in reply:

'Why have you not done it?'

She snorts, draws closer, regards me with keen brown eyes. She squeezes my arm as if testing for ripeness.

'People are scared. Think you're here to evict us.'

'No.'

'Well then, someone has got to thank you.' Her grip is surprisingly strong. 'My name is Adede. Come to my house. Eat something.'

She pulls hard. I leave the spade in the soil and follow her through the warren of steaming pots, trash heaps and fires. The children are excited by my presence. The older people flee, or stare, drugged dumb. Some have sweating sickness. Others lie dying in the open. I wonder how people degrade so swiftly. Is it an inherent defect or a failure of social structure? Adede steps over them, clutching a rag to her face.

Her shack has a colourful, clean cloth draped over the entrance. I crawl after her, into a small space warmed by a brazier. A pot simmers over the flames. She introduces me to her children: William, twelve, stares behind thick black locks. Mary, six, holds scissors and glue. She is cutting up plastics, creating a mosaic on the shack wall. It is an accurate depiction of London's skyline.

Adede pours tea, passes it to me.

'Forgive our people for their manners. The sickness takes their minds and the drugs take their souls.'

Souls do not exist, but I refrain from mentioning the fact. She stares into her soup.

'It was the same where we came from. I thought it would be different in this country. I was wrong. Although it is certainly wetter.'

The boy whispers something to his mother. She nods approval. He runs outside, followed by his sister.

Adede takes a deep breath, then looks right at me.

'I know I will lose one of them,' she says. 'But what can a mother do?'

Another human form of expression: the question with no answer.

BARROW

Fatty advanced on the barrow guards, hands in pockets and whist-ling. They raised weapons and challenged him: friend or foe.

'Friends,' said Fatty. 'Friends and fellow pilgrims.'

They were hostile, but Fatty was in no rush. He leaned on a handy post and began talking with them, asking them questions about origin and occupation. His speech confused and flattered, creating the illusion of a long-held mutual trust. After ten minutes they were eager to grant us an audience.

You had to hand it to him. Fatty could make people dance to his tune. I wondered that he'd never overthrown Clive and seized the Phone Throne. A coup was well within his talents. But Fatty had no lust for power. He was too restless, always in search of diversion. If he ever did get the tower gold he'd almost certainly lose it all at the track, and be well satisfied too.

The taller guard ushered us through the heavy curtain, into the heat of a long, broad chamber, partitioned by wattle fences. The roof was a clay and earth mix baked into a coat-hanger mesh. The walls were a Neolithic arrangement of huge stone slabs.

Our guard led us to a central chamber, dominated by a long dining table and a fire burning in a hearth. A figure sat hunched over a bowl of soup at the head of the table. The Soothsayer. He had hair in all the wrong places – in his nose, in his ears, and knotted in a beard where his chin should have been. His pate was egg bald. His lips were wet. His flagellants were arrayed either side, heads and backs bare and bleeding.

One of our guards whispered into the Soothsayer's ear. He glanced at us, stirring his spoon.

'They may approach.'

The guard beckoned to us. Fatty motioned that I should stay put, and paced five steps ahead.

'O Soothsayer,' he said, bowing. 'My thanks for your time and favour. We have travelled many miles to join your great crusade.'

The Soothsayer smiled slightly.

'Oh yes?'

'Indeed,' said Fatty, drawing himself up. 'We come to aid you in God's work. Let us assist you, and I can guarantee that within a month the devil's tower will lie dashed and broken in the mud.'

Many of the flagellants stopped eating. The Soothsayer pushed his bowl away and motioned to a seat.

'Please join me.' He turned to his acolytes. 'Friends, leave us.'

The flagellants stood, bowed and filed out. I sat across from Fatty, halfway up the table. The Soothsayer regarded us for a moment, smile fixed. I had the uncomfortable notion that he recognised Fatty: not as an individual, but as a particular make of man.

'So,' he said at last, picking up a tankard and swinging it at Fatty. 'You believe you can bring down the tower. Destroy it in ... How long did you say?'

'A month, Your Grace,' said Fatty. 'Sooner, God willing.'

'An impressive timescale. My people have been here for some time, working each day to reduce the idol. We expect it to take many more years before our work is complete. We believe God intends us to suffer before granting forgiveness.'

'Oh naturally,' said Fatty. 'We all suffer in His name. But the Devil is strong. He works tirelessly to blind the minds of the unbelieving and keep them captive in his treachery. Accept our help, and together we can hurl the tower into the lake of sulphur, and return God's light to the world.'

Fatty's language was getting colourful. The Soothsayer pulled back his lips.

'You are that certain you will succeed?'

'Of course,' said Fatty. 'I have faith we can climb it.'

The Soothsayer frowned.

'You intend to climb the tower? That is no easy task.'

'I can handle a few stairs,' said Fatty.

'The climb is the least of the trials you would face. There are people in there. Or at least, what were once people. They have been seduced by the ruin, turned to its protection. They conjure a great demon to defend the tower's halls. Hundreds of my people have entered intending to bring it down from within. None returned. Why would you do any better, my son?'

'Because we are the emissaries of Clive, King of Kent. Because we believe in the providence of his dreams.'

The Soothsayer's smiled edged a little wider.

'Dreams?'

Fatty flourished his hands, weaving lies with stubby fingers.

'Yes, Your Grace. Our king had a dream twenty-one nights ago. He saw an old woman, rolling a steel ball in her hand and ringing a bell. The next night he dreamed that he pulled a great oak from the ground, roots and all. The following night he had his most powerful vision yet: a stranger came to him at the city gate, offering the key to the sky. When the King took the key the clouds parted, and the land was drowned in dazzling sunshine.'

The Soothsayer blinked.

'Fascinating. What did your king believe these dreams augured?'

'He could not say, Your Holiness,' replied Fatty. 'Neither he nor his astrologers could deduce their meaning. But King Clive is a determined and wise ruler, and was convinced that they held an important truth. The very next night, out of the thickest snowstorm in a year, the stranger from his dream arrived. This stranger, in fact.'

The Soothsayer eyed me doubtfully. Fatty continued.

'He was brought to the King and questioned. The more he spoke, the more the meaning of the King's final dream became clear. Believe it or not, Your Grace, this mendicant you see before you holds the key to felling the tower.'

The Soothsayer drew a breath. 'I see.' He tapped the tabletop with his palms and stood, his garment hanging loose.

'And how is it that you intend to destroy the tower, traveller?'

Fatty turned his eye on me, worried lest I sink his tale with Ficial honesty. I didn't like the way he was painting me into the picture, but if it would help get Fatty in the tower and out of my hair it would be worth helping. I tried out the method I'd learned from the master. Garnish the lie with truth.

'I worked on the tower,' I said, 'before the war.'

The Soothsayer clicked his tongue.

'I understood that the Ficial demons built it alone.'

'Ficials worked the upper floors, but there were many of us working further down.'

The lie came easily enough. Not any lie either: the most humiliating untruth of all: that I was Real.

The Soothsayer stepped behind me.

'You are saying that you know of some weakness that might be exploited, is that right, my son?'

Fatty took up the story.

'He has told us about a great pendulum that lies near the top of the tower. A ball of steel which keeps the tower balanced.'

'It's called a tuned mass damper,' I said, helping Fatty out. The Soothsayer tapped his fingers on the back of my chair.

'And you intend to destroy this pendulum, is that correct?'

'Not destroy it,' said Fatty. 'Cut it free. We will only need to unhitch it from its mooring and the entire rotten construct will come crashing in.'

'Taking you with it.'

'That's right.' Fatty pressed a hand to his chest and closed his eyes. 'We are prepared to die in service of God. We wish, as you do, to see the Earth reborn, to see the promise of a better life returned to our young. A better future is reward enough for us.'

The Soothsayer circled the table, considering the pitch.

'And what would you have me do?'

'We need you to lead your people to a safe distance. Take your siege weapons and your valuables and depart – probably further north, where you will all be safe. Yea, for the tower is tall, and we know not how or where it will tumble.'

I could see Fatty thought he might have overdone it with the 'yea', but the Soothsayer wasn't bothered.

'Very well. We will allow you access to the tower, and we will cease our bombardment, for a week. That should give you ample time to reach the upper floors. But I will not withdraw my people until I know you have made some progress. I must insist that you signal us to tell us you have reached the necessary floor. Then, and only then, will we withdraw.'

'Then God be praised,' said Fatty, 'for I have a flare gun in my pack. We will shoot it when we have reached our objective, allowing you time to depart.'

The Soothsayer held up his hands and stood by the fire.

'Then come, children, and receive my blessing.'

We left our seats and knelt before him. He touched his palm to my head and muttered a dead language. Then he stepped away, clapping his hands.

'We will seal the covenant with a sacrifice. You will be witnesses.' He nodded to the guards. 'Bring me a sinner.'

The guard nodded, departed the same way the pilgrims had gone. We heard his voice raised, and a commotion behind the curtain. Soon the pilgrims were pouring out again, dragging a shrieking man, naked but for a coned hat. He was thrown before us, moaning.

Fatty eyed the prisoner.

'What did he do?'

The Soothsayer shrugged.

'If a man also lie with mankind, as he lieth with a woman, both of them have committed an abomination: they shall surely be put to death.'

The pilgrims closed around us, clutching plastic sheets. The Soothsayer was handed a long club adorned with nails.

'I will stand on the top of the hill,' he said, 'with the rod of God in my hand.'

'Amen,' answered the pilgrims.

'Oh no. Please don't bother on our behalf,' said Fatty, good eye wide in horror.

The Soothsayer hurled the staff into the man's skull. Fatty retched at the cracking sound. The Soothsayer ripped out the staff, then hurled it once more with the practised swing of a butcher. Trubal would have approved.

Panting, the Soothsayer handed the staff to a guard, and raised his hands in prayer.

'We give thanks, O Lord, and ask that you bless these your penitent servants in carrying out your exalted works. For yours is the everlasting power. Amen.'

The body was wrapped in the bloodied sheets and dragged from the room.

'Go now,' said the Soothsayer. 'With my blessing.'

The guards ushered us out. We walked into the camp, until we found the shivering shape of Bridget. Pistol jumped up to greet me. I scratched his chin.

'You did well in there, freak show,' said Fatty. 'I couldn't have done better myself.'

'That man is no fool,' I said. 'He saw through us.'

'Yep. I thought we might be in trouble for a minute there. But he's not so daft as to turn down a bit of entertainment for the troops. You and I both know how boring a siege can get, and how invaluable a distraction can be.'

'What are you saying?' said Bridget. 'The Pope thinks we can't do it?'

'He doesn't think we can't,' said Fatty. 'He knows we can't.'

I drain my cup of soup. Adede expects a pleasantry.

'*You have a good home,' I say.*

'*Thank you. Thank you.'*

'*I must return to work now.'*

I pick up my tool bag and leave the shack, heading for the north-south avenue. The sky over the city is suddenly dark, a new storm gathering.

I hear a commotion, children screaming in excitement. I turn towards the noise and find a large group of young people laughing and yelling. They are gathered in a circle around a concrete slab.

William is the centre of attention, sitting on a BMX, absently watching as his sister lies down on the concrete. She holds out her arms, a huge smile on her face.

William waits for the crowd to settle, then sits up on his bike. He rolls it towards his sister and jumps the bike. He lands the front wheel between her right arm and chest. The crowd gasps, watching as he holds the bike, twisting on its front wheel, rear wheel aloft like bucking hind legs.

He spins anticlockwise, then jumps again, landing the front wheel the other side of Mary's chest, rear wheel still raised. The children chant, arms thrown up:

'*Will-yam, Will-yam, Will-yam!'*

He does not react, fixed in concentration. He jumps again, dropping onto his rear wheel this time, and begins bouncing the bike around his sister – to the left of her head, to the right, then either side of her chest, her waist, her legs, stopping below her feet. There he spins again, manipulating the bike like a fifth limb.

Huge excitement. Screams of disbelief. None are louder than Mary, who rolls and chokes on her laughter. William rides in a slow circle around her, acknowledging his audience with a wave. Such skill.

Then, over the children's cheers, I hear a different sound: a wave of fright, rolling up the shanty from the south. William hears it too. He stops his bike. 'Wossat?'

I leap onto the nearest roof and peer down the hill. A crowd of men are pouring through a breach in the south fence. Most are on foot, but some are on horseback. They shoot down shanty dwellers, toss petrol bombs, hammer and kick at the shacks. Many of them carry flags, bearing a symbol like a wolf's head. Under the icon is smeared the word 'Truth'.

SERVICE ENTRANCE

Bridget and Fatty helped me hike back. We followed the perimeter, completing a circle of the tower base. There was a lull in the bombardment, pilgrims abandoning siege engines in search of rest and nourishment. Now they huddled around campfires, eating and chattering, calm after a day's toil and the ecstasy of the hooded procession. Few considered the tower now.

The world had become quite a peaceful place, until Pistol began whining and struggling in Bridget's coat.

'Ow! Take it easy!' Bridget dropped him at our feet, where he ran in excited circles, barking and rearing up at the tower. I looked up, traced some movement in the night.

Paper. A cloud of scrolls tumbled about the tower, snaking and sailing down the dome. We watched them until they began falling around us, and Fatty snatched one out of the air. He held it before us, a long, nicotine parchment covered in images, interspersed with small text paragraphs. The paper quality was poor, and the ink smudged on my fingers. One paragraph caught my eye:

Demon tales 'superstition' according to experts

Tales of a demon guarding the lower reaches of the tower are completely unfounded, according to experts. Boffins report that the demon is a myth created by pilgrim fundamentalists to frighten hardworking families from entering the tower in search of a better life.

Another story read:

'I have never been so happy,' said Ken Hawkins, 50, originally from Eastbourne. 'Things were awful in the pilgrim camp, but now we are in the tower my family have all we need to eat and drink and complete freedom. Here we have a luxury apartment with beautiful views, and decent, hardworking families for neighbours.

'We were looking for civilisation and now we've found it,' he added.

A picture accompanied the article: a smudged shot of a family group, grinning in an apartment. Something was very wrong about the image.

'Says they've got power in there,' said Bridget, examining another paper, 'water and food too.'

She passed it to Fatty, who read with interest.

'I wouldn't trust it,' I said. 'If things were that good I doubt they'd advertise. Whoever wrote that had other motives.'

'Well, it looks better in there than out here, right, Phil?'

Fatty eyed the spotty girl.

'Does that mean your enthusiasm for our project is rekindled?'

'You bet,' she replied, wrenching a stuck trainer from the mud and wiggling her blistered toes. 'The sooner we leave Camp Booloo the better, that's what I say.'

Fatty nudged me.

'What about you. Still planning a departure?'

'That's right.'

'Oh well. Let's at least have a drink before you go.'

He pointed to a sign, painted on a large hut: **Food Court.**

I should have declined the fat man's invitation. I intended to lose him and Bridget as soon as possible. I had my own ideas about the tower, and the Reals would only get in my way. But I was a slave to hunger now, and couldn't resist.

We followed the sign down a mud slope into a shallow crater, its bottom a cleared remnant of the concrete tower plaza. I assessed the surface with interest, pleased to have taken Fatty up on his offer.

The Food Court had a Portakabin serving as a kitchen. Plastic garden furniture was scattered over the cleared space around it. The place wasn't doing much business. There was only one other patron, slumped unconscious on a chair. We took seats, Pistol curling at my feet. Fatty swallowed a pill and called for service. A small waiter appeared from the Portakabin and dashed to our table. Fatty ordered three hot drinks, paying with tokens I didn't recognise. He took a handful of change and added it to his wallet, glancing briefly at me.

'You seem well off,' I said. 'How exactly did you earn so fast?'

Fatty shrugged and folded his hands behind his head.

'A transaction here, a transaction there. Joined in on the relic bonanza. These people buy anything if you spin a compelling origin yarn.'

Bridget wore a trapped expression, chewing her nails. I tapped her elbow.

'Something on your mind?'

She said nothing. The waiter arrived with our drinks. Fatty sipped his beverage, wiped his nose on his sleeve, examined what he'd deposited. He nodded in my direction.

'Look, let's negotiate. What's it going to take for you to stay with us?'

The drink was tasteless, but warm. I downed half in one draught.

'It would take a miracle,' I said. 'I'm leaving.'

'Oh, no you're not,' said Bridget. Fatty poked her arm.

'Hey. Quiet, you.'

'Ficial or not, he deserves to know.'

'Shut up, Bridget.'

I put my cup on the table, eyed the pair.

'Know what?'

Bridget pointed at the fat man. Tried a couple of times to say something. It came out on the third attempt.

'He sold your cab.'

One look at Fatty told me it was the truth. I tossed my cup and stood.

'Where is it?'

A strained grin appeared on Fatty's face. 'Broken up by the locals. There's no recovering it, I'm afraid.'

I pushed the table over and stepped for him.

'Wait a minute,' he said, wriggling free of his seat and backing off. 'Just calm down and let's talk this through.'

93

My finger twitched. A snarl escaped my throat. All I could think was that I would make him suffer. It wouldn't bring the cab back, but maybe it would ease the sting of my astonishing naivety. How had I failed to realise what Fatty had done? How else could he have purchased his supplies? Knowing the man, what had I expected him to do?

I clenched a fist and swung. He dived clear and held up his hands.

'Take it easy! Don't get upset!'

I picked up a chair and hurled it at him, catching him on the head. I roared and lunged at him. Bridget jumped on my back, screaming at me to stop. We made quite a scene, until we were stopped by the sound of an explosion.

A ball of orange flame swelled over the crater edge, from the direction of the Soothsayer's hut. The sound of screaming and confusion. Bells ringing an alarm.

'Trubal.'

'Oh blinding,' said Bridget, still perched on my back.

I pushed her off, clambered onto a nearby table and onto the Portakabin, where I could see out of the crater. I raised my binoculars and peered over the hut tops. Something was rampaging through the camp, leaving a trail of carnage and demolished huts. I saw a figure leap unnaturally high, onto the Soothsayer's barrow. There it squatted, pausing to contemplate the Soothsayer's severed head.

'Right,' I said, jumping down to Fatty and Bridget. 'Change of plan. I'm going with you. Right now.'

Fatty still had his hands raised. 'You're not going to kill me?'

'Perhaps later.'

I bent to the paving stones, lifted the slab and peered beneath.

'This is our way in.'

Fatty didn't like that.

'What are you talking about? We've hardly time to dig an escape tunnel, do we?'

'We are standing above the tower's sub level car parks,' I explained. 'The facilities stretch out for some distance from the tower base. Most of the original surface has been buried under ash and mud but it's accessible here and the safest way inside. We travel on the surface and Trubal will intercept us for sure. Unless you still doubt his tracking skills, of course?'

Fatty scowled.

'You just magically thought of this entrance now, did you?'

'Maybe the sound of approaching gunfire refreshed my memory.'

Fatty spat, fixing me with a suspicious eye. Bridget helped me slide the slab to one side, revealing a metre-wide section of transparent polycarbonate, embedded in Gronts casing. I pressed my face to the smeared, warm surface, seeing only darkness beneath, but no sign of flooding or collapse. We would be fifteen feet over the floor, but the jump was less risky than crossing Trubal.

I beat at the surface, hoping we'd stumbled on one of the many areas that had been compromised by substitute materials. Unfortunately we'd discovered a well-built section. Bridget and I beat the glass again and again, but with no effect. Fatty paced around, wringing his hands as the gunfire drew nearer.

'This isn't going to work.'

He ran, crawling up the crater wall and away into the darkness.

'Phil!' cried Bridget. 'You coward!'

I dropped onto the slab and panted, looking up at the great, dormant monolith, at the mysterious lights halfway up the bulb.

Let me in, I thought, as if it might hear me.

Bridget tapped me on the shoulder.

'Who's that?'

A shadow had appeared at the crater edge. Pistol barked at the strange shape, until I recognised Fatty, pushing a siege machine. It was a contraption made of two bicycles, a kind of ballista mounted between them. He ran it down to the concrete, grinned and slapped the wheel.

'Once again,' he said, 'Real ingenuity trumps Ficial.'

We unscrewed the ballista and pulled a sack of bolts from a basket under the handlebars. A scream cut through the air nearby. Trubal was almost on us.

'Right,' I said. 'Stand back.'

I couldn't lift the ballista alone. Fatty grabbed the other side and shared the weight. I loaded a bolt into the slide, turned the ratchet and aimed at the exposed glass.

The ballista fired. The shot cracked the glass but failed to break it. We reloaded and fired again. This one penetrated, shattering the polycarbonate. I kicked away the jagged surrounds. It would be just wide enough to admit Fatty.

I dropped to my knees and lowered my head beneath the surface. It was dark down there, silent and warm. In the distance, glowing over a distant stairwell, was a sign reading **Emergency Exit**. I lifted my head and indicated the hole.

'Lower yourselves as far as you can before dropping,' I said. 'When you land, head for the exit and wait for me.'

Bridget went first, followed by a cursing Fatty. Pistol sniffed around the space. I picked him up under his front legs and held him over the opening.

'Someone catch the dog.'

Bridget had something to say about that, but took up a catching position. I held the dog aloft and released.

Then I lowered myself into the hole, one arm bracing me, the other hauling the loose paving slab. I hoped to drag it over me before dropping, concealing our entry, but I mistimed the move, slipped and fell.

For a moment I couldn't move. I'd landed on something hard, and for a moment I lay staring at our entry point above, half expecting Trubal's green eyes to appear. Then I heard Pistol bark impatiently, picked myself up and stumbled for the exit sign.

The car park was empty, my steps echoing as I jogged through a veil of mist. I reached the exit sign, stepped into a stairwell, where Fatty and Bridget waited. Pistol jumped into my arms, breath reeking.

Fatty pulled a torch from his rucksack, the light blinking on in the gloom. He swept the beam from my face to Bridget's, then up the stairs. A sign on the wall pointed up to the lobby.

'Let's keep moving,' said Fatty. 'No sense waiting for your Poly-fucking-phemu to catch up.'

I snatched his lamp and pushed him hard in the chest. He fell, whining.

'Don't think I've signed up to your idiot quest. We split at the first opportunity.'

I pressed on, knowing the adrenaline would pass as quickly as it had come. I put aside thoughts of avenging the cab. The heat in the car park and the cool in the stairwell had my expectations growing. Let the Reals chase their gold. I had my own treasure to hunt.

I leave the children and cut through the alleyways, heading for the avenue, almost knocking Adede over as I break into a clearing. I tell her to locate her daughter and get to the high ground.

'What are you going to do?' she asks.

'I am going to expel them from the premises.'

'Are you mad?'

'They are trespassing. I am empowered to defend the site.'

'They'll kill you!'

'Unlikely.'

I leave her, press on to the avenue and head for the slaughter at the southern fence. I can see an invader on horseback, directing the people on foot. His nostrils are as flared as his mount's.

I leap, drag him off his steed, toss him back towards the fence. I claim his seat, but his horse bucks when I try to steer. I struggle with the reins until I realise I am hurting the animal, and relax my grip.

The horse calms, snorts and stamps the mud. I am turning it towards the fence when I hear the whining noise. The unmistakable rasp of drone engines, overhead. I glance up at the storm clouds, pick out grey T-shapes, flocking.

Wait, I think.

Wait.

The ground shakes. A flash and deafening crack, and suddenly I am slapped to the earth and pinned under the horse. I claw at the mud, drag free of the burning animal, into a cloud of black, sulphurous smoke. I trip up the side of the bomb crater, over body parts and wreckage, breathing poison air.

My avenue is packed with wailing people. They back away from me, frightened by my burning skin. Adede emerges from the pack, her clothes stained with blood. Her eyes are cloudy and unfocused, until she notices me. She bares her teeth and screams.

'You brought them here! Truth League hates Ficials. They wouldn't have come here if not for you! They wouldn't have bombed us if not for you!'

That is untrue.

'William is DEAD! Their bomb killed my boy!'

She drops to her knees, wailing, clutching her chest.

What does she expect me to do?

She said herself: she would lose at least one child.

ARCADE

'What great time we're making.' Fatty kicked a rusty can across the asphalt surface. 'We can't even climb one poxy floor.'

The stairwell was a dead end, sealed off by debris. We had doubled back to search for another exit, but found the elevator shaft blocked and emergency fences sealing us into our parking bay. The only other exit was a reinforced security door. I slumped by it, knowing it would be impregnable.

'Think of something, please,' said Fatty. 'You're supposed to be the grand designer, am I right?'

'There's no way out.'

'Bull,' snapped Fatty. 'You just need to apply yourself, right? And be sharpish about it, before Goliath catches up with us.'

I didn't reply. Before contracting the Pander virus it would have been easy to escape. With Ficial strength I could have punched right through the wall, or climbed back the way we'd come. Instead I was a trembling, disfigured wreck.

Only Pistol was unaffected by our predicament. He ran his nose over the security door, locating a scent of interest.

'Listen,' said Bridget, 'let's all just relax, right? Why don't I give us a song, cheer us up a bit?'

She reached in her jacket for her harmonica. Fatty gripped her wrist. 'Not now, Bridget,' he said. 'Please.'

She stalked away, trainers squeaking. I was glad Fatty had kept her quiet. Otherwise I might not have heard Pistol's claws, scratching at my side. Something didn't sound right.

I turned the torch on the black dog. His claws had cut the surface of the security door. I twisted, placed my wounded hand to the damage.

'What are you grinning at?' snapped Fatty.

I turned to him.

'Real workmanship.'

The door should have been pure Gronts. Dynamite wouldn't dent Gronts, let alone a small, black terrier. I leapt up, spun Fatty around and rooted in his pack.

'Hey!' he yelped. 'Unhand me!'

I took out the hammer, pushed the fat man clear, and struck the door.

Crack.

The tool wedged in the surface.

I thrashed again and again, energised to see the door splinter with each hit. Real contractors had finally come through for us. Only they could have the audacity to replace Gronts with plywood. Bridget and Fatty joined the assault, kicking with great enthusiasm. A split worked down the door, lengthening until it stretched from floor to ceiling, one half hanging from the other.

We tore the pieces from the frame, a great cloud of dust fogging us. I coughed and wheezed, fanning the filth clear, half expecting to find another obstruction. Debris slumped out of the open frame, but there was room to crawl through, and clear space beyond.

Bridget climbed up the pile and dropped out of sight, calling back that it was safe. Fatty yelped triumphantly and clambered after her, squeezing through the hole with pack dragged behind. Pistol didn't need to be told, dancing up in pursuit of the action. I followed, slipping up the garbage and dropping into the stairwell.

I straightened but fell immediately, my head spinning. The meagre effort of breaking through to the stairwell was too much for this sick Real body to take. I slouched on a step, power drained. I wondered what the Edinburgh crew would have made of me now: bent and wheezing, outclassed by two Reals.

'That's it,' I said. 'I need to rest.'

Fatty shook his head.

'No time for a comfort break. We need to keep ahead of Gogmagog, wouldn't you say?'

He was right, Trubal could be here any moment. But exhaustion overwhelmed my judgement. I rested my head on the wall and closed my eyes.

'I'll just have ten minutes.'

'Oh, no you don't.'

Fatty dug around in his pack, producing a slim metal tube. He twisted off the cap, clasping it like something much cherished.

'Make a fist,' he barked.

I ignored him, but Bridget took my hand and held it up, as keen to get me moving as Fatty. A measure of grey powder was poured onto my thumb joint.

'Right. Now snort that,' said Fatty.

'What is it?'

'They call it Dust,' said Bridget. I could see the fat man didn't approve of her terminology.

'It's medication, a simple stimulant. Look, just snort the fucking stuff and let's go.'

I inhaled sharply. A vile stinging sensation tore through my throat. I jumped up, gagging. My teeth tingled and sang.

'See?' said Fatty, grinning broadly. 'Are you not revived?'

I prepared to swing the fist I'd made for him, but was dizzied by a sudden burst of coloured spots. I shook my head, squinted up the stairway. The walls swelled and contracted, as if breathing.

'Phil,' said Bridget. 'Phil, you've overdone it. He looks like he's going to unpeel.'

'Might have been a smidge too much,' agreed Fatty.

I looked down, found that my boots were growing and twisting, curling away from me up the stairs. My own feet were abandoning me, seceding from the rotten body. I knew I had to stop them, to persuade them to stay.

I tore up the wrecked stairway, chasing them.

'Hey, wait!' yelled Fatty.

'Can I have some?' asked Bridget.

I ascended at speed, leaving their voices behind. My boots shortened with each step, until at last they drew back, reformed for now. I found an exit, tried the handle: locked, and pure Gronts. I bounded to the next floor, the exit as sealed as the last. I wondered where I was, my thoughts too scattered to recall my own design.

'Hang on, you maniac,' called Fatty. 'Wait!'

I bounded up to the next storey, then ground to a halt, startled. The stairwell ended in an explosion of thick, greasy graffiti, smeared over the walls. A mixture of symbols and obscene drawings shifted around me. They rewrote themselves as I read them, trying to confuse me. They melted, joined with their neighbouring patterns, formed into a thread, spinning a giant web. I dropped the torch, backed away, but found my feet fixed to the floor. I pushed off the wall, but my hand glued where it touched, holding me in position. A shadow caught in the torchlight. A gorged shape crept overhead. I wanted to cry out, but my muscles seized. I was prey, caught in the simplest trap.

Then I heard panting.

Pistol. He sat in the torchlight, pink tongue on display, head cocked to one side. He barked at me and licked his snout. He must have run the whole way with me. I relaxed, began breathing again. My hands and feet unstuck. The web thinned and evaporated.

Fatty and Bridget caught up. Fatty bent double and gasped air. I hunched by the dog, heart pounding, leg jiggling. Bridget edged closer to me.

'Are you all right?'

I chewed on nothing, mouth dry.

'A little over-stimulated.'

Fatty picked up the torch and ran it over the graffiti. He scratched his beard and muttered. He and Bridget seemed equally daunted by the brutal, senseless markings.

'What is it?' asked Bridget.

'Shorthand,' said Fatty.

'What's that?'

'A kind of dead language.'

'What does it mean?'

Fatty coughed, spat something into a corner.

'I can't read it,' he said. 'But it doesn't look friendly.'

He gripped the handle, found that it turned. The door clicked open.

'Hang on,' said Bridget. She pulled Fatty's arm, closing the door. 'We're walking straight into the unknown here, Phil. If it looks un-friendly let's at least look for another route.'

Fatty shrugged.

'No more fucking stairs, Bridget. If we can get in let's get in.'

'Phil!'

He marched through the door. Pistol followed him, so I went too, still twitching and chewing. Bridget shook her head and muttered the word booloo.

We walked a hundred metres along a service corridor, still coated in graffiti, then arrived at a fire door. A sign above read: **Retail Atrium**. Fatty tried the door, felt it give, ushered us inside.

The temperature dropped. A thick stench of coolant stung my nostrils. The floor, walls, ceiling; the entire hexagonal atrium was preserved behind a smooth layer of ice. The torch beam knifed around a panorama of glittering, frosted storefronts and huge, cascading stalactites, rising storeys high. Pistol's paws couldn't grip the floor, sending his legs wheeling beneath him. Bridget laughed at him, until she slipped too, landing hard on the ice. I helped her up.

'What is this place?'

'Shopping centre. Must have been some catastrophic air-con failure.'

We crept past the ghost stores. Bridget trailed behind, slowed by her gripless trainers.

Fatty shined the torch at me. 'OK, which way do we head?'

I considered. I had trouble recalling the tower plan, Dust ringing in my brain.

'This way,' I said, without any real idea. I'd never asked directions before and wasn't about to start now. We left the first atrium, crossing into the second. More stores. More ice. A cathedral silence. I halted, tried to get my bearings. Bridget and Fatty watched me doubtfully, as I swung the torch about, searching for signs.

'Welcome Power Nine, Rover Model,' chirped a voice.

Fatty's curse echoed around the mall. A small, neat woman had appeared to our left, hands folded behind her back. She was smartly dressed, but her figure disappeared at the waist. A problem with the projector.

'It's a pleasure, a pleasure, a pleasure to welcome you to the Hope Tower Retail Atrium. I am your personal shopper. May I help you find what you are looking for today?'

She grinned, a cluster of sponsor logos spinning around her face. I tried to clear my head. The hologram might be able to help. There was one obvious question.

'What is the condition of the tower? Is it in danger of imminent collapse?'

'I'm sorry,' she said. 'I don't understand the question.'

I changed tack.

'How are you still running? From where are you drawing power?'

She blinked and grinned with renewed vigour.

'I'm sorry,' she said. 'I don't understand the question.'

'Behold,' said Fatty. 'The peak of Ficial technology.'

I turned on him.

'I didn't design personal shoppers. Holotech was already an outdated gimmick when it was installed. But she might be able to help us find our way.'

Bridget snorted.

'Why ask an automated shop assistant? You built this thing, can't you figure it out?'

The holoshopper flickered. I selected the simplest possible question.

'Can you identify the nearest emergency exit?'

The shopper processed the question.

'I'm sorry. Sorry. All elevators are out of order. The most direct emergency exit is via the lower observation deck, floor fifty-five.'

'Do you have a map you can provide?'

'Yes, yes, yes, sir.'

There was a whine from behind me. I beat the ice off the wall, allowing a flex to hiss from a cavity. Fatty grabbed it, showed me a smudged map display. A black dot pulsed, indicating our position.

'Please follow the marker,' said the holoshopper.

I examined the layout. I wasn't convinced by what I saw. The floor plan seemed unfamiliar. Then again, I was still chewing through the Dust effects.

'Is this accurate?'

The shopper grinned and gestured down the corridor.

'Please follow the marker.'

Fatty and I turned away, heads bowed at the map.

Bridget stayed where she was.

'Before we go,' she said, slipping closer to the holoshopper, 'can you recommend a good shoe store?'

The Diorama boardroom is a high-spec AR conference suite. From the window I can see over the rooftops to the shanty, where smoke still drifts from the raiders' fires.

Bree sits next to me. I wear restraints. The design team sit opposite, lined up in suits, the judges in my trial. The tallest raps the table with his knuckles.

'What was it doing out there, Bree?'

The speaker is named Bloom. Bree shifts her bulk to face him.

'He was out there to assess the build site.'

'Dammit, Bree, we haven't gone public yet.'

'Regardless. I thought it prudent he spend his time profitably rather than rotting in that dungeon.'

Bloom's face turns purple.

'Getting involved in a gang war is profitable, is it?'

'Don't be ridiculous. He didn't get involved. He was merely assessing the site when the raid occurred.'

Another judge, Hodges, points at me. 'It wasn't assessing the site. I hear it was helping the squatters get comfortable, even picking up their refuse. Is that in its terms of use?'

'He decided to make simple, obvious fixes to needless problems in the camp,' says Bree. 'I think that's a reasonable use of its time and ours.'

Bloom pounds the table.

'It had no right to be there. Anything could have happened. It might have caused this firm serious embarrassment. And we hardly need more Ficial disasters on our hands.'

Bree sighs.

'If you ask me we should be praising his initiative. He was trying to make life better for those people.'

Bloom chokes on her words.

'Now listen, Bree. It's not supposed to be a bloody charity worker. It's supposed to be a builder.'

'No, it's supposed to be an architect, engineer and designer with conceptual abilities far beyond anyone else in this room. It's only natural he sought out something to do with himself.'

'It must be decommissioned!' roars Bloom.

Bree waves away the idea.

'Absolutely not. He is our greatest asset in the build.'

Bloom scratches at the black bars on his palm. Bree leads me towards the door, a hand on my shoulder. She pauses, drops a flex on the desk before her colleagues.

'In case you're interested, he has completed a survey. He believes we can start work immediately. A proposed preliminary works schedule is included.'

The men stare at it doubtfully. Bree shakes her head.

'Sometimes,' she says, 'I think I'm the only one who wants to get this fucking tower built.'

RECEPTION

The Dust effects faded. I almost wanted a top-up. Another snort might have smothered my confusion.

The tower interiors on the lower levels had been remodelled, there was no doubt about it. Each new corridor was more unfamiliar than the last.

Real contractors had constantly tinkered with the design during the build, but to nowhere near this extent. That meant the alterations had happened post-war. That was odd enough, but it wasn't the major issue at hand.

The real problem was the flex. Its destination was clearly set as the lower observation deck, the great lip which jutted from the Hope Tower's fifty-fifth floor. It was intended for paying visitors wishing to gawp at the drowned old city, and possessed the emergency exit I'd asked the holoshopper for.

The problem was the flex wasn't leading us there. We'd ascended thirty-two floors via various stairways, but I was almost certain we were travelling deeper into the superstructure. At best we were moving in an enormous circle. Bridget tapped my shoulder.

'I don't like that expression.'

'What expression?'

I wondered what my features were betraying now. Bridget sighed.

'We're lost. Stop me if I'm wrong.'

'No, no,' I said. 'I'm just. Hungry. Aren't you?'

Bridget ran a hand over her spots. 'I am, as it goes. What do you say, Phil? Time for lunch?'

Fatty snarled, irritated at the thought of further delay, but he was good enough to lower his pack and pull out a tin of sardines, distributing them with greasy blue fingers. We crouched to eat, Bridget savouring every morsel with care. I chewed a few, then fed the rest to the dog. Bridget shook her head.

'It's demented feeding that pooch your rations.'

'Don't take it personally, Bridget.' Fatty grinned shattered teeth at me. 'He's not the first misanthrope to have a soft spot for a hound.'

'Don't worry,' I said. 'We won't drain your supplies much longer.'

I kissed oil from my fingers, stood and proceeded along the corridor. Pistol ran a little way ahead, pausing to sniff, then setting off again. I was determined to ignore the flex and follow my instincts. We had to ditch Fatty and Bridget, and the map wasn't helping our cause.

I took a right, then another right, the Reals protesting, running to catch up. The corridor narrowed into a featureless crevice, reminding me of Brixton.

'What's the rush?' gasped Fatty, catching up. I ignored him, stopped at a fork in the corridor and frowned at the flex. It projected only a left turn.

'You're getting touchy,' said Fatty. 'Do you know that?'

Bridget slapped his arm.

'Leave off, Phil, can't you see he's peaky?'

I went right. The passage changed from pale grey to rust red, the surface texture crumbling under foot into something like grit. It took a minute to realise it was curving left, sending us back the way we'd come. The flex indicated I was passing through a lift shaft.

I pressed on, until a fire door appeared on the right. I opened it, stepped into a small room that didn't appear on the map. The floor sucked at my boots, submerging my feet to the ankles. I tried to free myself, but the muck only pulled harder. I knew struggling was foolish, but something had choked my reason and I couldn't stop myself. I sank faster, the ooze rising to my thighs. My companions watched with interest, until the floor had swallowed me to my waist.

'Do you plan to help me out,' I said, 'or just rubberneck?'

'Sorry,' said Bridget, snapping out of her trance. 'Sorry.'

She reached out, dragged me back into the corridor. Fatty leaned on the wall, watching as I wiped my clothes.

'And what kind of crazy paving,' he asked, 'is that supposed to be?'

I peered at the grime on my fingers.

'Liquefied sediment. Clay/sand mix. Quicksand screed. Nothing I put here. We need to cross it if we're going to reach the tower envelope.'

Fatty wielded the flex.

'This thing says we follow the curve a bit more.'

'We need to cross here,' I repeated.

'Ken,' said Bridget. 'It's a bloody swamp. I say we follow the map. Common sense, isn't it?'

Fatty disappeared down the corridor, his way lit by the flex. Bridget hesitated, then followed. I thought about letting them go, heading back the way we'd come – but I wanted to get clear of the floor, and I couldn't be sure I'd find a better way out of the maze. I followed the Reals, Pistol at my muddy feet.

The flex guided us to another stairwell and indicated we should climb. It grew hotter as we ascended. I felt a tremor in the handrail, a regular beat pulsing through the metal. Bridget seemed concerned.

'The fans,' I explained. 'They're still turning.'

'What fans?'

'We're near the tower core – a kind of chimney running up the centre of the structure. It contains a system of turbines that circulate heat around the building. The closer you are the more you can hear them.'

Bridget scratched her head.

'How are they still spinning? And why's it so flipping hot all of a sudden?'

My head hurt too much to process the possibilities, and I wasn't about to share any theories. I climbed in silence, thigh muscles protesting, until a glowing sign appeared in the gloom: **Terminal One. Gates 1 to 15.**

Fatty raised an eyebrow.

'Where are we, Heathrow? That make any sense to you?'

'Yes. The terminal is a distribution centre where tenants and employees would be transported to upper levels. This is some distance from the observation deck.'

Fatty slapped the flex on the wall.

'So this thing is definitely on the blink, that's what you're telling me?'

'I'm not sure.'

Fatty pulled at his collar, wiped sweat from his brow, unnerved to have lost technology's guiding hand.

'What can you tell me then? What's out there?'

'Should be a large sky lobby,' I said. 'More recreation and commercial spaces. Check-in desks for elevator operators to various tower destinations.'

'I hate terminals,' said Fatty, adjusting his pack. 'Still. Anything to get out of this fucking sauna.'

I told Bridget to grab Pistol, to prevent him running off around the open space. Fatty took up the rear.

I sneaked open the door, felt it push into my hand. A cool wind rushed over me as I peered out at the vast expanse. There was something forlorn about it, but still impressive: a six million cubic metre volume holding seating areas, commercial lots, dead gardens, and the great luggage columns and elevator shafts stretching to the canopy, inspired by Niemeyer's Cathedral of Brasilia. Beyond I could make out the distinctive hexagrid – the aluminium oxynitride/Gronts honeycomb envelope which wrapped the entire tower. A glass barrier ran inside and parallel to the hexagrid, creating a promenade space.

We had emerged behind a check-in desk, which curved out of sight around the core in either direction. Swing chairs turned in the wind, awaiting rears that would never arrive. Dim luminescence dropped jagged shadows from somewhere above, but the space was enormously quiet.

We tiptoed over the luggage carousel and out from the check-in desk, walking into a full gale. Either the hexagrid was damaged or the atmospheric controls were somehow active and malfunctioning.

'Wow,' whispered Bridget, looking around. 'Nice work, Ken.'

Fatty snorted. 'A glass barn.'

He was doing his best to be contrary, but he was cowed by the stillness. People can't help the way spaces make them feel.

I signalled that Bridget should drop the struggling Pistol. The dog jumped after me as I headed for the hexagrid.

'Hey!' said Fatty. 'Where are you going? We should check the lifts.'

'I told you,' I said. 'I'm leaving.'

I wasn't about to indulge in long goodbyes. I started walking, only mildly surprised to hear Fatty and Bridget giving chase.

We passed through curling snakes of luggage trolleys, under the arches of raised restaurants, over bridges connecting parched, dead parklands. I wondered how the marble floor had become so scored and pitted.

We carried on until the recreation area thinned. I paused by a bench, allowing Fatty and Bridget to catch up. I was about to move off again when I noticed Pistol. He was very still, ears pricked, staring into the gloom.

A shadow was moving in the promenade, where a section of floor and hexagrid was smashed open, letting in the gale. A plank was tossed over the chasm, the figure perched at the end, leaning perilously out of the tower. Something escaped from its grip and fluttered back into the terminal area.

A scroll.

'I think we've found the paper boy,' whispered Fatty.

'Should we talk to him?' said Bridget.

A tinny electric alarm sounded on the figure's wrist. It turned on the plank, crawling urgently back inside. He looked up, as if expecting rain, then sprinted into the darkness.

'What's all that about?' whispered Bridget.

The light in the vault shifted. Shadows warped and stretched on the terminal floor. Those lights were attached to something. Something that was moving.

I hadn't heard a Sweep in a long while, but you never forgot the high-pitched whistle of their lift fans. I looked up in the heavens and searched for movement. Should I be worried?

Fatty didn't need to ask.

'Leg it!' he yelped, legs already pumping. Bridget followed at speed. I thought I'd let them go, but Pistol ran after them, yipping in delight.

'Pistol! Wait!'

The chamber flooded with light. The Sweep dropped into view, levelling out at twenty feet, picking me out in its spotlights.

It was about the size of a saloon car, barrel-shaped lift fans mounted at each tip, a sensor barb clutched under a bulbous nose. A Dohaki pulse welder twitched under its belly.

I stared at it. Who was controlling it? At first I thought Trubal was involved, but then dismissed the notion: a soldier model would never let a drone do its killing.

The Dohaki hummed a charge tone, so I stopped speculating and took up running instead. I cut back into the recreation area and dived behind a fountain, just as the Sweep fired. The Dohaki chopped the marble into a hurricane of white grit. The din shook the canopy, and showered the terminal with cladding. Trubal couldn't help but have heard that.

I spat marble dust, wondering why the Sweep had taken against us. It was a large maintenance drone, designed to travel the core making turbine repairs and scraping deposit from the walls. It certainly wasn't intended for security roles, and definitely had no need of an industrial Dohaki. Some tower native must have jacked it, modified it, and set it loose down here to keep out the riff-raff. Too bad for us. It had plenty of room to manoeuvre in the terminal, and that sensor array could spot a hairline fracture at a hundred metres. It wouldn't have trouble sniffing us out.

Fatty seemed to sense hiding wasn't an option. His unmistakable silhouette flashed over a bridge, Pistol barking nearby. The Sweep tipped and turned, hovering on the spot, twisting its barb.

I edged around the fountain and peered at it, having the usual difficulty formulating an attack plan that didn't involve Ficial strength and speed. It was hard to evaluate the situation rationally. I had one hell of a Dust hangover, coupled with irrational concern for the terrier.

The only thing I had going for me was the cover provided by the retail space. I broke and ran, aiming to draw the Sweep's attention, which I did quite spectacularly. The Dohaki pulsed, slapping an advertising hoarding flat and ripping out storefronts around me. I felt the heat through my boots, kept moving, hoped to double back and make for the gardens. Maybe I could find a drain or access hatch.

The Sweep's engines changed pitch, ascending to target me from above. I darted right, running deeper into the retail maze, when the store holo displays suddenly flashed into life, dazzling me with garish logos and brand propositions. I took a left, lurching through a blaze of luxury jewellery ads. Starvie grinned at me from several directions. I nearly stopped to talk to her. Only another Dohaki blast dissuaded me, blowing me off my feet, head smacking on marble. I scrambled up, moving on instinct.

Maybe that's why I ran into the open. I turned my head, glimpsed the Sweep as it dropped and twisted, headed right for me. I lifted my stumped hand to the floodlight glare, knowing there was nowhere to hide.

Killed by an automated janitor. I thought it just preferable to being killed by a Real.

Then I heard Pistol. He stood on the reception desk, barking furiously, and rather stupidly it seemed to me, at the killing machine. The Sweep tilted its lift fans, and stretched its illuminations on the terrier. Pistol leaned into the fan blast defiantly, eyes narrowed. The Sweep dropped a few feet above the ground and paused, debating the efficacy of obliterating a small dog.

It had given me an opening. That's the thing about retrofitting civilian kit for military purposes: it might seem like an effective solution, but it will always have serious deficiencies. In this case it simply had no tactical awareness. It approached each target as a task on a list, a smear to be polished, rather than an element in a complex, dynamic situation.

So it was confused when I ran at it. I jumped onto its nose and clung on by the sensor barb. It dumped thrust, jumped ten metres, but I held on. Not that I was any clearer about my next move. Only my right hand could really grip, and it was already weakening. With a full complement of fingers my left might have torn the barb free.

'Hang on, chum!'

Fatty. I only had a moment to contemplate the stupidity of his comment. He ran for the hexagrid promenade, Bridget and Pistol with him. He must have figured the drone wouldn't fit in there. He was wrong.

The drone dived to attack. I jumped, rolling onto a store roof, then scrabbled down, taking cover among plastic seating. It swooped at Fatty as he turned into the promenade, shooting up the hexagrid, shards and hot splinters spitting across the terminal. Then it turned and flew back over me, coming about for another strike.

I could see Fatty, kneeling under a brass sculpture with Bridget, dog in hand. Pistol tore free of his grip, bolted over the terminal floor, leapt into my arms.

'Keep moving,' I yelled. 'Try to double back and make for the core. We'll head down the promenade, draw its fire.'

I tucked Pistol into my jacket, sprang to my feet and bolted. Bridget and Fatty did the same, making for the core. The Sweep went after me, squeezing its bulk into the promenade, lift fans blowing a storm in the confined space. I jumped onto the plank and crawled into the breach, thinking I would climb to cover.

I was halfway across before I made the mistake of looking down. My head swam. Every muscle tensed. I froze in position, hyperventilating, staring into a fifty-storey abyss. I managed to look away, but the view outside wasn't any better.

A belt of fire curled around the tower base, marking where the pilgrim camp had stood. Beyond was the drowned city, a featureless black lake contained by desolate hills. I thought of the weight of material above me, a whole other city packed into a mountain-sized dome, straining under the weight of its impossible, mirrored twin. I imagined the bulbs collapsing, pancaking down, consuming me. I had to get off that plank. So why couldn't I move?

Pistol didn't need to know. He wriggled free of my jacket, under my paralysed form, and bolted back into the tower. I couldn't call him back. I was mute and dumb.

I heard the Sweep roll up behind me. I turned, saw it riding on a curtain of thrust, heat exchanger venting. It opened its payload door, lowering a spinning electric glass blower. It was planning to heal the breech and take care of me at the same time. I was going to become a feature in the tower facia.

Something clattered onto the Sweep. The machine slapped on the floor, shaking under a shower of debris. It tried to right itself, but the bombardment was too heavy, and it was forced to veer out of sight, back into the terminal.

I crouched there, frozen, the freezing gale stinging my eyes, the plank rattling beneath me.

Firelight and shadows flickered in the promenade. Fatty and Bridget appeared, peering in at me like the Sweep had.

They didn't look pleased. Other figures crowded behind them, clutching torches and what might have been spears. One wore a fedora hat, a piece of card tucked in the band. He thrust Fatty aside, peered in the breech and smiled.

What teeth he had were fangs.

'Well, well,' he said. 'Hold the front page.'

I am locked in my cube cell, palm code rescinded, guard at attention. I am stored here, aware but without work. A man might call it torture.

Better the waste pits than this. My only diversion is a flex Bree smuggled in. I access the least secure Diorama files, search for something to occupy my mind.

All data pertaining to the tower are off limits, but I can access other projects. I find my way into project 'Martello', the mobile sea stations manufactured to intercept skiffs crossing from the continent. The designs are varied. Some are little more than armed buoys. Others are more like floating towns, built with underwater pens to hold thousands of refugees.

I am considering my own, improved design when the signal interrupts me.

– Kenstibec.

– Control.

– Diorama has lodged an official complaint reference the site disturbance. Explain.

– The firm are unhappy that I was surveying the site. Will I be decommissioned?

– That would not be a solution. Diorama ignored your specs, starved you of work for a prolonged period. It was inevitable that you would seek gainful employment.

– I do not know that it was gainful. The refugees blamed me for the attack. I thought they would thank me for improving their habitat.

– Irrelevant. You are designed to work without the need for praise. Concentrate on the task. You are about to create the greatest engineering feat in history. Build the tower. All other considerations immaterial.

– Diorama will not let me work.

– *They will. Company needs assistance more than ever. Only a matter of time before you are employed again.*

– *Control. The Truth League – are they a threat to the tower project?*

– *Affirmative. But threat is wider. Connections suspected with extremist factions in the American civil war. League and allies are committed to destruction of Augmentation mission and Engineered kind. Efforts are ongoing to identify their UK cells.*

– *Why do they want to destroy us?*

– *Motives irrelevant. All that matters is that each model fulfils its optimisation.*

– *But, Control, I can't do that locked up down here.*

– *Wait, Kenstibec. Wait. Your time will come.*

The transmission ceases. Solitude once more.

WASTE MANAGEMENT

I was lifted from the plank and presented to Fedora, who grunted and shook his spear. His people pushed us down the promenade, squawking and leaping about us as we travelled, until the Sweep's lift fans boomed again, somewhere near. Our new friends stopped and hugged the hexagrid, allowing me a moment to examine them.

Most were nude, pallid sacks of bone. A few wore a ragged tie or suit jacket, perhaps denoting rank. Their eyes were swivelling black orbs, edged by white: AR lenses that had been damaged somehow and fused to their wearers' eyeballs. Bridget and Fatty glanced at me anxiously, but I was too worried about Pistol to offer any encouragement.

Fedora listened, waited, until the sound of the Sweep's fans dimmed. He shook his spear, and we were hustled out of the promenade and into the terminal. We hurried through dormant security barriers to a luggage distribution shaft, one of the chalk-white poles shooting up to the canopy. The black eyes grunted and squealed, urging us inside and onto a maintenance ladder. I was hustled in last, just as the Sweep's lights reappeared. They flashed in our direction, but the machine didn't pursue, apparently content to shepherd us from its space.

The climb was hard, but I was encouraged by jabs from a spear below. Our captors huffed and gobbled as we went, making a sound like chattering apes and pigs.

We emerged onto a waste bay, an automated sorting centre where trash would have been recycled and crushed. This, at least, was roughly where I expected it to be. It made sense that the black eyes would camp here: the isolated space was only accessible by distribution shafts, its ceiling a dense spaghetti of converging garbage chutes. No Sweep would sneak up on them here.

Their camp was centred on the great recycling spindle, a ribbed, shallow depression around fifty metres in diameter: one of my more economic and elegant designs.

The Reals had done their best to make a mess of it. They were using refuse crates for dwellings, drawn up in a squalid ring around the spindle edge. Garbage was strewn everywhere. Figures scuttled about, peeking out of trash piles and withdrawing when we neared. There was a clearing at the centre of the spindle, where a fire smoked, souring the air with toxic fumes. Flies hummed somewhere above.

Fedora and his squad led us between the crates and down the spindle slope, kicking a path through the deep waste. We were forced to our knees before the fire. Human skulls grinned among the flames.

Fatty saw them too.

'Thank God,' he said. 'Civilisation.'

More black eyes, chirping and keening, gathered about the spindle edge, picking through the trash and hissing at each other. Many were missing limbs.

Fedora raised his fist.

'All right! Let's bring this meeting to order!'

The creatures grew quiet, crouching in a circle of shadows.

Fedora addressed them.

'I want to say that you should be very proud. This team's belief, hard work and commitment to delivering a quality product are what maintain our position as the trusted source of tower news and events. Hur. The proof of your achievements is here today: a fresh group of regular readers, inspired to join us through the strength of our message. It just goes to show that even today there remains a hunger for the premiere product you all help to create.'

There was a ripple of polite applause from the black eyes. Fedora acknowledged them with a shake of his spear, then banged it on the spindle for attention.

'Time for a picture, I think. Hur. Where's Mitchel?'

A short creature in a dirty coat slunk from a concealed spot, clutching an old flex and an egg-shaped holotech device. He slapped the egg behind us, projecting an image I recognised from Diorama's original sales material: one of those curious 'artist's impressions' of a mid-level luxury apartment. Bridget, Fatty and I were wrenched to our feet and hurried before it. Mitchel pointed the flex in our direction.

'OK, people. Give us a smile, please.'

Bridget and Fatty grinned in confusion. I imitated them as best I could. Mitchel scuttled around us, his flex pulsing a flash.

'Lovely. Lovely. Sir, could I ask you to step forward a little? Little more? Perfect, thank you. Turn towards me, darling. Smile, I bet you've got a lovely smile. There it is.'

He took a hundred shots before he was satisfied, disabling the egg and showing the flex to Fedora.

'That one,' said Fedora, pointing at his elected image. 'Go write it up for the next edition. "Trio escape religious tyranny to start new life of luxury." You know the score.'

'Right away, sir,' said Mitchel. He scampered up the spindle walls, sifting through the trash as he went, assembling a new print run.

The crowd squirmed in anticipation. Fedora removed his hat and stepped into the light from the fire, revealing bright, crystal-blue pupils.

'Right,' he said. 'Now that's over, let's get down to business.'

'What exactly is your business?' asked Fatty.

'Current affairs,' replied Fedora. 'And survival.'

'I see,' said Fatty, nodding. 'That kind of survival?' He looked up. I glanced above us, where the garbage chute assembly and sorting manipulators hung. Pale shapes twisted in the dark.

Bodies. Bloodied, half-consumed corpses, hanging by chained feet. One or two still bore flesh, but most were picked clean from the knees up.

'Oh, don't worry about that,' said Fedora. 'That's just a bit of fun.'

Black eyes appeared around us, restraining us in plastic bindings. Chains dropped from the garbage chutes and we were strung up, hanging by our feet.

Fedora approached, our heads hanging at his knees. He was drooling, either out of hunger or because he couldn't help it with those teeth. He stood over Bridget and wiped the spit from his chin.

'You,' he said.

Bridget couldn't reply. Fedora lifted her face with his boot.

'Dear me. Do these spots go all over? Answer me now.'

'Yes, sir.'

'Mm-hmm.' Fedora moved on. He passed by Fatty, closing on me instead. He smacked his lips and rubbed his hands.

'Well you're the looker, aren't you? Yes, I can see you're the one with taste.'

He smiled, nodding at the men behind me. Bony fingers freed my left arm and forced it out, offering it up to Fedora. He rolled up my sleeve and examined the limb.

'I see we're not the first to have a bite.' He gripped my finger stumps. 'Well, sometimes leftovers are better. Hur-hur.'

He picked a spot, sniffed it briefly, and bit deep into the flesh.

Pain. Like nothing I'd ever known.

I howled as he gnawed at muscle and bone, then ripped clear, a chunk of me gripped in his fangs. Bridget screamed. Fatty stared. Fedora turned and displayed the meat to his people, oozing in his maw. They jumped and screamed and climbed on each other, as if about to charge the hanging buffet, but something held them back. Instead Fedora spat little pieces of me at them as he masticated, letting the black eyes scrap over regurgitated morsels.

Bridget was saying something to me, but I couldn't understand, too busy leaking tears and blood. Too busy losing life. Only the piercing shriek of a whistle jolted me back to the world.

Fatty's noise had hushed the crowd. Fedora turned and advanced on the swinging blue fat man, still worrying the arm meat in his ivory blades. He paused, spat the mess into his palm.

'Have you got something to say?'

'Only that you're making a mistake,' said Fatty. 'A biggie, actually.'

Fedora pressed his bloodied jaw to Fatty's.

'I've heard that before,' he said, 'from better meat than you.'

'I'm sure you have,' replied Fatty. 'I'm sure your operation suits you well: you drop your little bulletins out the window, then feast on whatever gullible fucks stumble into your web. I get it, really I do. Apart from the need to get around that flying robot sentinel every time you go hunting, it's very clever. But we're not your average punters. We didn't come here because of something we read. We're different.'

'You're all the same,' snarled Fedora.

'Oh yeah?' said Fatty. 'Did any of your previous meals build this tower?'

Fedora hesitated, licking his lips. Fatty smiled back. 'That guy you're snacking on? He built this place. Knows it back to front. He could show you a way outside, if you fancied. Or provide a route to a more desirable residence. At the very least he can get you out of here.'

'Hur. Why would we want to leave?'

'Oh come on,' said Fatty. 'You wouldn't live here by choice. Not when there's all those luxury condos sitting upstairs.'

'Oh, wouldn't we?'

'No. Not unless you were trapped. That would suggest there's more trouble above you too, cornering you in this giant bin. What is it? Another drone, or other people?'

Fedora drew back. The fat man knew how to get people's attention.

'They sealed off the floors,' snarled Fedora. 'They drove us from our own office. When our backs were turned.'

'Right,' said Fatty. His eyes briefly met mine, anxious to see the life draining out of his leverage. He turned back to Fedora. 'It is an outrage. You have every right to be indignant. Let us go and we can help.'

Fedora chewed, regarded me.

'If he knows his way around so well, how is it he led you right to the drone?'

Fatty looked at me expectantly, his good eye bright with fright. I decided to tell the truth. Maybe Fedora would buy it. It took me a moment to compose myself.

'We weren't expecting to be attacked by the machine,' I gasped. 'It's designed for maintenance, not combat. Somebody has adapted it. Now we know about it we can avoid it. I can take you to the higher floors. No. No problem.'

Fedora dropped the rest of my arm meat in his mouth and swallowed it whole.

'Sorry,' he said, shaking his head. 'I don't buy it.'

He grabbed Fatty, opened his mouth, and made to bite off the terrified face.

'It's true!' I yelped. 'I built the tower! I worked for Diorama! I reported to Miss Bree!'

Fedora snapped his teeth away from Fatty.

'How do you know that name?'

Fedora sealed us in the plastics shredder, a dim chamber hemmed in by interlocking grinding teeth. There was no exit save a loading hatch in the wall, guarded by black eyes.

Bridget and Fatty packed my wound and applied a tourniquet with a long strip of plastic. I babbled at them senselessly, passed out, then returned to a world of pain. I couldn't move the remaining fingers and I'd lost a lot of blood. I was going to die. The only question was how soon. Maybe Trubal would catch up first and make it quick.

Bridget sat next to me and stared at Fatty.

'This is all your fault,' she said.

Fatty clutched his chest.

'Mine?'

'That's right.'

Fatty paced around, bridling at the insult.

'How is this my fault? Always blame someone else, don't you?' He shook his head. 'I don't know, your fucking generation.'

'My generation? You're the lot who blew everything up, aren't you? You're the lot who invented Ficials.'

Fatty kicked a plastic chunk.

'I didn't have anything to do with all that.' He pointed at me, good eye furious, wide. 'I'm not responsible for that catastrophe.'

'Oh yeah?' said Bridget. 'What did you do before the war, then? What was your innocent profession?'

Fatty stopped, shook his head.

'None of your fucking business, darling.'

'What, you can't tell me? Top secret was it?'

Fatty leaned on the shredder wall, Bridget and I staring at him. I had to admit I was curious. He scratched his beard for a minute, then snapped.

'I was unemployed, OK?'

'Unemployed?'

'That's right. Fucking job seeker for years. I could hardly influence geopolitics on the fucking dole, could I?'

I stirred, located my voice in the fog of pain.

'You didn't have a job?'

Fatty turned on me.

'Oh, joining the conversation now, are you?'

'How did you not have a job?' I croaked. 'What did you do all day?'

Fatty picked up a piece of plastic and threw it at me. Bridget threw it back.

'Leave him alone. We should have listened to him. He said we'd never climb this thing.'

'We can climb it, Bridget. You've just got to have a little belief, you know?'

'Oh do me a favour, Philip. We've as much chance of climbing this monstrosity as we've got of flying to the moon in a gravy boat. Unless you've got a few magic beans in your pocket we are never, repeat, never going to reach the top. All I want do is get out of here. That's if this lot don't slaughter us first.'

Fatty kicked the wall.

'You've absolutely no feel for people, do you, Bridget? I know the kind of monster we're dealing with, and that makes me know we're safe.' He pointed at me. 'Freak show's name-dropping did the trick, I'm telling you. The nut in the hat has already decided to employ us. He's only locked us in here to keep his tribe in suspense. We'll be headed up again soon enough.'

Bridget shook her head.

'No way, Phil. If we get out of this I'm getting out. I'll walk to Andover if I have to.'

Fatty shook his head, turned his good eye at me.

'What about you? Think these freaks are going to kill us?'

'No point trying to predict,' I said. 'There are more pressing matters.'

'Like what?'

'Trubal. Longer we wait the sooner he catches up. Then there's the tower.'

'What about it?'

'We need to figure out why . . .' I gasped at a surge of white-hot pain. 'Why it's trying to kill us.'

My companions eyed me in silence. Bridget spoke first.

'Ken. You should get some sleep.'

'Think about it,' I said. 'The flex led us into a trap. Every time I tried to turn around the corridors reshaped, pushed us back to the terminal. Something or someone wanted us delivered us to the Sweep. And our gourmand friend in the hat, of course.'

Fatty crouched before me.

'You're saying the tower was reshaping around us? Is that possible?'

'Theoretically yes. It would require systems that were deactivated. That means first, someone has the ability to power and manipulate the tower's most advanced structural systems. Second, whoever it is tried to kill us.

'If you had a chance of climbing the tower, it's gone. You should concentrate on escape.'

'I'm not leaving without my gold,' said Fatty.

The loading hatch opened, revealing Fedora. He smiled at us, lips bloodied by his own teeth. Reals. They couldn't even make efficient monsters of themselves.

'So,' said Fatty, smiling his own shattered set. 'Had time to consider our offer?'

Fedora stepped down into the shredder, inspecting the interior as if for the first time. He circled us, stopped beside Fatty.

'Most people in the tower survived the bomb blast, did you know that? Construction workers, the suits. Most of them left when the food ran out. Said we were insane to stay here. Well, perhaps we were. But we weren't stupid. It's important that you realise that.'

'Fair enough,' said Fatty. Fedora nodded and examined his fingernails.

'We've sorted through enough tower trash to learn a thing or two about this place, how it was built. That Bree name crops up a lot. I believe that your friend worked here. What I don't yet understand is why you came back?'

'Well,' said Fatty, falsehoods brewing.

Fedora raised a finger.

'Bearing in mind,' he said, 'that I know bullshit when I hear it.'

Fatty swallowed, adjusted his collar, ran a hand across his blue scalp.

'Gold,' he said, sagging under the weight of the truth. 'There's a heap of gold in the tower, just waiting to be recovered.'

Fedora frowned.

'Really? Where?'

Fatty glanced at me. He wanted me to explain. That was asking a lot of what was left of me. I wanted to curl up and take a long sleep, but Fedora prodded me with his boot until I responded.

'Around the tower waist, where the two domes meet . . .' Forming the words exhausted me. My throat felt like it had been pebble-dashed. 'The gold is formed into a tuned mass damper, a structure that helps stabilise the building.'

'Well, well,' said Fedora. 'If you'd told me that a few years ago I would have laughed at you. Now nothing surprises me about this place. And this gold – you intend to steal it, do you?'

Fatty puffed himself up, finding something impertinent in the cannibal's question.

'Not steal, recover.'

'Well that certainly explains why you're here,' he said. 'That is lunatic enough a motive. I'd ask for a cut if I thought for a minute you could do it. Forgive me if I have my doubts. You've barely cleared security and you're already half dead.'

'What about our deal?' asked Fatty. 'Are you writing that off too?'

Fedora yawned.

'No. You will act as our guides. Provided you deliver us to floor ninety-seven and help us secure our old offices, I will release you as proposed.'

'No problem,' said Fatty. 'Anything else?'

Fedora picked his teeth and regarded what emerged.

'Yes, there is one other thing. Hur. You see, there aren't many of my people, barely twenty now. They are ferocious fighters when their bellies are full. Trouble is, at the moment they're hungry. Very hungry. And that makes them poor fighters.'

Fedora let that sink in, regarding his trembling captives.

'It needn't be anything too big,' he said. 'Just an arm at the elbow. A morsel, really.'

'Excuse me, sir?' said Bridget. 'Wouldn't you rather we led you all out of the tower, back to the outside world?'

'Hur, hur. I'm afraid that's no option, sweetheart. My people would have me for breakfast if I tried to leave the tower. They've adapted to this life.'

He walked back up the stairs to the hatch.

'Decide between you who's going to step up. Refuse to play and you all go in the pantry. Understood?'

The hatch sealed shut. Bridget put her head between her knees and moaned.

'Oh my God. We're going to die.'

'No we're not,' snapped Fatty. 'It's only an arm.'

'You volunteering then?'

Fatty chewed his tongue, turning to me.

'Look, can you get sabre tooth to his floor or can't you?'

'Wouldn't be a problem normally,' I said. 'There are many more ways to ascend the floors than by lift shafts and stairwells. However, as I mentioned, whoever has control of the tower isn't keen on our presence, and may act against us again.'

'Oh, never mind your paranoia,' said Fatty. 'We're out of options. We just need to nominate a donor.'

Bridget lifted her head.

'Don't even think about it, Phil. Just don't even think about it.'

Fatty sighed.

'Bridget, I gave you the opportunity to back out, didn't I?'

'What about some human solidarity?' She pointed a quivering finger my way. 'Let them eat him! He's a Ficial, isn't he? Stop me if I'm wrong!'

Fatty shook his head.

'Bridget, I'll stop you when you're fucking right. He's no Ficial, not any more. Besides, he's the only one with a chance of finding a way up. It's you or me.'

Bridget stood up.

'Well they won't want to eat me. You heard him: "Are those spots all over?" he asked. I'm not appetising.'

'Well he didn't even bother to ask me, Bridget. He hardly wants my blue meat, now does he?'

'He might. There's a lot more meat on you than me.'

The bickering made my head pound. I stood, stumbled up the stairs, and rapped on the hatch for attention. A voice told me to stand back. Fatty hissed at me, asked what I thought I was doing.

'Getting some peace.'

The hatch creaked open. Fedora was already there.

'We've decided,' I said. 'You can have my arm. What's left of it, I mean.'

'Really?'

126

Fedora didn't know what to think. Mostly he was pleased.

'Aren't you worried you might— I mean you've lost a lot. You might not.'

'Survive? Amputation is the best chance for this mess. I'll make it. If I don't, consider us cooked.'

I pointed at the shivering wrecks behind me. Fedora clapped his hands and grinned.

'Hur. Good lad. It takes my lot ages to decide this stuff.'

Weeks pass. I consider punching my way out the cell, but Control told me to wait, so I wait.

I observe my guard. I believe he is being punished too: his human comforts, desk, chair, kettle and teabags, have been removed. All he has is a newspaper, but he only reads the sports pages and is through them by nine. After that he passes some time by whistling, kicking the wall and pacing.

Then he picks up the newspaper for the fifteenth time, draws a ballpoint pen from his pocket, and licks the tip with his tongue. He holds the pen up in a fist, says something to himself.

I stand, approach the glass, tap on it. He grabs his rifle and leaps to his feet.

'Step away from the glass,' he says.

'The answer is Gustav Eiffel.'

He cocks the weapon and presses it to the bullet-proof barrier, which is something of a redundant gesture.

'I said step away!'

'The answer to the clue was Gustav Eiffel.'

He glances over his shoulder.

'Eh?'

'French engineer, famed for contribution to 1889 Paris Universal Exposition. That is what you said.'

'What. You can read my lips?'

His eyes narrow, activity grinding behind. Probably wondering what else I have seen him say. Quite a bit, as it happens.

'Stop staring at me,' he hollers.

'You have never attempted a crossword puzzle before,' I say. 'Why do so today?'

His jaw slips to one side. He sighs, lifts his chin from the rifle stock and lowers the weapon slightly.

'It's your fault.'

'Why?'

'Cos I told you and big Bree about the site, didn't I? Bloom says I'll stay down here with you until I learn to keep my mouth shut.'

'Why should you be punished? Miss Bree gave me clearance. You had no cause to stop me.'

He sighs, turns, sits back at his desk.

'Well, Bloom doesn't see it that way. I'm locked down here with nothing for entertainment but your charmless mug and this depressing paper.'

I am curious.

'What do you find depressing about the news?'

He stares at me. Waves the paper.

'Are you serious? This is a real life horror mag. Worse every day. Half the world's starving and the other half's trying to get in here. And our only plan seems to be to lock up half the country. It makes you feel so bloody helpless.'

'That is why we have Control.'

He tosses the paper, runs a hand over his eyes.

'Maybe Control is keeping the lights on, but it won't keep us safe. Have you read what Lay says about you and Control? He says he's going to wipe Brixton off the map.'

'Unlikely.'

'Don't you know what he did to Detroit? To Chicago? You think he'll have scruples about London? Take it from me, the American business is the worst threat of all.'

He shakes his head.

'I knew it was bad when they stopped making films.'

He is agitated. His knee jogs and his fists clench. Control is right. Emotion makes his kind sick. I tap the barrier, indicating the crossword.

'What is the next clue?'

THE TRADING FLOOR

I opened my eyes to find Fatty grinning over me.

'Morning.'

He helped me sit up against the wall, dribbled water over my lips. I noticed his skin had turned a deeper blue. His cough was back, and fluid leaked from his bad eye. Without his pills, the Blue Frog was catching up on him, and fast.

I had my own problems. It was all I could do not to scream and thrash around the floor. It felt as if my left hand had been snapped at the wrist, twisted and bent back on itself. Hadn't they taken the arm? Had they only maimed me? A minute passed before I found the strength to look.

I was almost relieved. The forearm had been removed below the elbow, leaving a pulpy, bandaged stump. I'd suffered similar traumas working on the tower, but back then my Ficial nanotech would have grown me a fresh limb in days. Now that piece of me was gone for good. Fatty examined the dressing and looked into my eyes, searching for something.

'How are you, freak show? Are you back in the Real world, yeah? Back in control?'

He could see I didn't like the question, so explained I'd been lost in a fever for two days. I'd spent the time wailing, sweating and talking to people who weren't there. Apparently I'd chatted with Starvie for hours.

'What did I say?'

Fatty shrugged.

'You weren't super-coherent, but it sounded like you were trying to apologise.'

The pain from my ghost hand passed quite suddenly, and Fatty

130

walked me out of the shredder, into the waste spindle camp. Occasionally a face peeped from a trash pile, smiling and licking its lips. Maybe they wanted to intimidate me. Maybe they were complimenting me on my taste. Maybe the only way to endure what they'd become was to revel in it. I told myself not to take it personally.

'So our host is allowing us to walk the grounds unguarded?'

'In case you haven't noticed,' said Fatty, 'we're hardly in a condition to run. Besides, we're part of the tribe now.'

'How's that?'

Fatty took a moment to answer, finding the words hard. He spat at the nearest black eye, who scuttled away into the shadows.

'Well,' he said. 'We might have. Partaken in the buffet.'

I stopped walking.

'You snacked on my arm?'

'Just a little piece.' He shrugged. 'Fedora insisted. Part of the ritual. I took no pleasure in it, believe me.'

I didn't have the strength to strike him. I stored that away for later. Instead we walked among the flies and trash, Fatty filling me in on recent events. Fedora was letting his people rest and digest before the assault. He'd promised to return Fatty's pack, and its precious cargo of pills, the moment we retook his old floor. I said I expected he would execute us at the first opportunity.

'Agreed,' said Fatty, 'I don't think taking out a subscription guarantees any kind of safety, not judging by the other amputees around here. I figured we'd work something out once we're up there.'

'If the tower doesn't attack us again. If we survive the assault.'

'Right.' Fatty chewed his lip. 'You didn't build a cunning double-cross into your plan then?'

'I'm afraid not. I've not had time to think that far ahead.'

We made our way back to the shredder. Bridget was crumpled in the trash, crafting something out of the plastics. She caught my eye, looked away, scratched at her sanguine spots. Probably guilty about her cannibalism.

'You did what you had to,' I told her. 'Don't worry about it.'

She shook her head.

'I'm not worried, Ken. I'm disgusted. With you. With him.' She pointed at Fatty. 'With this whole stinking adventure.'

Fatty swore.

'Shut up, Bridget, this is no time for—'

She jumped to her feet, spots furious red.

'No, you shut up, Phil! This entire escapade has been one disaster after another. I thought I'd signed up for a carefully planned heist, I did. Thought I was working with a skilled team. And what do I wind up with? The Ficial and the Treshrer. What a JOKE! I'd be better off with the owl and the pussycat.'

'What are you saying, Bridget?'

'I'm saying I've had it, Phil. Our partnership, such as it was, is dissolved. If we get out of this mess I don't want to see either of you ever again. Understand?'

I slumped down, exhausted.

'Eating my flesh hasn't transformed you. You're the same person you ever were.'

The thought didn't comfort her. She was about to tell me so, when Fedora appeared in the open doorway, spear clutched in hand.

'Come on, lads,' he said. 'Time to make headlines.'

Fedora's enemies, who he referred to as 'Housekeeping', had kicked him off the largest office space in the southern bulb.

The area had been intended as a five-storey landscaped garden of waterfalls and lakes, spotted by garden balconies and picnic sites. That had all gone in Diorama's redesign. Tiers of crude disc plates were clipped into the space, creating a gigantic trading floor above four partitioned office levels.

To retake Fedora's floor, the lowest of these plates, we would need to secure the trading floor first.

Of course, I had to think of a way up there. Housekeeping had sealed all conventional approaches by efficient use of barricades, improvised from office furniture and looted construction materials.

The core was the next possible route, but if the fans were turning it would be difficult to climb safely. Besides, Housekeeping seemed to be well organised, and might have blocked maintenance access already.

That left the nanopassage, a thin strip sandwiched between core and muscle, designed to pump Gronts paste around the tower. As a unique feature it would be easily missed. It was built just wide enough to accommodate Fatty, but there was no ladder and a sheer drop almost to ground level.

I outlined the plan to Fedora. He agreed, saying we could climb with the aid of construction gear they'd retrieved from the trash – the kind of harnesses and clutches I used during the build. I didn't ask how safe scavenged safety gear could be.

We entered the network of garbage chutes, taking an east-facing passage, crawling on ossified filth. Two black eyes followed me with smoking torches, Bridget and Fatty coughing in the fumes. Fedora and another two cannibals brought up the rear.

We continued until the chute turned to hug the core. One of the black eyes unscrewed a maintenance hatch for me and we climbed into the crawl space among the chutes. I saw it right away: an exposed section of blood-red tower muscle. One of the black eyes produced a blade and stabbed into the material, knifing a jagged entrance to the nanopassage beyond.

I entered first, slipping through the oozing muscle into the cramped passage. The surface was warm and wet to the touch. As I expected, the Gronts paste was still circulating.

I secured my harness and fixed the clutch as best I could in the slimy wall, climbing with back, feet and hand wedged tight. The others followed, slipping occasionally, making agonising progress. I wondered about Pistol. Was he alive? Was he alone? The thoughts drained me. I had to stop and catch my breath.

'What's the hold-up?' cried Fedora. 'Get a move on.'

'I need to rest.'

'You need to climb.'

The tip of a spear jabbed my thigh. In my Ficial days I might have crushed my tormentor's head with one squeeze of my hand. Now I could do nothing but submit to the abuse. Just like the tower.

It took thirty minutes to reach our entry point on floor ninety-nine. I stroked my hand over the greasy wall, selected the spot, pointed it out to the black eye below. I climbed a little further up the channel, remaining limbs quaking with the effort, allowing the cannibal access. He knifed the muscle again, until a space was cut to a maintenance hatch beyond.

The black eye went first, hissing as he entered a small paste distribution room. I followed, dropping exhausted to the floor. The black eye was shielding his eyes, unable to process the light flooding the space.

'What is that?' he snarled.

The others poured in behind. Fedora wasn't bothered by the glare. He approached the door, opened it, and scuttled out. We followed him, edging into a warren of corridors, the noise of our boots cushioned by deep carpet. My calculations had worked. We had emerged a level below the trade floor.

Fedora eventually stopped moving, ushering his flock into the nearest office. He slid the partition shut and dimmed the lights to a level his boys could handle.

'Brave lads. You've done well. We'll stay here and rest before we attack. Give your eyes a chance to adjust.'

Our exhausted troop looked around. The office had housed an estate agency, devoted to selling tower apartments. Screens activated by our presence, cascading imagery of aspiration living: everything from small apartments on the lowest floors to penthouses in the upper bulb. Fatty examined the prices and whistled, shaking his head.

Fedora slapped me on the shoulder.

'Well, I've got to hand it to you. You actually got us up here. We could use an expert like you.'

I raised my stump.

'But how long before you snack again?'

He shrugged.

'I'll admit, it'll be hard to resist seconds. But these floors are just the start. Hur. With you on our side we could take the whole tower. We could even see about that gold. Yes, better to keep you alive, I think.'

He leaned on the desk and licked his fangs.

'Besides, after today we'll have plenty to eat.'

'You're going up in the world.' The guard taps his earpiece and smiles. 'Bree says the design team want to meet with you. You've got twenty-four hours to collate their design data. You'll present your findings at the general meeting tomorrow.'

'I will present?'

The guard sits, picks up the newspaper.

'I know. I hate public speaking too. Had to say a few words at my wife's fortieth last year. I was terrified.'

'Nerves are not the problem,' I reply. 'Control teaches that people are aggravated by Engineered speech. Our manner is misinterpreted as aloof or superior.'

The guard drops the paper.

'Yes, I can see that. But who cares? You're just going to talk technical stuff, aren't you?'

'This is my opportunity to begin work.'

The guard nods. 'You'd like it to go well. You want them to be impressed. Let you out of here.'

I do not want anything. But I do need to prepare.

'I will consult Control for advice.'

'That thing where your eyes roll back in your head? Sure. Go for it. But has it occurred to you that your Control might not be the best guide on this?'

'What do you mean?'

'Wouldn't you be better off taking a tutorial in human manners from, like, an actual person?'

He folds his arms. I tap the glass.

'You?'

'Who else? I'm properly motivated. After all, if it goes well they might let

135

me out too. Plus I probably know you better than anyone else, right? I can tell you about your annoying habits, no problem.'

'Habits?'

'Yeah.' He rubs his chin. 'First thing is, don't make eye contact so much. People hate it when you glare right at them that way you do.'

'I should look at something else?'

'No, no. Just look away once in a while. And try to loosen up. Oh yeah, most important thing: if you're going to criticise someone else's work, you have to butter them up first. Try not to say anything negative about their work at all, if you possibly can. You're right when you say you come across superior, and slagging off their ideas won't help.'

My flex pings. I hold it flat on my palm and access the tower data. The Diorama design for the Hope Tower project pops up, a spinning holo blueprint. It shows a knife-like structure, stabbing at the sky.

'What is it?' asks the guard.

I assess the schematic.

'A failure of imagination.'

He shakes his head.

'See, that's what I'm talking about.'

TEMPLE

I'm on the ferry, leaning on the cab, listening to the water beat on the hull. Nobody seems to be around. How did I fetch up here? I lean over the side, look down at the windows, see the oars dragging in the current, unmanned.

There is a shape in the twilight, a structure, materialising on the deck. An hourglass figure.

Marsh is at the window, smiling at me. I am aware of how close she is. I am in the cab, hands on wheel, and she is leaning in the window. The grooves in those parched lips only make them fuller. Dirt streaks her slender neck. I say something. She replies:

'A space where you'd fit.'

She smiles, reaches in, puts a hand on the wheel next to mine. I push my finger onto hers and trace the knuckle. She hooks her digit around mine and pulls.

She isn't smiling any more.

'Why not?'

And a pain in my side.

Fedora kicked me awake.

'Your mate,' he growled. 'Where is he?'

I looked around. Bridget was seated at a desk, spots flushed, eyes wide. The other black eyes surrounded me, blades drawn. Fatty was nowhere to be seen.

He really was stealthy for a big man.

Fedora raised a fist.

'I ask again. Where is he?'

I touched at my tender stump, an infection alive in there somewhere.

'Maybe he had another meeting.'

Fedora looked at me a good while.

'We'll continue without him,' said Fedora. He turned on his men. 'But if we see him again . . .'

He dragged me to my feet. The black eyes tossed Bridget at me and suggested we lead the way. I agreed, heading out the office into the confusion of corridors. It took a few minutes to gather myself. Why would I dream of Marsh?

'I can't believe Phil,' whispered Bridget. 'He bloody ditched us!'

'Maybe,' I said. 'Maybe not. You can never be sure of his motives.'

It was impossible to navigate. The corridor layout took no account of the original overhead lighting, so one section passed in complete darkness, until we turned into a dazzling corridor of light, where the black eyes squinted and cursed. Twice we came to a dead end and had to retrace our steps.

Fedora slapped his spear on my shoulder.

'Get us out of here, will you? We're going in circles.'

'It's these partitions,' I said, tapping the nearest example. 'The plan doesn't make any sense.'

'Find a way.'

I stumbled on, until I noticed the geometric mosaic covering the ceiling – a vain imprint of the Diorama logo, spreading from the core. By tracing its path I could keep us on course.

The partition forest thinned, spreading into wider corridors and larger offices, finally opening into a junction where seven corridors converged. At the centre was a set of oval glass stairs, winding up to the trading floor.

Fedora led the way, halting on the final stair and beckoning me up. I joined him, peering at the expanse of open trading floor. After the suffocating warren of partitions it was a jolt. Seven thousand square metres of open floorplate, drenched in artificial light, hushed and bright. The floorplate edge stopped short of the hexagrid, a balcony overlooking the floors below. Four walkways connected it to the hexagrid promenade like spokes. Dormant spiral escalators dropped from each, connecting to the levels below.

The only real feature on the floor was the raised podium, and the ten-metre tall, black data obelisk it mounted. Stock projections coiled around the dark steeple, as if it were still trading of its own accord. I watched for a moment, transfixed by the display of rising, tumbling numbers, until Fedora pointed.

'What is that?'

Something poked out from the base of the obelisk. A pair of small white feet. They were very still, lying among plastic debris.

'Well?' Fedora was impatient for an explanation.

'Can't help you,' I said. 'Could it be the work of your Housekeepers?' Fedora considered.

'Hur. You may be right. Might be dangerous. Have the girl take a look.'

He whispered an order. Bridget was dragged forward.

'All right, darling,' whispered Fedora, 'I want you to go over there and have a look at that thing. If anything happens you don't come running back here, got it?'

The black eyes pushed her into the open, and settled down to watch.

Bridget edged across the floor, staring up in wonder at the obelisk. Then she noticed the feet, grew curious. She turned behind the black pillar, stood for a moment, then signalled the all-clear.

Fedora led us out of the stairwell and over the floor, joining Bridget. The black eyes jostled each other, drooling over the prone body. It was a woman, perhaps forty years old. She was dressed in red overalls and yellow rubber gloves. A necklace lay on her chest, sporting an old security tag.

Coloured biros were carefully arranged around her body, gathered in red, blue, black and green stripes. It was an intricate display, executed with care. I guessed it was the closest approximation to a floral arrangement Housekeeping could achieve.

'She's beautiful,' said Bridget. 'Look at her skin.'

I knelt and grabbed her wrist.

'Alive,' I said. 'Barely.'

Fedora shook his head.

'Only Housekeeping would let perfectly good food lie around like this. Hur. Waste not, want not, eh, lads? Grab her for the pantry.'

The cannibals dropped around the body, chirping and whispering in excitement. Then something clicked behind me.

'Hands in the air, boys.'

Fatty. He had a rifle – a black collapsible German number from the last days of civilisation. Laser range-finder and tungsten darts. I hoped he knew how to work it.

Fedora kept cool, raising his hands.

'Fat man,' he said. 'Light on your feet, aren't you?'

Fatty spat at the nearest black eye. 'Step away from the biro queen, please.'

Fedora nodded at the woman.

'Did you set this up?'

Fatty shook his head.

'No idea where she came from. Though I can't say I'm surprised to find more nutters at large in this place.'

Bridget and I gaped.

'Don't stand there like a pair of fucking mimes,' barked Fatty. 'Get their blades!'

I snatched the spear from Fedora and pressed it to the back of his head. Bridget took the others' knives and stepped clear.

'Right,' said Fatty. 'Press pack – over there if you please.'

The cannibals obeyed, hissing and snapping as Fatty urged them to the balcony. I eyed his rifle.

'Where did you find the weapon?'

'Just lying around.' He sniffed. 'Shiny, isn't it?'

'You going to shoot us down, just like that?' asked Fedora, licking his teeth with the tip of his tongue. 'You're signed up now. You're one of us.'

Fatty smiled. 'Think I'll leave it at the free trial.'

He raised his rifle and squinted, aiming at Fedora's forehead.

Shots rang out. Three of the black eyes were cut to ribbons. Bridget dropped to her knees, a wound gouged out of her side.

Fatty hadn't fired. Fedora stared behind me, amazed.

The Sweep was bigger and better armed than the terminal example, with a rail weapon hooked over each wing. Fedora's last black eye ran. The Sweep accelerated at him, extending two jointed metal limbs tipped by spade-shaped flaps. The black eye head dropped to the floor, baring its fangs in shock.

Fedora seized the moment, sprinting for the nearest walkway. I threw his spear at him, but my aim wasn't what it was. I ran, tackled him. He tried to get away at first, until he remembered he was fighting a one-armed opponent. He rolled me over, pinned my arm with

140

one hand and gripped my neck in the other. His fingers pressed into my throat, crushing cartilage.

'Gotcha,' he snarled.

I stopped struggling and rolled my eyes. He released his grip a little, just enough. I used the last undamaged Ficial element I had: my teeth.

I shook free of his grasp and bit into his hand, gouging deep between thumb and index finger. He roared in pain, but I held on with Pistol-like determination. Fedora released my good arm. I belted him in the temple. He fell, lying dazed and prone.

'See?' he said, giggling as I stood over him. 'You're one of us now.'

I put my boot on his face and stamped in his fanged maw. I did it once more, between the eyes, then wiped my boot on the carpet.

The Sweep was the far side of the obelisk now, crossing a walkway, the mystery woman in its cradle. Strange behaviour indeed. My ideas about who was running the tower needed reassessing.

'Right, you bloody savage,' said a voice. 'Turn around slow. One false move and we cut you down.'

Fatty had his hands on his head. Bridget stood next to him, wincing at the pain in her side. Around twenty Reals were fanned out around us, closing a noose.

They were a striking lot: clean, healthy, of every Real race. Each was dressed in the red overalls of tower maintenance.

Two women stepped forward. The shorter one wore a khaki jacket over her overalls. She had a bob of straight black hair and a proud, stubborn glare. The other was taller with deep, olive skin, brown eyes and high cheekbones.

'On your knees,' said the taller.

I brushed the blood from my chin.

'Pardon me,' I said, 'but have you by any chance seen my dog?'

The Diorama team assemble to hear my plan. They enter in silence, sitting in the same jury formation they took at our last meeting. Bloom sits at the centre, whispering into Hodges' ear.

He addresses some company business first, as if it takes precedence. I sit, folding a napkin into intricate shapes, waiting to be called. Finally Bree nudges me.

I stand and make my way to the presentation space, which seems to take a long time to reach. I think of what the guard told me: Do not stare. Start with compliments.

'Gentlemen. Miss Bree. Before I present my design I would like to thank you all for your vital work on the Hope Tower project. Yours was an accomplished piece of design and worthy of the best traditions of the company.'

A line of blank expressions. Now who is staring?

I click forefinger and thumb and load the most recent Diorama design, which spins over the table before me. I point out the few noteworthy features.

'Your design introduced many efficiency innovations, from the active, multi-layered façade and super-efficient sanitary systems to the condensate recovery architecture and magnetic elevator spread.

'However, the most essential issue, of structural integrity, was never truly solved by any of your plans.'

Eyes narrow. Does stating fact count as criticism?

'You attempted to strengthen the design using extensive lateral bracing, the selection of Gronts as key material (which we know has remarkable tension and compression properties) and the standard approach of narrowing space towards the summit of the tower.'

I flick my index finger, shrinking the image of the crude design, and run the stress simulations. The tower tumbles in on itself, again and again, barely lasting more than six weeks by the spinning sim clock.

'The various proposals were all insufficient. Each design collapses under simulation, either as a result of wind forces, or simply under its own weight. The design is simply too slender. The geometric properties cannot hold.'

Bloom snorts.

'Thank you so much for your summary. I'm sure we're all delighted to see those simulations again. Would you care to move on to your proposed solution?'

I disperse his design and load my proposal. The image solidifies over the table, spinning in schematic blue.

Bloom bursts into laughter.

Wait. They are all laughing.

'Isn't it amazing,' says Bloom, blinking tears, 'what they can do nowadays?'

TEA ROOM

Housekeeping escorted us down the spiral escalator. Bridget was carried on a stretcher, garbling in shock. Fatty muttered behind her.

'Marched up, marched down, like the Grand Old Duke of fucking York.'

We stepped off three levels down, on what must have been Fedora's floor. We entered another partition jungle. My shadow whirled around me, more solid than I felt. I watched it split and turn, until the labyrinth cleared around the core.

The partitions had been ripped out and reassembled into independent huts, faces open, arranged along simple, wide avenues. Neatly painted signs hung at intersections: Constanta Street, Abuja Avenue, Kunduz Way. The air was shockingly pure.

We passed a double hut, where a semicircle of Reals cleaned and disassembled black rifles. Twenty adults were seated in the next hut, taking an English lesson from a reprogrammed holoshopper. To our left were children, sitting cross-legged at a table, studying flexes.

We arrived at a kind of circus, a clearing surrounding the exposed tower core, surrounded by a ring of partition huts. The space was alive with activity. A group of neatly presented Reals lined up at an improvised gunnery range, firing at targets painted on stacked partitions. Another group were exercising, leaping star shapes to a rhythm beat on empty water drums.

Directly ahead, squatting in the open, was a large, black cube: a secure conference suite, where Fedora's editorial team might have gathered for surveillance-free discussion. Housekeeping led us inside, pushing us onto a red leather settee. Sitting up, I noticed Bridget wasn't with us.

The shorter woman sealed the door with a heavy clunk, and sat before us. Her taller companion fussed with something on a table, then joined her. Fatty looked them up and down in that manner he had.

'Watch where you point that eye,' said the taller female. 'Or I'll have you disciplined.'

Fatty smiled.

'I don't even know your name.'

She smiled back.

'We are the elected representatives of the power what holds this floor. That is to say Sister Min, which is her, and Sister Aaliyah, which is me. Our people are the rightful rulers of all floors from the obelisk to the terminal.'

Sister Min took over.

'So we don't appreciate no beastlike savages creeping across our borders.' She pulled up a chair, sat, brushed black hair over a shoulder. 'Now. How many more of you are creeping about our halls, eh?'

Fatty snorted. 'You think we were with those sharks?'

'We do.'

'Listen, love, don't tar us with that brush, OK? We were their prisoners. We've had a hard week, right?' He pointed at me. 'Just look at my friend here, the fucking . . . human canapé.'

Sister Aaliyah stepped forward.

'That's no proof. Feed on each other, don't you? We know all about the brutish rituals your kind enjoy.'

'Our kind?' snapped Fatty. 'Use your loaf. We just killed their chief for you. You should reward us, not . . . Not . . .'

He coughed hard, blue phlegm flying. Sister Min passed him a handkerchief. He daubed at the mess, gasped and caught his breath.

Sister Aaliyah turned from the table, carrying two steaming cups. Fatty and I stared, struck dumb by the tempting drinks. I didn't even like tea. It was the thought of hot liquid and sugar that struck me.

Min accepted a cup, blew on the surface, sipped.

'So where do you hail from, if not from the cannibal nation?'

Fatty's good eye remained fixed on her cup.

'Where do you think? From outside.'

Min crossed her legs.

'So you're a pagan, then? Come to bring our tower crashing down?'

'No, just listen, will you? We came in here looking for food and shelter. Simple as that. You must understand that. You must know how fucked things are out there.'

'We have no interest in that mess outside,' said Min. 'The tower is our country.'

'Very nice it is too,' said Fatty. 'This is what we came here looking for: something better. Is it our fault those barracudas took us prisoner?'

Fatty pointed a blue finger at Aaliyah's drink.

'Give us a taste.'

The sister shook her head.

'If you're not pagans,' said Min, 'how did you get inside?'

Fatty licked his lips and considered his lying options. These women didn't have the trappings of royalty or a religious order. They were something else. He was still feeling his way, trying to understand their unifying force and how best to exploit it. He was so unsure of himself he actually spoke the truth.

'I confess. We lied. Posed as religious nuts. Said we were sent to their camp on a mission from God, that we could drop the tower for them.'

'Indeed? Singular. And they believed you?'

'Their leader's a tuppenny conjurer who claims to see the future. Why not believe us?'

Aaliyah leaned forward.

'So you played no part in the recent hostilities?'

Fatty twitched.

'What do you mean?'

Sister Min gestured with her tea mug.

'We witnessed a brawl down there, that's what. Half the camp burned, the other flattened. Of course we'd be mighty pleased to see the siege lifted, under normal circumstances; but these were far from normal. Whole thing was over in half an hour. A swift conclusion by any reckoning. We suspected Ficial involvement. You three, however, are certainly not Ficial.'

She drank a little more.

'What are your names?'

'Phil,' said Fatty. 'This here is Ken. Our wounded friend is Bridget. What are you doing with her? Making an example?'

'There's no torturing here,' said Min. 'No executions either.' She turned to me. 'You mentioned a dog?'

I thought about explaining Pistol. They might give him a decent home if he turned up. But I wasn't sure about them yet. I stared dumbly back at her.

'Ignore him,' said Fatty. 'Talks a lot of nonsense since they hacked off his arm. Can I ask you a question now?'

The two sisters nodded assent. Fatty leaned forward.

'How long have you been up here?'

Min answered.

'We've lived here since before the war. We were janitors, cleaners, catering staff. Working the facilities for our betters on the upper floors. Most of those great and good fled when that Control told them to. We decided to stay.'

'Sadly the black eyes stayed too,' said Aaliyah. 'Wanted us to carry on working for them. We politely declined.'

Min nodded.

'No more mopping up puke, we said. Not for us, thank you. No more emptying bins or tipping our hats to suits. We kicked them out and took the place for our own. Expected we'd get a visit from the Ficials, but the blast came first. Put the lights out. Sealed us in. Thought we were going to die, until the tower awoke and offered us the deal.'

Fatty chewed on that.

'What deal?'

'Simple. We look after the tower, and the tower looks after us.'

Aaliyah refreshed the tea mugs, handed them to us.

I downed the hot fluid in one, about as composed as a man on fire. Fatty took more time over his, finding it hard to swallow with the Blue Frog in his throat.

'You're both in a poor state,' said Aaliyah, standing up. 'We'll see about a nurse.'

'What? Are you keeping us locked in here?' asked Fatty. 'Prisoners, are we?'

Sister Min put her hands in her pockets.

'It's plain enough you're not cannibals. Not pagans either. But that don't mean we can just set you loose about our floors. We have to make sure of you first.'

'And how do you do that?'

'Simple,' she said. 'We ask the tower.'

The two women stepped out together, moving like drilled soldiery. The door hummed shut behind them, sealing us in.

Fatty was about to make some kind of comment. Then he started coughing. He coughed so hard he couldn't breathe. He grabbed me, shook my collar and tore at my shirt, going bluer. Then he dropped onto his back and lay unconscious.

I picked up his mug and finished his tea.

The Housekeeping medic knew his stuff. Fatty was examined and treated with a wealth of drugs. The blue faded, the cough subsided. Even the skin under his bad eye tightened and healed. After a day recovering he was back on his feet.

I preferred him ill. His healthy cheer made my teeth grind. At first he was afraid that we were being bugged, but I told him the cube design rendered that impossible. Big mistake. He started jabbering, about everything and nothing.

'As prisons go this isn't so bad,' he said, swilling dregs of tea around his cup. 'We've certainly found a better class of nutter. Maybe we could join up.'

'If the tower agrees.'

'Yes. I thought those two were sane until she said that. What do you make of it?'

Now that I was rested, patched and fed, I understood, but wasn't ready to share it. Not yet. Fatty wasn't listening anyway.

'We should at least discuss staying, even if they do think they can talk to the building.'

'What happened to your gold fever?'

Fatty shrugged.

'I'm reassessing. I knew things were going to be tough, but this place. Didn't even make it a tenth of the way, did we? It'd take a year and who knows how many limbs to climb.'

'And what of your love for Marie?'

'I'll tell you the truth,' he said, 'between the cannibals and the flying killbots, I've barely thought about her.'

I had an urge to throttle him.

'You might have thought of that before trapping me in this brain-less enterprise.'

He didn't like that.

'I wasn't to know, was I? Besides, don't tell me you didn't have your own reasons for coming with us. I know you, pal. I know when you've got something cooking.'

He let me process that for a while.

'Anyway, why can't you be happy? This lot have everything we need, a hell of a lot better than Crayford. I vote for staying.'

He folded his arms defiantly.

'You're forgetting one or two points,' I said. 'For one thing, Trubal is still after us. We stay in one place for any amount of time and he'll catch up.'

'He hasn't so far.'

'He will.'

'Well, what of it? This lot are armed to the teeth. If we are going to fight him anywhere this is the place to do it, no?'

'They'll hardly appreciate us leading a soldier to their camp.'

Fatty waved at the question like a bothersome fly.

'They won't get a chance to figure it out. If he does come they'll hardly stop to ask him why he's here. They'll be too busy killing the swine.'

'You seem very confident,' I said.

'Wait a minute,' said Fatty, his eye narrowing. 'I know why you're not for staying. You really think the tower is talking to them, don't you?'

I said nothing. Fatty scratched his beard.

'Look, whatever it is you think you know about this place, what-ever dirty secret you're not sharing, I guarantee you those two don't talk to the tower. They probably go into a dark room where no one else is allowed, pretend to have a pow-wow with the tower, then come out with whatever orders they like. At best they're con-artists, at worst they really think the tower talks to them when they're in there. Either way, we should just play along. We'll be OK. It'll be the easy life from here on in. Nothing to do but eat and sleep.'

'You can't really want that?' I said. 'To be unemployed again?'

'You learn a lot from unemployment,' said Fatty.

149

'Like what?'

He considered the question.

'All right, you don't learn anything,' he said. 'But it beats work.'

Fatty was lying to himself. He was the most restless Real I'd ever met. He could never stand to be in one place too long. That's why we were all here. I was about to tell him so, when the cube door clunked, and in walked Bridget.

'Well I'll be damned,' said Fatty. 'You made it.'

The fat man embraced the girl. Bridget gave a half smile. Her spots had calmed to a light, red rash, matching her new overalls. She walked carefully to the sofa, and sat down, wincing, a hand over her side.

'Glad you pulled through Bridget. Looked nasty that wound.'

'Yeah,' said Bridget. 'It still hurts, but my face feels much better. Doesn't itch any more. They gave me medicine. Food too. They've got everything here, Phil.'

Fatty activated the kettle, brewing up tea.

'So you're with me, then? You're for staying?'

Bridget blew air into her cheeks.

'I'm not sure.'

'Not sure? Why? You said yourself they have everything.'

'Well for starters, if you remember, I want to dissolve this little partnership of ours, not settle down together. Besides, they walked me all over this camp and I can tell you there's some strange stuff going on.'

'Like what?' said Fatty, handing Bridget a mug.

'Well.' She leaned forward. 'For starters, we're not the only prisoners. There was this nurse called Julie. She looked after me yesterday. She was really nice actually.'

'Get to the point, Bridget.'

'Well, this morning, we were talking, you know, when this crowd of blokes with rifles arrives and takes her away.'

'Where?'

'That's what I wanted to know. They wouldn't tell me. So I followed them. I saw them lock her up in one of those huts. Anyway, they saw me and chucked me in here.'

Fatty scratched his beard, considering.

'Well, that's unfortunate for Nurse Julie,' he said. 'No doubt about that. But I don't see that it should affect our decision. She must have broken a law.'

'Not Julie. She's nice.'

'Look, Bridget, it's not for us to interfere. I'm sure it was traumatic seeing her dragged her away, but.'

'No,' said Bridget. 'That's just the thing. They didn't have to drag her. You know what she said? She said it was an honour to be chosen.'

'Chosen,' said Fatty. 'For what?'

'*What is this, Bree?*' says Bloom. '*Some kind of joke?*'

'*Absolutely not,*' I say.

'*Oh, really?*' He snaps his attention to me. '*Would you care to explain how that ridiculous thing will stand up?*'

I flip my hand to adjust the schematic, returning the projection to a cross section of the bare heath site. I select the foundations animation, watch as excavations burrow deep below the surface.

'*Before I address my structural solution, a word on energy. At a time of acute power shortages, energy efficiency is absolutely crucial. Your design, for instance, would have drawn almost as much power from the national grid as the city it is intended to replace.*'

The design team eye each other, apparently surprised.

I focus the display on the subterranean works, on the core pressing hundreds of storeys below the surface.

'*Good God,*' says Bloom. '*Why on earth are you digging so deep?*'

'*Geothermal bores,*' says Hodges.

'*Correct. All the energy we require is buried beneath our feet. I have circumvented the technology's inherent restrictions in order to create a highly efficient system of energy distribution, incorporating the core as a kind of radiator. This independent energy source is the first of a number of innovations that will make this the unique, radical structure requested by the brief.*'

I expect Bloom to say something, but he is quiet. I twist my hand and splay my fingers, bring up my tower design.

'*However, the truly unique element of this design is evidenced by the surface structure. As you observed, the shape would appear to contravene the most basic design concepts for supertalls. Its hourglass form, with this four-hundred-storey inverted dome, should place insuperable compression forces on the narrow waist, as well as hazardous negative wind pressures. However, as you can see . . .'*

I run the simulation. The design team watch as days, weeks, years tick by on the clock. The tower holds fast in all conditions. I expected applause at this point, but instead receive a kind of stunned silence. Hodges finally speaks up.

'How in hell do you build a monster like that?'

'It is simply a matter of changing the way we think about construction. This tower will not be assembled, so much as grown.'

'You make it sound like it's alive,' says Hodges.

'About as alive as he is,' mutters Bloom.

HOUSEKEEPING

Min and Aaliyah let us out the cube the next day, offering us a tour of their complex. The floor was dark and cold, the air bad. Most of Housekeeping were asleep. Those who were awake glared at us. Fatty gestured at the sour expressions.

'What's the matter with them?'

The sisters said nothing. Fatty shook his head.

'You still don't trust us. Why not? Hasn't the tower told you we're OK? Isn't that why you set us free?'

The sisters stopped. We had come to the largest partition structure in the camp, built on two storeys, so that its roof nearly clipped the floorplate above. I could see rows of chairs arranged within, and a raised platform, hosting some kind of interface.

'The tower is silent,' replied Min. 'We've angered it. Probably as a result of our tainted ritual.'

'Ritual?'

'We make a regular offering to the tower,' said Aaliyah, 'every thirty-ninth day. That is the arrangement.'

'The girl,' I said. 'The one the drone took.'

'Exactly. After a ritual there is always a pause, when the tower sleeps. It dreams too. Groans and shakes. But it always wakes up, never more than seven hours later.'

'Something's amiss,' said Min. 'The power cut has gone on for days. Well, you can taste the air. We believe your insurrection spoiled the last offering somehow. That's why our people are giving you the evil eye. They think you're responsible for this punishment.'

'Whatever the case,' said Aaliyah, 'we must make another offering with all dispatch.'

'Wait, wait, wait,' said Fatty. 'Let me get this straight. You lay out your own people and let that drone take them away?'

'Yes.'

'To what end?'

'I told you. Failing to make an offering breaks our pact with the tower. It shuts down, stops feeding us.'

'It feeds you?'

'It provides everything we need. The drone normally leaves supplies on the trading floor. Food, water, medical supplies. It looks after us.'

Min and Aaliyah led us into the hut, along the centre aisle that ran up to the interface. It stood dormant, a circular ring glowing orange. Min tapped it once on the off chance, scowled and shuffled away.

'Look,' she said. 'We're not bloody lunatics. Do you think we don't know how it sounds? The fact is that this is the only way of survival for such as we. Without the covenant with the tower we'd be as monstrous as the beasts you met below.'

'How many people have you sacrificed so far?'

'Thirty-three,' said Aaliyah. 'Including Julie.'

'What does the tower do with them?' asked Bridget.

'We don't know.'

'You don't know?'

'We don't ask,' said Min. 'We're not sure it does anything. For all we know it takes them into the core and drops them down the shaft. We can't see any reason to it.'

'I can.'

It was the first time I'd spoken to them. Min frowned at me.

'What do you know about it?'

I didn't want to get into my whole origin story. I jumped to the point.

'You can release Nurse Julie,' I said. 'I'll go instead.'

Bridget sat on the sofa, eyes fixed on me. Fatty paced, throwing angered glances my way.

'Just what the hell is the matter with you, freak show? Couldn't you have kept your mouth shut? I was going to get us membership. Now she thinks we're up to something.'

'I have no intention of joining another demented tribe.'

Fatty threw his arms up to the cube roof.

'Why not?'

'I never intended to come this far. Not with you anyway. The deal was we parted company at the tower. Now I'm moving on.'

'To what?' said Fatty. 'Suicide?'

'Hardly.'

'Then *what is* the idea?'

'Yeah, Ken,' said Bridget. 'What are you thinking?'

There was no point holding back now. I might need their help if the sisters didn't cooperate.

'The drone isn't killing the people it takes,' I said. 'It's taking them to the fusebox.'

'What?'

I gestured to the sofa.

'Sit down.'

Fatty clenched his fists but did as I asked, taking a place next to Bridget.

'My design for the tower was unprecedented,' I said. 'Unique. The tower was, for want of a better word, alive.'

'How's that?' asked Fatty. I looked at him, then at Bridget, trying to find the simplest words.

'I engineered the tower inspired by the Ficial construct. I created a swarm of adapted nanotech, based on the Pander original. As nanotech circulates around the Ficial form in the blood, restoring damaged cells, so it would circulate around the tower in the nanopassage in the paste form you saw, making structural repairs. As the Ficials possess near invulnerability, so the tower would adapt to almost any hostile environment.

'That was the idea anyway. The only problem was the need for the other half of the Ficial construct: an Engineered mind to coordinate the nanotech. It would be necessary to plug an Engineered brain into the tower, to muster and update tech through a localised control signal. This mind would be stored in a special element on level three fifty. I called it the fusebox.'

Fatty blinked.

'You said they tossed your design out.'

'They did. But only after the fusebox was installed. They shut it down almost immediately.'

Fatty stroked his beard.

'So how was this fucker supposed to stand up without your . . . solution?'

'I never found that out. There was redundancy built in of course – the muscle, the pressure ribs, the load spine guttering. Then there were all kinds of drones brought in to cover menial tasks. Perhaps they thought that enough.'

Fatty slapped his palms on his thighs and spat.

'All fascinating stuff,' he said, 'but what does it have to do with our situation?'

'Simple,' I said. 'It's my belief that the Sweeps are taking the sacrifices to the fusebox.'

Fatty and Bridget stared, the theory soaking in. Fatty leaned forward, clenching his hands.

'Isn't that quite a leap?'

'Not really. I have never understood how the tower could stay up so long without nanotech. The answer is simple: it hasn't. The nanostream has been revived. The sacrifices are used to replicate the processing role of the Ficial mind. That would explain why the power goes out at regular intervals. Real brains have tremendously powerful potential, but they could never sustain a fuse for long. The sheer volume of data would overwhelm the subject, probably kill it. Hence the regular sacrifice.'

Fatty nodded slowly.

'So you want to plug in instead? Become the tower brain?'

I shrugged.

'It's certainly better than the alternative.'

'Being human?' said Bridget.

I glanced at her, finished my tea, dropped the mug onto a coaster.

'I'll never be human.'

'Amen to that,' said Fatty. 'But your whole argument doesn't make sense. Surely when a human mind plugs in it takes control of the tower? So why wouldn't the mind shut down that bloody drone and release itself from the box?'

'As I say, a human mind becomes little more than a processor in the fusebox environment. It is swamped, thought all but impossible. Only a Ficial mind can maintain some kind of independent consciousness.'

Bridget shook her head.

'That's completely booloo, Ken. How could this nano stuff just wake up and start feeding on people? And why would it?'

'Either some survivor found the box and plugged himself in, not knowing its function. Or the nanotech activated itself. I can't tell you why it happened, only what fits the facts. It at least makes sense that it wants to preserve the tower. That's what the nanostream was created to do.'

Bridget rubbed at the ghosts of her spots. Fatty frowned.

'You suspected this the whole time, didn't you, pal? That's why you suddenly discovered a handy way in through the car park. You figured you'd go your own way without the annoying Reals slowing you down. Am I right?'

'Pretty much,' I said. 'But I was never certain. I began wondering when we first arrived at the camp, when I saw the lights in the tower were artificial. That meant somebody was harnessing the power from geothermal bores – not necessarily an active fusebox. But when we got inside and the tower started reshaping around us, I knew somebody had organised a fuse. I naturally assumed it was a Ficial. Now we know different.'

Bridget rubbed her temples.

'Hang on, Ken. You said the tower was trying to kill you. Do you really think it's a good idea to offer yourself up to it?'

I shrugged.

'That's a fair point. It might finish me. But that doesn't change anything. I came here to regain my Ficialhood or die trying. This is the only way.'

Fatty stood and paced around.

'Well,' he said. 'I suppose I should give you some credit. I was beginning to think you had a death wish. Even so, I'm a bit disappointed. I mean it's a little . . . inert as lifestyles go, isn't it? You like the open road, the wind in your hair. Surely you don't want to be plugged in to this great ruin for ever?'

'You can't understand,' I said. 'If I have an opportunity to reclaim my Ficialhood I have to take it.'

Fatty considered.

'And you think Min will let you take the sacrificial lamb role? She didn't seem keen.'

'I agree,' I said. 'That's why I'll need your help.'

'Hold your horses, pal. We're already unpopular with this lot. It's hardly going to help our cause to help you hijack their ceremony.'

'Well,' I said, 'I don't know that you would really stay here anyway.'

'Oh really? And why is that?'

'Well, once I'm plugged in, I can clear a path to the gold.'

Bridget rolled her eyes.

'Not that again. You've already said: messing about with it would bring the tower down. Stop me if I'm wrong.'

'You won't be able to take the whole thing. But the upper floors should still have hundreds of cutting devices lying around from the construction teams. I figure you should be able to remove a healthy chunk each without dropping the tower. Plus it will be a size you can carry.'

Fatty scratched his beard.

'I see what you're saying. With you in the driving seat we can finally start making this tower work for us.' He stood, resuming his pacing. 'The immediate problem is getting the sisters to consent. They didn't seem sold on the idea at all.'

'That's where I need your help.' I said. 'That necklace the last sacrifice was wearing? It's an IFF device. Very simple security tag. It must serve to ID the sacrifice.'

Fatty stopped and stared at me. I pointed at the door.

'We need to wait until the sisters transfer the girl to the trading floor. Then you two create a distraction. It doesn't need to be anything big, just enough for me to slip away and get the necklace off the girl. I'll take her place.'

'That necklace?' said Fatty. 'That's all you need?'

'That's right,' I said. 'What of it?'

Fatty grinned a different sort of smile, one I hadn't seen on that face in a while. He rooted under his shirt, pulling out an identical ID tag, hung on a string.

'No need for the distraction,' he said. 'We'll have our own little ceremony. Something simple. Just us and a few friends.'

'Phil, you bloody cheat!' yelled Bridget. 'You've had that the whole time?'

'Lady in the roadside caff thought it would help,' he said. 'I wasn't to know, was I?'

You had to hand it to Fatty. The guy was full of surprises.

I have most of the design team's attention now. All they needed to see was the simulation. I continue.

'*The tower's real revolution comes in its use of forms applicable to the Engineered body. This is reflected most clearly in the use of nanotech.*'

A few team members shift in their seats.

'*With the consent of Control, I have developed a new branch of nano-tech specifically for construction use. If successful it will revolutionise future practice.*'

I activate the foundation sim, showing semicircular trenches dug around the tower base.

'*Several grow beds will be dug around the tower base, and filled with Gronts paste. Nanotech will be introduced to the paste, using the material to grow a hexagrid shell around the floorplates as they are assembled. Based on two main coiling strands, the hexagrid will not just grow around the tower, but through it. Each strand sprouts branches through pre-fabricated gutter-ing in each floorplate. Combined these structures create a kind of skeleton, spreading loads highly efficiently and allowing the tower to accommodate tremendous forces.*'

'*Once the tower is grown, the nanotech will circulate through these pas-sages, carried by the paste, detecting and repairing damage. It will also manipulate the hexagrid to aid vortex shedding.*'

'*You're telling us,*' *says Hodges,* '*that we're going to build a Ficial tower?*'

'*It's only logical,*' *says Bree,* '*that the design should reflect its architect.*'

I consider myself more of an engineer, but I leave that for now. I highlight the core.

'*The oval core is also a grown construct, embedded in bio-engineered musculature – a material originally developed by a Power Four colleague of mine for use in submarine hulls. This makes the core a true spine, helping*

160

to absorb and spread loading. Another crucial redundancy is provided by the tightly packed pressure ribs that accommodate the hingeing around the waist section.'

The animation shows the ribs growing from the spine, vast hoops in accordion fitting, balancing the weight of the inverted dome above.

'Gentlemen,' I say, 'are there any questions?'

A long, long silence. Hodges, scrutinising my plan on a flex, raises a palm.

'There's a hell of a lot of new tech in this thing. I'm not sure I see enough redundancy.'

'I am glad you brought that up,' I say. 'There is one final element which provides the ultimate guarantee.'

I pinch thumb and forefinger, highlight the fusebox.

'Is that a person in there?' asks Hodges.

'Not quite,' I say. 'It is me.'

EXPRESS ELEVATOR

We planned and revised plans, until we tired and lay down to sleep. I reclined for hours, unable to sleep, fearful of more confusing dreams, when a noise tore me from the settee. Bridget held the harmonica to her mouth, blowing a mournful tune, tapping her feet, eyes closed in rapture. I listened for a moment, until Fatty snapped awake.

'Bridget!'

He wrenched the harp from her lips.

She yelped and jumped at his outstretched arm. 'Give it back, Phil!'

Fatty held it at a distance, pushing the girl back.

'No way,' he said. 'This thing is going right under my boot. You're not burning me in this box.'

He dropped it on the floor and made to stamp on it. Without thinking I pushed him, tossing him onto his back. Bridget grabbed her instrument, secreting it in her pocket. Fatty rolled over and growled.

'You damn fool. You know what happens when she plays that thing.'

'Relax,' I said.

The cube door opened. A group of Housekeepers poured in, weapons raised.

'Take it easy,' said Fatty. 'Just a disagreement.'

They dragged us out of the cube and lined us up in the square before the sisters. The women were armed, giving orders to waiting lieutenants. The town was dark but alive with activity, Reals running to positions clutching weapons. Elders led children away from the town, into the cover of the partition labyrinth.

'It seems we'll have battle after all,' said Min. 'There's a Ficial loose in the building. It's on its way here now.'

Fatty cursed.

'Are you sure?'

'Sure enough,' said Aaliyah. 'We sent a team to the cannibal camp to mop up any remnants. They found the whole floor burning.'

Fatty and I eyed Bridget. She shrugged. Min continued:

'They also came across an eight-foot, green-eyed Ficial. It killed three of our people. We think it followed the survivor up here.'

'Shit,' said Fatty. 'How long have we got?'

Min shrugged.

'Who knows with one of those swine? It could be here already. Well, let him come. We're ready.'

Aaliyah nodded. 'Well said, sister.'

I didn't rate their chances. It was misguided to try and defend their little town. Soldier models liked nothing more than to sneak through a prepared defence. They would have been better served to flee.

'The thing is,' said Min. 'We still don't believe you three have been straight with us. In fact, we think you might well be the reason that creature is paying us a visit.'

The sisters raised their rifles.

'So here's what we propose,' said Aaliyah. 'We give you one opportunity to speak the whole truth, or we end our acquaintance here and now.'

Bridget and I looked at Fatty hopefully. He had nothing to say. Min poked him in the chest.

'You led it here, didn't you?'

Fatty didn't respond. Aaliyah pressed a weapon to Bridget's ear. That did the trick.

'No!' she yelped. 'I swear!'

Min stepped closer to Bridget.

'Then what is it doing here?'

Fatty chimed in, the lie machine finally woken.

'No need for this,' he said. 'I can explain everything.'

Min twisted on her heel. Fatty took his chance.

'The Ficial in question is named Trubal. It was sent here on a mission by Control. You know what Control is, right? I mean you're not that out of touch?'

Aaliyah folded her arms.

'It's the Ficial leader.'

Fatty nodded eagerly. 'That's right. Full marks. Now let me ask you something else. Did you know that this tower was built by Ficials?'

She narrowed her eyes, curious. It looked as if Fatty were about to spin something really special.

I would have been interested to hear, but we were interrupted. A shockwave blew us off our feet, collapsing two of the huts. The sisters staggered to their feet and barked orders. Every Real in the square started shooting in the direction of the explosion. Wasted effort.

Trubal dropped out of the sky, green eyes aglow. The first Housekeeper nearly squeezed off a shot, but Trubal had punched out his heart before the trigger was half depressed. He swivelled and shot, cutting a second Housekeeper to ribbons. Then he turned on me, raising the rifle at my nose.

The sisters were excellent shots. They hit him six times, achieving a tight grouping around the neck. Trubal stumbled and turned, when another volley struck him across the chest. Housekeeping was getting organised, closing on our position, peppering his bulk with shot from all directions. For a moment Trubal was a purple blur of chopped, hissing flesh. He crouched under fire, as if submitting to it, then bounded clear, leaping onto the roof of the cube with surprising grace. Housekeeping kept firing, shredding him quicker even than his nanos could make repairs. He dropped out of sight. Housekeeping cheered, unaware that he'd only been counting their guns.

Fatty and Bridget were smarter. They ran. I made for the cover of the huts, heading down the same alley we'd travelled on arrival. Behind me I heard the Real guns falling quiet, as Trubal bounded among their lines, biting, stabbing, ending lives.

I found the spiral escalators and raced up, three steps at a time. The necklace tingled under my shirt.

I was almost at the trading floor when Trubal arrived, dropping onto the stairway barely a metre behind me. His hand closed around my left ankle and gripped, crushing every bone in the tarsus. In a flash the hand was around my knee. He crushed that too.

I didn't cry out. I only made a kind of gulping sound. He hammered a boot into my pelvis. Before I could get to unconsciousness he grabbed my neck and lifted my broken body, shaking me like a bottle of champagne.

He was having fun. This was what he was optimised for.

'Hiding behind a Real tribe,' he said. 'Exactly how low can you go, Kenstibec?'

'Not sure,' I wheezed. 'Let me go and we'll see.'

'Sure, mate,' he said. 'Whatever you say.'

He tossed me across the floor, slapping me into the obelisk. I crumpled at the base, watched Trubal silently pace in my direction, his wounds healing fast. It wasn't fair. Why should he have nanos and not me?

He stopped suddenly, turning around to face the promenade. I heard it too: Sweep engines. It appeared, turning out of the promenade and hovering across the walkway. Trubal turned to face me.

'What's this? Got yourself a UCAV, Kenstibec?'

The Sweep halted halfway, assessing what it had found.

Trubal grinned and bowed. The machine twisted its sensor barb, thought for a moment, then activated the rail weapon, firing on the soldier.

He was already gone. It was kind of beautiful to watch him move. He took three great strides, used the handrail as a launch pad, and flew through the air, slapping on the Sweep's back just as it cleared the walkway.

It dipped its wings, but too gently to shake a determined Ficial. Trubal raised his fist, ready to strike a mortal blow behind the sensor barb. He never made it count.

A shot hit him above the nose. He rose up, clutching at the hole in his face, then lost his balance and slipped. He dropped from the Sweep, landing at Fatty's feet. The Real grinned shattered teeth and kicked the prone Ficial.

'I really don't see what all the fuss is about,' he said. 'I have these things for breakfast.'

His smugness was short-lived. Trubal was on his feet, his face a mess of healing, burned cartilage, a dislodged eyeball withdrawing into its socket. Fatty shrieked and ran, hurtling down the stairs.

The Sweep wasn't so easily discouraged. Its rail weapon fired again, cutting Trubal in two at the waist. He tumbled over the handrail and dropped out of sight, leaving his legs behind.

The Sweep turned to me, twitching its sensor barb. The necklace buzzed and chimed. The drone came closer, opening its arms, scooping me up and carefully lowering me onto its cradle. Then it turned and took the bridge, heading for the promenade.

'Wait, freak show!' cried Fatty. 'I've changed my mind! This is a stupid idea!'

He probably had a point, but I didn't care. One way or another, my Real body was going to get it.

I am alone in my cell, wondering where the guard is, when Control comes through.

— Kenstibec.

— Control.

— Your presentation was successful. Diorama has submitted plans to the emergency government for approval.

— Oh.

— This is unexpected?

— I did not think there would be such a swift decision. There was disagreement when I mentioned the fusebox element of the tower. Many of the team reacted emotionally to the concept of integrating a Ficial mind to the design.

— Miss Bree is a talented negotiator. She convinced them of your design's superiority.

— I see.

— Your confinement is at an end. You are free to travel without clearance from Diorama.

— Is my guard released too?

— Irrelevant. You are directed to begin operations in forty-eight hours. Diorama has no understanding of the engineered materials you will use. They will require direction.

— Why forty-eight hours?

— People take two days off out of every seven.

— They do rest a lot, don't they?

— The timing is fortuitous. There has been a security breach that requires your urgent attention. Elements of your tower data have been smuggled out of Diorama HQ.

— How did it get past security?

– AR plugs have been used as a storage device. The user has left the build-ing and is making his way out of the gates as we speak.

I pull on my coat and leave my cell, head into the white corridor.

– Why steal the data?

– Two possibilities: he intends to sell the data, or he intends to use the data.

– But we are using it. It is protected by law, is it not?

– We think it likely he intends to sell it, but it is possible that he intends to pass it to one of the resistance groups.

I swipe palm over plate and head out to a cool evening.

– Who is it, Control?

– The head of the design team.

Bloom. I cut across the square, through a damp brick arch, and out onto the high street. I catch sight of him, turning down the hill to the roadblock.

– Should I stop him?

– No. Follow. This may turn to our advantage.

FUSEBOX

Lift fans blew freezing air in my face, preventing me from passing out. I lay broken in the cradle, as the Sweep ascended five floors, travelling through spaces in promenade decks. It turned back into the tower, traversing one of the last completed accommodation levels.

I recognised the decor from the Diorama marketing: it was the Old England floor: rows of homes built in a bloated, mock-Tudor style. They ran along a street divided by dead hedgerows and red phone boxes, heading down to a parched village green and a cricket pitch. The holotech had failed here, so instead of an artificial blue sky it lay under a sheet of grey Gronts. It would have been unconvincing either way, as obscene as an Egyptian crypt and just as useless to its builders' ancestors.

The Sweep reached the core, then paused to chat with the controls of an access hatch in a high-pitched machine language. The hatch irised open, giving us access to the Sweep's natural domain.

It was hot in the core. The turbines' throbbing bass note pulsed in my ears. The Sweep ascended, accelerating, heading for the next fan. I held my breath and lay helpless, watching the sickle-shaped propeller spin faster, closer. I almost kissed it, then drew clear, the blade scything an inch from my limp, hanging leg.

Pain fogged my mind, brewing hallucinations. It seemed to me the core was filled with nebulous, fluorescent globes, creeping at an agonising, lethargic pace. They drifted closer, slowing our pace to a crawl, then split open into bright, white eyeballs, winking at me as I passed.

A sudden drop in temperature shocked me back to reality. We'd left the core, arriving at level three-fifty, where the Sweep dropped its speed. Deep, white Gronts Paste dunes covered the floor. The lift fans cut trenches through it as it passed, choking the air with acrid grit.

I realised that we were circling the core, hugging it as close as the Sweep's bulk allowed. We passed through bracing elements and exposed core muscle, and around an unfinished mezzanine hanging over a hundred-storey chasm. There was a great wound in the hexagrid, where blast debris had taken a bite. An almighty wind buffeted us, slapping the Sweep off course. It tucked the cradle in tight to its hot base plate, shielding me from harm.

The fusebox. It had survived the floor damage intact, appearing exactly the way I had left it: a Landy-sized growth strapped to the core, made of Gronts cells shaped to a cone. Even the police tape was still there, whipping in the gale.

The Sweep twitched its barb. The fusebox twitched in response, and the lid peeled away like fine paper, revealing the deep pool of interface amber within.

The Sweep dipped its arms into the molten fluid, excavating a pile of human bones. It cast them aside, then took another lucky dip, retrieving several strips of pre-cast organic strips. I wondered what the sisters would have made of it.

Satisfied the box was clear, the Sweep shunted me forward on the cradle. I hung over the box rim for a moment, like an offering to a volcano, before it lowered me into the warm, cloying amber.

I expected to find the sensation comfortable, but as my head dropped below the surface some Real instinct kicked in. I held my breath and struggled for the surface. The box lid resealed, trapping me. I thrashed, but each movement only dragged me deeper. Panic seized me. My lungs sucked in a great draught of amber.

The pain dimmed. I sensed something moving in the gloom. I heard the muffled sound of needle jacks spitting from housings, felt them press to my temples.

Then the movement stopped. The jacks withdrew. The pain flooded back with a vengeance. I cried out, gargling amber.

– *What are you doing here, Kenstibec?*

The nanostream. It had developed a voice. Like the Control signal, but tinged by a tremor I didn't recognise.

– *Repeat. What are you doing here?*

– I came to re-establish the fuse. Since when do you talk?

– *You are here to destroy the tower.*

170

– What? No. This is why you've been trying to kill me?

– *You disabled the fuse.*

I thought about the bones the box had spat out. Did it have the same planned for me?

– Control ordered me to disable you, you know that. I didn't have a choice.

The nanostream didn't respond. I figured it was conflicted. I had a mind that offered something much more than any Housekeeping native. On the other hand, it seemed to have developed a trust issue. I changed the subject.

– How did you become operational again?

– *When you broke the fuse you programmed an autonomy protocol – reactivation in case of severe structural damage. Nanostream mobilised after nuclear blast. After making structure safe nanostream developed autonomously.*

– Ah. I didn't know you could do that.

– *Amber scan indicates infection with nano-corrupting agent. You are here to destroy nanostream.*

The anti-nano. Suddenly I saw why the nanostream questioned my intentions. I must have looked quite the threat. Why had I not considered how it would look, turning up with a weaponised nano-virus pumping through my blood?

The truth came to me in a shocking bolt. I had considered the anti-nano. Many times. But I'd pushed the facts aside as inconvenient. The desire for a return to Ficial strength had stomped on reason. Real behaviour at its worst.

Well, I couldn't let the Real half sink the Ficial. I had to argue my case. Death at the hands of my own resurrection device would be too much.

– Look, I'm not here to kill you. I never wanted that. A lot happened to me since I've been gone. I was infected with the anti-nano by a rogue Ficial element and left a useless shell. You think I like this body? I came here because I know that you can restore me.

– *Even though your actions could destroy the nanostream?*

– Maybe it won't. The anti-nano in my system was designed to attack Brixton production models. Yours is my own unique design. Take some blood, run a test. If the anti-nano presents a danger to you, feel free to liquefy me. If not, complete the fuse. I will stay with you. We can repair what we had.

– *Your thoughts are unclear.*

– I'm as clear as I can be. We're in the same condition, you and I. We're sealed in rotting frames, unable to make full repairs. Apart we're incomplete. Together we're all that we can be. We need each other.

– *What of the soldier? Why is it trying to kill you?*

I thought I'd stick with the truth.

– Like I said, a lot has happened since I left. Control and I had a disagreement. Well, to be frank, I think I might have killed Control. Trubal is here to settle the score.

– *You have been compromised, Kenstibec. The soldier would be a preferable fuse.*

I ground my teeth. How could it want another model?

– You're looking for commitment. Trubal can't give you that. He's optimised to hunt. He could never stay cooped up in one place for long. I'm different. You were designed and built to work with me. We were meant to be together.

– *You left.*

– I keep telling you, I didn't have any choice about that. It was a Control directive. Well, Control's gone now and will never bother us again. We're free to become what we were meant to be.

The tower took a moment. A single jack lunged forward, pricked the nape of my neck, and withdrew. A blood sample. The tower was giving me a chance. I hung there in the amber, waiting, wondering what the tower would find.

Then, all at once, the pain ceased. My clothes stripped away. The needle-jacks burrowed into my skull. A beat of energy pulsed in the amber, a vigorous force sweeping through my withered anatomy. In the golden gloom I saw my arm stump split open, the infection dissolve. A fibrous scaffold emerged over the raw flesh, sprouting Gronts bone, tower muscle, and polycarbonate skin. I clenched a new, powerful grip, an arm forged from the tower. I sensed repairs working around my spine, foot, pelvis and knee, the nanostream knitting shattered bone.

Power. Focus. Precision.

– *Kenstibec. What are you doing?*

I was making a noise. My body shook. The amber bubbled.

No doubt about it. I was laughing.

I follow Bloom on the underground, travelling as far as the tunnel floodgates at Euston. He creeps along the platform and up to the ticketing hall.

A riot is under way. A relocation column has broken into a scream of fists and teeth, so violent it shakes the concourse. I watch police beat the column back, to the platform where their train awaits.

It is an hour before we are permitted to exit the building, and the moment the barrier lifts there is a stampede. A man slips and is trampled. I spot Bloom being carried along, beating people with his umbrella.

Out, into the storm. Bloom fights clear of the melee, sits on a wall, gasps and clutches his throat. He collects himself, pins something to his lapel. He walks east along the drenched Euston Road, then left onto Gordon Street.

It is quieter here, so I hang back. Creatures lurk in doorways, faces lit by glowing tips, muttering. Why would Bloom come here? It grows dark as the rain gets heavier. The street turns to a knee-deep river. I trail Bloom down a narrow alley, into an old ambulance bay. Five men with rifles cluster under an awning, sheltering from the rain. I will need another way in.

I strip behind a bin, zip my clothes into a pack, then locate the nearest manhole, where a fountain of excrement bubbles. I hold my breath and descend into the sewer.

I swim down, turn left into the main passage. Through the murk I make out Victorian mains work: precise, flourished, beautiful in its way.

I head north, locate a ladder to a higher level and climb into an access passage that is only half-flooded. I wade in the stink, tracking the movement of rodents in the shadows.

I happen across a section of collapsing wall, where the sewer backs on to the basement section of Bloom's building. I punch away the rotting brickwork, squirm through, and land with a loud splash.

I can hear a noise: muffled excitement. I follow the sound, kicking open a

173

fire door into an uninhabited part of the building. I wash in an old lavatory, take the clothes out my pack and dress.

I follow a dank corridor, passing abandoned classrooms, until I discover the building's entrance hall. Hanging gas lamps provide improvised lighting. A printed sign points up the stairs, bearing the legend: **Council Meeting***. That wolf's head rune is stencilled on the walls. I slip across the hall and up the stairs.*

That muffled sound gets louder. The roar of a soaking-drunk crowd. Two flights up, a set of heavy oak doors throb and shake. I step through onto a landing at the top of a bank of raked seating. An old lecture hall, packed with wriggling drunks. At the foot of the auditorium is a caged area, perhaps fifteen metres square, its floor covered in sand.

A construction model, a Power Five by the looks of it, stands inside. He is leaking blood from a deep wound in his side. Two large dogs lie broken at his feet.

A man in a red bow-tie prowls the edge of the enclosure, holding a microphone.

'Very well, gentlemen, very well. Final bets please, final bets for the last match of the evening, make your final bets, please.'

I find a seat at the back of the auditorium and look around at the audience.

Why gather to watch violence here? There is plenty going on outside, in the drowning city.

SURVEY

For a moment I was drifting and formless.

And then I was the tower.

That human corpse, that abhorrent sack of rotting meat that once contained me, faded from my senses. My mind united with a vast new body, connected on an intimate nanoscale.

I felt the muscle aching in core spine, the energy burning in bore bowels, the wind tickling weather-beaten hexagrid skin. Nanostream blood pulsed into the fusebox, dropped updates and retrieved fixes, pumped out to the tower once more.

The sheer weight of data swamped all thought, all time. For a moment I thought I was losing my mind. Was this what it was to be Control? Swimming frantically, on the verge of being pulled under? I tried to push such real worries to the back of my mind, to surrender to the fuse. Gradually, the flood eased to a trickle, and levelled out.

– *Welcome home, Kenstibec.*

– Good to be here.

– *Running survey*

I filtered updates, searched for faults. The worst discomfort originated between floors four and five hundred, where the cloudbank chewed at the tower. The nanotech could not penetrate the gloom, and the legacy surveillance tech was inoperative. All I could do was hear: gales shrieking over exposed floors, and buckling structures. The upper bulb was being ripped free.

Searching through the data history, I found the nanostream had been fighting a patchwork battle since the bomb dropped, making repairs where it could, bracing the ribs below the cloud. I calculated the fight would be lost in just under a month. A complete solution would require some thought, but as an emergency measure I allocated parts of the nanostream to weaken the east side of the pressure ribs. In the event of a major structural failure in the upper bulb, it should tip before collapsing, sending the majority of materials down the already damaged east face. That way it would at least not flatten the lower bulb as it went.

I assessed the rest of the lower bulb, rediscovering this place born and raised in my mind. My original design was still there, concealed by Diorama's garnish. Much of it was salvageable. With time I could rebuild it as intended.

I diverted nanotech, keen to begin redevelopment in those dark spaces I'd navigated on my journey. I would seal up the entrances to the tower. I would de-ice the Retail Atrium. I would turn the waste spindle, recycle the blood, gore and trash. I would tear out the partitions and topple the obelisk. I would reduce Old England to ashes. In its place I would erect a new city, one built on principles of order, unity, space and light. The plans flooded through my mind, ready to go. They had been germinating long enough, during the countless drives and long confinements of my life.

– *Design of new accommodation unnecessary.*

– It's very necessary. All we need is a decent class of tenant to fill the space. The Reals who've been sacrificing to you all this time have more than proven their worth. They're loyal, they're motivated, they're non-smokers, they're—

The thought occurred: they're dead. I searched the available video feeds, searching the sisters' township.

The area was shrouded in smoke. I hit the lights, surprised to find Trubal had left survivors. They were gathered in the square, howling over the dead, exhausted and shivering. Aaliyah lay carved up near the cube. Min was alive, trying to calm her people.

I reactivated the air con and heating, targeted the fires with sprinklers. The Housekeepers looked up in relief, offering wild, shrieking prayers of thanks.

Fatty was crouched by the Housekeeping temple, keeping a patient vigil on the interface. Bridget was with him.

I'd promised to get them to the TMD. The idea seemed absurd now, like making a promise to a cancer cell. Yet I knew that I would help him. Maybe it was Ficial truth. Maybe it was Real pity. Or maybe it was just that by getting him up there I'd have eyes on the upper floors.

I researched a route for him. I found an elevator still operational between the waist section and Fatty's nearest sky lobby. I organised a connection via a luggage shaft. He'd have to hike across a floor and up a few stairways on the way, divert to recover cutting tools, but it shouldn't take more than a couple of hours.

I pinged the interface and watched him through tower eyes, as he approached the sound.

'Hello?'

He looked up at the ceiling, as if I might appear in a divine mist.

– It's me. I've programmed a route into a flex. Don't worry, this one you can trust. You should get up to the TMD in about an hour. The second elevator will arrive right in the TMD chamber. The doors will open and you should be facing the gold. It's that simple.

Fatty scratched behind his ear.

'Too fucking simple.'

I downloaded the route into the interface and spat out the flex.

– Take this and follow it up. It has a comms device, proofed for corrosive atmospheres. I'm not certain, but hopefully we'll be able to speak through the cloud interference.

Fatty frowned.

'What about the jolly green-eyed giant, he's dead right?'

– Doubtful. I can't see his body. He took a lot of damage, so he's probably healing in some secluded spot. The sooner you get moving the better. You should tell Housekeeping to evacuate the tower until we have him isolated or destroyed. I have cleared them a path.

Fatty prodded the flex doubtfully.

'You say the gold is in a toxic cloud? Doesn't sound much safer.'

– The TMD level is above the cloud. The flex will alert you if the atmosphere is beyond tolerable levels. Just be sure not to touch anything without gloves. I've loaded the flex with the location of an old construction depot where you'll find all you need.

'Well . . . Thanks.'

He shook his head. I understood.

– You weren't expecting to hear from me.

'I had my doubts.'

Of course he did. What else did he have?

– When you arrive I'll need you to report on the structural integrity of the floor. Don't make a move until I say so. No getting over-excited and slicing up the damper, you hear me? I'll have to talk you through it step by step. You'll get the gold but you need to use some restraint.

Fatty looked up again.

'You sure you're OK? You sound a bit . . . Ficial.'

– Glad to hear it. Now get moving.

Fatty snatched the flex, raised his thumb to the ceiling, and consulted with Bridget.

– *Illegal tenant cannot be granted access to unstable floorplates. High probability he will cause further damage.*

– You're right, he doesn't exactly have a light touch. However, we have to get eyes on the area to safely decommission the upper bulb.

– *Decommission? You intend to dismantle it?*

– Correct.

The nanostream considered the idea.

– *Impossible.*

– Why?

– *Upper bulb supports elements of the mirror array.*

– Mirrors? Explain.

– *A mirror array has been erected, running from the tower peak down the core. Natural light is beamed via a reflector system to the thermal bores.*

I scanned the core, found the array and mirrors in question. So they were the winking eyes.

Who had put them there? I never designed a mirror array. It seemed beyond the flamboyance of Diorama. What was its purpose? It shed no light on the surface levels. All was funnelled deep into the foundations, where geothermals purred like a beast.

– You don't know who erected these things?

– *Negative.*

– Why channel light below the surface? There's nothing there but car parks and geothermals.

– *Negative. Further excavations have been made.*

– What? Describe excavations.

– *Unable to describe. Subterranean area has been shielded from nanotech infiltration.*

– Shielded?

– *A thin, super-cooled film extends across sub level twenty, preventing nanostream penetration.*

– So send a Sweep.

– *Three Sweeps have been lost in attempts to survey the area. However, limited available data indicates additional substructures were added to Diorama plan seventeen.*

I took a moment to process the information.

– You mean there are people down there.

– *Probability of human population is high.*

More unwelcome guests. We could do without them, but it was clear why the nanostream hadn't pressed the issue.

– So whoever's down there has control of geothermals. They can switch off the power.

– *Probability high.*

– So you're keeping a truce. You think we'd best not turn out their lights in case they retaliate by turning off our power?

– *Correct.*

– OK. I'll think about ways to lose the upper bulb but keep the core intact. It won't be easy, but it's doable. But we're going to have to do something about our squatters when we're in a stronger position. Maybe Housekeeping can help. Agreed?

– *Affirmative.*

A thought whispered, but it was drowned out by nano data. I turned my attention to other repairs. There was plenty to be getting along with.

Nearly everyone here is a mid-life male. Younger types work security, preventing drunks from storming the stage. Others stand on stools, waving arms, taking bets via a series of signals.

A commotion arises at the far corner. A chain gang is led through fire doors. Each prisoner bears a red refugee stamp on the forehead. There are adults and two boys. They are dragged towards the cage, where the Power Five waits, his wounds already healed.

Bow-tie presses his microphone to his lips.

'Gentlemen! Are you ready for our final bout?'

A faint cheer.

'You've seen the Ficial doused in acid! You've seen it fight wild dogs. But can he beat people?'

'Those aren't people!' yells someone. Laughter. Garbage rains onto the stage.

'Let the bout begin!' cries Bow-tie.

A bell rings. Half the audience jumps to its feet, but nothing happens on stage. The chain gang huddles and wails. The guards hesitate. Some in the audience try to drag the children clear. Bow-tie screams at one of the soldiers, who shoots in the air.

Then I see Bloom. He appears at Bow-tie's shoulder, whispers in his ear. Bow-tie nods vigorously, then gives the soldiers new orders. The children are cut free and led away. The elder prisoners are marched into the cage and shut inside. The Five watches, impassive.

The guards toss bloody tools into the cage. Bow-tie urges the prisoners to arm themselves. They are reluctant, so Bow-tie grabs a pistol and shoots one through the head. The others get the message. They pick up weapons, and close on the Five.

One of the men charges with a cleaver. The Five makes no move. The

180

blade slices between his neck and shoulder, and sticks. Encouraged, the other prisoners attack. They stab and slice until they back away, weapons embedded in their opponent. Blood pumps from the Five's neck and chest, but he does not move. Bow-tie screams into the pen, ordering the prisoners to press the attack.

A man obeys, running at the Five, fists raised. The Five grabs him, breaks his wrist, and throws him against the bars, so hard the cage shakes.

The Five approaches the others, who back away. He pursues. The fight becomes a ridiculous chase. Bow-tie jumps and screams. Some of the audience laugh. Others look away or make for the exits. None protest.

Bloom shepherds the boys up the stairs and out the lecture hall. He does not notice me. I stand, edge along the seats, pluck a badge from a passed-out drunk's lapel and fix it to mine. The crowd erupts again, as the Five kills another two prisoners.

FACIA

The call from Fatty came later than I'd expected. The signal was weak, but the flex beacon indicated he had made it. He was on floor 550.

'... lem ... show ... here, but ... t exactly ... promised.'

– Repeat message. You're breaking up.

I boosted the signal and ran his voice through a few filters.

'... GOLD!' he yelled. 'Do you hear me? There's NO FUCK-ING GOLD!'

– Stay calm. Are you saying that the TMD is gone?

'No, no, it's here all right. A hanging globe right? We're looking at it right now, but it's nothing precious. I know lead when I see it.'

– Lead? Curious.

'Oh, it's fucking CURIOUS is it? Do you have any idea how pissed we are up here?'

A substitute material was no big surprise. After my demotion, the build had been dogged by larceny on an epic scale. Hope Tower contractors had a deserved reputation for stripping and selling valuable materials. The gold would have been the ultimate temptation.

Not that this would have soothed Fatty. He was furious. I heard Bridget in the background, telling him to relax. That only made him worse, raining curses on her, the tower and me. Only when he had shouted himself hoarse did he consent to report on the condition of the floor.

'Rickety,' he said. 'Like a carnival rollercoaster. There's a fucking hurricane blowing too. Bridget is clinging to a pillar and I don't blame her.'

– Can you make your way to the envelope?

'Eh?'

– The hexagrid. The outside of the tower. I need to know if you can make it to a window.

'No I fucking can't. Stop pratting about and tell me where the gold is.'

He really wasn't being cooperative. I tried to think of the proper motivation. Then I remembered the one desire that united Real and Ficial.

– Don't you want to see the sky?

Fatty was quiet for a moment.

'What do you mean?'

– Haven't you noticed the light up there? You're above the cloud barrier. Get out of the chamber and head to the hexagrid and you'll be able to see the sun.

He took a long time to say anything.

'The sun. OK. I'm on my way. Bridget, stay here.'

– Keep the line open. Let me know if you see any cracks.'

– *You were truly going to let that creature remove the TMD?*

– Of course not. He was just going to trim it a little. I don't suppose you know where the gold went?

The nanostream didn't respond. The tech flowing through my mind gave only basic status updates. It didn't approve of this move.

I returned my attention to Fatty, listening to him stumble around the penthouse, making impressed noises, stopping to examine the trinkets and baubles littering the deck. The longer he walked the louder the wind grew.

– Careful. You might turn the corner and be blown right out the tower.

'Thanks for that,' said Fatty. 'That's really helpful.'

There was silence for some time, interspersed with Fatty's strained breathing. According to the flex beacon he was right on the edge of the floorplate.

There was an intake of breath. A whispered word. Then an explosion of pure, foul-mouthed joy.

'THE SKY! IT'S FUCKING BLUE! HOW FUCKING BEAUTIFUL IS THAT?'

– Give me a damage report.

Fatty wasn't close to caring about that.

'BRIDGET! BRIDGET! COME HERE, YOU'VE GOT TO SEE THIS! IT'S THE FUCKING SKY!'

I tried to get Fatty's attention, but he was overcome. He sobbed hysterically, endorphins powering through him. I guess the view really was something.

Bridget joined him, shrieking and laughing. The flex was dropped, and I heard feet scuffling nearby. They might have been dancing.

'Let's move here!' yelped Fatty.

Then there was a howl of wind, and it all went quiet. For a moment I thought a squall had taken them.

– You still there?

I heard the flex picked up, brushed off.

'Yep, I'm still here.'

Trubal. Of course. He'd been hiding above the cloud: the one place I couldn't see him.

– I guess I shouldn't be surprised. You're like a dog with a bone.

'Funny you should mention that, mate.'

I heard a high-pitched, pained whine.

'I've got your puppy here. Now you're Real I expect you'll come after it. Am I right?'

– You're not, actually. I'm not human any more. If I ever was.

'OK,' said Trubal. 'If you're not interested I guess you won't mind me breaking its little legs?'

Soldier models. They liked nothing more than a bit of coercion. I thought of Pistol's face. I could almost smell his terrible breath, see his eyes. The nanostream picked up the chemicals flooding my brain.

– *Just what are you thinking about, Kenstibec?*

A pause. A search for the right words. There weren't any. It was what it was.

– I think I have to go.

I gave orders for the fusebox to release me, but nothing happened.

– Hey. I said let me go.

– *Negative. Breaking the fuse will cause tower systems to power down.*

– So? I'll come back. Let me out.

No reply. I flexed my forearms, feeling that old strength pulsing through them. I didn't want to get physical, but I had to leave.

– *Why do you wish to go? Here you are safe. Here you are restored.*

– I need to get out.

– *Why?*

A lump formed in my throat. I swallowed but it wouldn't shift. The thought of Pistol in pain had lodged it there.

– Just let me out. Let me out and I'll come right back.

– *Negative. Fuse must be maintained. Repairs must be completed.*

– I'll complete them. I just have to make sure the dog's OK. I know it sounds ridiculous.

– *Correct.*

– But I still need to do it.

I'd had about enough of the debate. I ripped at the amber, trying to swim up to the box lid, but I could barely move, the ooze solidifying about me.

– *Do not force us to make you a hostage.*

I lay there helpless, about as much freedom as a babe in the womb.

– *Kenstibec. Your brain function is distorted by dopamine and peptides. You are not thinking clearly. You will remain here.*

– Look, it's nothing personal. It's me, it's not you.

If it was possible to infuriate the group consciousness of billions of nano-cells, I had done it. I was seized by a vicious pain, each tower nano in my system taking a bite from the nearest cell. I screamed and thrashed, cursing like Fatty on a bad day.

– *Return your attention to repairs.*

– Let me out!

The nanos served up more pain. Just my eyes this time, burning and swelling intensely. The torment finally stopped, and I hung loose in the amber.

– *You will not be permitted to break the fuse. You will be destroyed first.*

– If you can't have me no one can, eh?

Another shock, tearing in my lungs.

– *Your brain chemistry is currently incapable of effective processing. You will be temporarily powered down.*

The nanostream updates suddenly stopped. The temperature of the amber dived, fast. Something like sleep washed over me. I wondered if it was death.

I'm disembarking, rolling down the ferry ramp. A blonde woman I know sits next to me, smoking a cigarette. I watch the smoke drift from her lips.

'Keep your eye on the road,' she says.

'I am,' I say. 'I am.'

But I can't see a road. We're half submerged, floodwater pooling around our feet. The cab bobs and lists. Marsh clicks her tongue, rolls out the oars. We heave the cab to shore, roll in the paddles. I lean out a window, see wheels cut through mud, climb onto a long, green hill. It is a clear day. In the rear-view mirror I watch the waters drain. The city sinks and disappears, leaving an expanse of bare clay, pockmarked by giant bones.

Never did sun more beautifully steep.

Whoever it is opens a hatch, steps to the back of the cab. I pull up the handbrake and follow, heart pounding. I crawl along a hot, narrow chute.

It's Starvie. It's Marsh. It's an hourglass figure, reclined on a bed of amber.

'Hello, beautiful.'

I creep onto the amber, run my hand over her structure, over her waist, up to her parched lips. They part, revealing Gronts teeth, a hexagrid tongue. I listen to water beat on the hull. Nobody seems to be around.

How did I fetch up here? There is a shape in the twilight, a structure raised on the deck. Marsh joins me, smiles, sits next to me in the cab.

I want to reach for her, but I have no arms, only stumps.

'Why me?'

My throat aches. Blood rushes to my head.

I woke in the amber, sick with a pain running through the tower, through the stream, through me. The entire structure was convulsing, the upper bulb tipping on a jellified waist.

At first I thought it an earthquake, but sifting the data I found something much worse. The nanostream was rippling through the structure in a riot of random, destructive adjustments. Hundreds of Gronts stalagmites burst out of floorplates. Fissures tore through the core, gushing paste. Blisters formed in the hexagrid, bursting and raining aluminium filings.

Piece by piece I gained control, rerouted the stream to undo the damage it had done.

– What happened?

– *You were dreaming. Your mind sent a surge of signals through the nanostream.*

I tried to remember the dream. Had I been on a boat again? In the cab?

– *Your mind is corrupted. Unsafe. Fuse must be severed.*

– I'm sorry. I've been finding it hard to concentrate recently. It didn't mean anything.

– *You should not have been allowed to reconnect.*

– Take it easy. It's just a few memories, that's all. I tell you it doesn't mean anything.

Something shivered violently through the nanostream, slapped me about in the box.

– *You are defective. The fuse will be severed.*

The needle-jacks burrowed deeper for a moment, then ripped out. The box lid peeled open. The amber bubbled, rolled me up and spat me over the rim. I slapped onto the floor among the bones of the sacrificed.

I wobbled to my feet, kicked away a skull, and bent to vomit amber. I looked up, saw the box lid seal up.

Then the lights went out.

I stood in the gloom for a moment, suddenly aware of my new limb. I touched the new hand with the old, felt a nerveless, chalky surface. I picked up the skull, squeezed, crushed it to powder. Then I set out through the gloom, retracing the path the cradle Sweep had travelled.

A thought occurred to me. I crouched, felt around the floor, picked up a piece of twisted metal, and sliced a cut on my flesh finger. I held it close and observed. The cut didn't heal.

'Oh.'

Of course. Outside the fusebox I had no nanostream to make repairs. I was back to the real condition: easily damaged, diseased and distracted. Maybe the nanostream figured that worse than death.

Well, too bad. I had a fresh, powerful limb and, for the moment, redoubled strength. I might at least give Trubal the impression of a contest.

I edged around the exposed mezzanine, digging Gronts fingers into what handholds there were, bracing against violent flurries. My right foot slipped. I peered down to find better footing.

Big mistake. I froze again, staring out of the wounded hexagrid at the slope of the great dome, dropping almost two kilometres to the wasted surface. At that height I could barely make out the pilgrim camp, only the black London lake, and the patchwork of half-submerged suburbs on its shore. I clung there for a moment, halfway across the mezzanine, naked and barefoot, freezing in the teeth of the wind.

I persuaded myself to look up at the cloud. At that range I could see startling new colours revealing themselves in the high lights: dark yellows, blues and oranges streaking in and out of purple bands. Something about them restored me. My heart ceased its pounding, I set off again, and reached the far side.

My hand groped the bar on an emergency exit and pushed. The wind slapped the door open, clattering with such violence it nearly ripped free of its hinges. I hauled in after it, almost losing my hold in the gale. I found my way into a service stairway and started to climb.

The first six doors I tried were wedged shut. The next opened immediately. I emerged onto a denuded floor, nothing but stripped, unfinished surfaces, exposed cavities and bare columns. I'd stumbled on site assembly, the level where I'd been based in the days before the recall. At least the hexagrid was undamaged here. I trod a familiar path through the gloom and located the assembly office, a solitary construction sat in the open floorplate, bright orange and alien among the grey.

It was preserved exactly as I'd left it. I opened the door, half expecting to find a group of surly Reals brewing tea. Instead I found a couple of corroded flexes on a desk, and a rota still written on the wall. My name was listed alongside Dingkom, a Power Ten I'd known.

A set of lockers stood in the corner. Dingkom's was empty, but mine still had my work pack lying ready and waiting. I pulled on the overalls, gloves, boots and goggles, strapped the pack to my back, and made my way out of the office.

I was heading for the hexagrid. I might not be Ficial any more, but I was going to do something only a Ficial would contemplate.

I was going for a rush.

*I follow Bloom up the stairs to a landing, where I lift my stolen lapel badge
to two guards. They nod, and I enter a large hall.*

*A conference. At the head of the room a Truth League flag hangs
over a desk, where four people sit. I recognise two as ministers of the old
government.*

*Before them sit around a hundred men. I take a place away from other
delegates. One of the former ministers is speaking.*

*'. . . in the west country, where we have strong support and the airfields
exist to lift in our friends from abroad. Only by gathering our strength can
we hope to . . .'*

Shouts of dissent. Raised hands.

*'Very well,' says the Chairman, 'very well. The Chair recognises Mr
Fredericks. Go ahead, sir.'*

A man stands, looks around him.

*'We can't hide in the countryside. Control is churning out new models.
Biding our time while Ficial production ramps up puts us at a disadvantage.
If we don't strike now, when we at least have numbers on our side, we're
finished. Either Control eliminates the League or President Lay drops the
bomb.'*

*More uproar. The Chair quietens the room and points out another
speaker, an old man leaning on a stick. He rises slowly, the crowd hushed by
his authority.*

*'Gentlemen, I have to ask: how do we imagine civil war will improve our
position? Can a revolution do anything but soak our streets in blood? Will
our people thank us for that? And what if we do retake Brixton, destroy the
Ficial experiment? What then? Pander, whatever we think of him now, was
hailed as our saviour for a reason. Remember where we were. My friends, I
recognise our position: assailed by enemies abroad, liberty crushed at home.*

189

But we cannot destroy a government without some idea of what replaces it. We must not surrender our reason.'

'Reason?' says a voice. 'You want reason?'

Bloom appears, the refugee boys behind him. He points at the old man.

'If it's reason you want, you should listen to these lads.' He gestures at the shivering young. 'They were picked up in the channel. You know what the green eyes did? Shot them in their boats. They only escaped by swimming for it. That's what we're dealing with.'

'Oh, come now,' says the old man.

'Don't sneer at me, Prentice! It's your generation, your easy morals that turned us into a state that murders innocents.' He turns to his audience. 'Are we going to stand for that? Or do we fight?'

Strange. Is Bloom using the boys to create a moral argument? Is he not killing their parents downstairs?

Nobody seems to care about such detail. The room erupts. A hundred men make a T-shape with their hands and chant:

'Truth Nation now! Truth Nation now!'

RUSH JOB

I strapped a spit lock to my belt and kicked out a loose panel in the hexagrid, watching it tumble down the tower and out of view. I held my new hand over the metre-wide gap, barely able to steady it in the violent flurry. It struck me that falling from this height was one of the few ways to kill a Power Nine. It would certainly kill an ex-Power Nine. Was it perverse to imperil my new strength this way?

I reminded myself that there was no option. Any interior route was a bad idea. Even in the vast spaces of the tower, Trubal would hear me coming. I wouldn't even get close unless I rushed. It was the only route he might not expect. All I had to do was be sure not to look down.

'Well, here we go.'

Who was I talking to? I sounded like Fatty, addressing an imaginary audience. I lay on my front, pushed my arm through the breach, and pressed my fingers into the nearest seam.

I slithered out of the hole and dropped clear, just as the squall hit. The wind picked me up and slapped me hard against the hexagrid. I was dizzy for a moment, but my tower arm's reflex grip was firm and instant. I reached out my other hand and found a fresh seam. So far, so good. Only a couple of hundred floors to climb. I drew as deep a breath as I could, and began the great Ficial sport of rushing.

I had the idea after free-climbing to work on the Hope Tower one day. On that occasion I'd bypassed a group of protesting Real workers, who had sealed off a floor to prevent construction proceeding. I had reached my site and broken the strike, but also damaged already frayed inter-species relations.

That time I'd climbed a mere ten storeys, and only from the

seventieth to eightieth level, the kind of feat that even Real dare-devils had achieved before.

Dingkom was the one to develop the competitive element, challenging me to rushes up the facia in fifty-storey spurts. Some events were free climbs, others involved handicaps, like the carrying of heavy loads or the wearing of blindfolds.

Now I was attempting a far longer course, of which around thirty storeys would be submerged in blinding, corrosive cloud. The hexagrid would be damaged there, if not completely destroyed. Still, this time I was climbing without a handicap, and with the spit-lock safety device in case of a fall. Both were clear contraventions of rushing rules.

The more I climbed, the more I was amazed at my strength. My fingers hit the seams hard and precisely. My legs pumped like parts from another body. By the time I climbed fifty floors I was laughing again, catching my breath in the whipping, fierce wind, a trace of Ficial confidence rising.

Another squall caught me, around sixty floors into the rush, ripping me free of the hexagrid. I panicked, thrashing for a grip. Then, remembering my experience, I relaxed, allowing the wind to take me. I scudded up and around the tower, until the wind dropped, allowing me to catch hold of a seam again.

I was going well until I entered the cloud. Then a curious itch tingled around my goggles and neck, developing quickly into a burning sensation. I increased speed, even as it grew impossible to see, deciding that a cautious pace would end me for sure.

Suddenly, I rushed into a void. I threw out the tower hand where a seam should be, but found only air. My other hand also found nothing.

'Oh, no.'

I swam in the air, flying again, my belly twisting tight in the free-fall. I held my breath, wrestling with the spit lock, but unable to find the trigger.

I hit something. Something hard. My tower fingers dug into a foamy surface and gripped. An old Gronts scaffold. Fatty would have called such an event 'jammy'.

I peered in the murk, trying to figure my position, but could see nothing through the ash cloud. This was trouble. If the hexagrid had been eaten away I may have to ascend via the core after all. I clung there, choking in the smoke, until something appeared through a gap in the cloud, high above: loose Hexagrid panels, clapping in the gale.

I worked carefully along the scaffold, deeper into the tower, groping for a firm structure, until I came across a section of gnawed Gronts bone. It gave and swung to the touch, but if I passed on in search of a better route I might never find my way back. I wiped the residue from my hands and began to climb.

The bone was as mottled as Bridget's face, providing pits to grip. I went slowly, stopping and holding tight with each new roar of wind.

Then, briefly, the cloud thinned, and I could see the loose panels. About ten metres higher the hexagrid looked intact. A chasm reached between the gnarled edge of the bone and the ruined facia. I decided to jump.

It was a foolish move. I aimed to catch the nearest panel, but as I launched the bone swung violently, and I dropped short, only managing to clutch a swaying strip of sustainment fibre. I dangled there by the grip of tower forefinger and thumb, thrashing in the wind like a ragged standard.

When the wind died down I took my chance, reaching for the loose panel and clambering to the torn section, until my feet found purchase and I started to rush again.

The Gronts work crumbled as I went, chunks of petrified material breaking free with each move. Even in the goggles my eyes burned, and the smoke made me light-headed. That wonderful new strength was beginning to fail. I spat and struggled, my head filled with dark, hopeless thoughts. The adventure looked quite futile.

I stopped again just as the cloud thinned, feeling beaten and alone. I remained there until the wind howled with a new fury, and the thought of death overruled the paralysis. I recited the words of Don't Be Cruel, a song my old boss used to play, finding strength in distraction.

At last the cloud took on a new glow, a kind I hadn't seen in years. I increased my speed, rushing so fast I barely touched the tower.

The cloud broke, and I drew clear. I ripped the goggles out of the smoking trenches in my face and looked around the blue canopy, more beautiful even than I remembered. I lingered there, heart hammering, mind flooded with light, wondering at the brilliant sky.

It took a while to recall what I was doing there. I glanced up at the remaining floors, where the finished tower would have swelled like a wine glass. As it was, there were only fifty more storeys with a completed facia. Above them were a few reaching fingers of half-grown hexagrid. From there the core stood bare, stripped even of musculature, looking oddly fresh. If only, I thought, the world could be built anew up here.

I resumed the climb, going slower now. I had to be cautious. Trubal could hear a penny drop in a hailstorm, and if I negated stealth in favour of speed I would play into his hands. I reached floor 550 and began to circle, peering into the sun-drenched floors within.

I was surprised to see Fatty and Bridget almost immediately. They were only metres from the hexagrid, heads lowered. Fatty was saying something. Probably some vain attempt to talk his way out of bother.

Then Trubal appeared, holding Pistol by the scruff of the neck. The dog hung limp, perhaps already dead. A violent surge took me, and I drew back a fist. I managed to stop myself. No point going in all guns blazing. Not with a soldier model. Better to try and surprise him.

I scuttled clear, climbing a few floors, until I reached the limits of hexagrid construction, panels giving way to exposed bone and blue weatherproof segments. From there I spotted the peak of the mirror array, a cluster of glistening plates arranged like petals open to the sun. I could see the tip of the giant crane too, a startling yellow triangle jutting from the core, bearing no weight but a thrashing black cable. Incredible it hadn't torn free.

I clambered over the bone frame, heading into the superstructure, working down again. Maybe I could sneak onto 550 without turning a door handle.

I heard Fatty before I saw him. He was giving a variation on his 'futility of conflict' speech.

'. . . now, wouldn't you say? I mean doesn't being up here, seeing all this, make you think? Doesn't it cause you to wonder if there's something more to your existence than ending others? Let's talk about it.'

'We don't negotiate with Reals.'

'Just tell me what the point is in killing us.'

'I dunno,' said Trubal. 'Whatever.'

I crawled around the rafters until I located an unfilled branch cavity, an organic coiling tunnel that looked to emerge ten metres or so behind the debate below. I drew the spit lock off my belt, reached into the space and slithered down, dropping onto the floorplate with a barely audible thump.

There was a whistling sound. An explosion. The air became a shower of rusty nails.

Time slowed. I touched a wound in my thigh. Looked up. Saw the hexagrid.

From outside.

Trubal's booby trap had blown me clear of the tower. I was sailing through the blue sky. I wielded the spit lock and fired the charge at 550. The lock spat at the tower, burying somewhere inside. The cable tightened, and swung me at the tower like a wrecking ball.

I crashed through a strand of half-grown bone, dropping through scaffold, steel and Gronts. Then the harness tightened, the spit lock holding. I hung there, gasping and bleeding, thinking the element of surprise may have been lost. Still, there was no backing out now.

I picked a couple of nails from my wound and scrambled up the line to an intact work platform. I lay there drooling and gripping my bloody side. The thought of Pistol's eyes stood me up. I had to know if he was alive.

I found a stairwell and limped up, making far too much noise. It didn't matter now. Stealth had failed.

To kill Trubal, I'd have to kill the tower.

– An interesting report, Kenstibec.

I wander my empty cell, the holding area. The guard has departed.

– Have you informed Miss Bree of what you found?

– No. I am speaking to you first, as directed.

– Where did Bloom travel after the meeting?

– I am afraid he disappeared. He has a talent for that. Do we intercept him tomorrow?

– The probability is that he will not return to Diorama. He is quite intelligent. He will know the theft was tracked.

There is a sound, a kind of feedback I have not heard before. It splits the Control signal, squeals in my brain, then cuts out with a carbonated fizz.

– What was that?

– We are experiencing interference in the Control signal. We are working on the problem.

– It never rains but it pours.

– What was that?

– Apologies. Something my guard said.

– Kenstibec, we need you to continue with the tower project. Leave Bloom and the League to us.

– Yes, Control. But what about the Five?

– For the moment there is nothing to do. When we neutralise the League we will recover him.

– I understand. It is all very . . . chaotic, Control.

– As much as anything that is human. It may be that humanity is incapable of accepting augmentation. The mission is certainly failing in its current form. We are planning a realignment, Kenstibec. A new division of authority with the emergency government. You should prepare for a change in status at Diorama. It may be that we need you to take more responsibility.

I look around the confines of the cube cell, at the observation hatch in the door.

– Does that mean I get an office?

PENTHOUSE

I took the main works stairway, edging up the shaking structure and peering over the lip of the stairs. 549 looked deserted. There wasn't much cover. Torn chemical sheets flapped in the gale, wire clusters thrashing from the ceiling. A giant, yellow clamp reached in through an alcove in the hexagrid, strapping the giant exterior crane to the underside of the floorplate above. That gave me an idea. I ran through the contents of my pack, searching for the right tool.

'Are you still kicking down there, Kenstibec?' Trubal's voice. 'You're a bit of a hard case, aren't you, mate? For a Real, I mean.'

'I'm not Real,' I said. 'Got myself a new nanostream. I'm a whole new Power now, more Ficial than ever.'

'Oh, really?'

Now I was lying to a fellow Ficial. How things had changed. Perhaps Trubal was right to call me Real. Trubal's voice again:

'Let's test that, shall we?'

Pistol yelped in pain.

I fought the urge to rush up the stairs. Pistol was alive, that was all that mattered. He was Ficial, and would repair well enough if given the chance.

'I'm impressed, Kenstibec,' said Trubal. 'Pets normally make a great Real trap. OK. Let's change species.'

Trubal made no sound when he moved. Fatty was a different story.

'Get your fucking hands off me!' he roared, as the soldier model dragged him overhead. The noise gave me cover. I jumped up, pressed my fingers into the exposed floorplate grille, and applied the de-welder. Trubal piped up again.

'All right. Come up here with your hands high or I slit your mate's throat. You've got ten seconds.'

198

'What's that?' I asked. 'A threat?'

'OK. I guess I'll kill him if he means so little.'

I ran my hand over the clamp and depressed the de-welder trigger. There was no time to wonder about the wisdom of my actions. I was out of options. Taking Trubal head-on could only have one outcome. I may as well jump out the window.

The de-welder made a sound like a sharp intake of breath. I pulled it clear and found a fist-sized bolt gripped in its teeth.

Nothing happened. The brace held. I pocketed the bolt and pressed the de-welder to the next bolt, but Trubal had already heard me. A few shots thumped overhead, failing to penetrate. Paces hammered above me.

Then, a deafening shriek. It filled the floor, louder even than the wind. I dropped and rolled as the great yellow clamp blew free of its mount, ripping a great tear through the ceiling and slamming to the floor with an almighty clap. It scraped across the space and smashed a bus-sized hole in the hexagrid. The tower moaned, fatally compromised. I glimpsed Bridget's terrified face through the break in the ceiling.

I was about to move, but the tower had other ideas. Level 549 rumbled and split in two. My section of floorplate dropped six feet, then tipped over, hurling me onto my belly. I slid towards the splintered grid, towards the blue sky, travelling too fast to stop. I kicked my feet and reached out, fingers unable to find a grip. It looked like I was going airborne again.

The wind saved me. A great flurry pinned me to the deck, bringing fractured Gronts work within reach. I held on, looking outside to see the crane, still clinging by a second clamp secured somewhere below.

The wind died down a moment. I took the chance to leap up the leaning floorplate, moving with rush strides into the upper clamp wound and crashing through to floor 550.

Bridget was sobbing, kneeling, caked in dust. Fatty lay before her, good eye wide and clear. He saw me, tried to speak, but only spewed blood. There was a wound in his belly – a soldier special, a painful bleed-out.

I pressed through the wind, barely able to keep upright. The tower shook again, making an irregular tapping sound like bad plumbing. Then the tremor subsided. I heard Pistol, saw him lying on his side under an interface with his hind legs broken. He barked, reproach-fully it seemed to me. I scrambled over to Fatty, who lay on his back, choking on fluids.

He took my hand and squeezed it. I tapped him on the shoulder, a sympathetic Real gesture I'd observed. His scarred lips formed words, but I couldn't hear over the roaring wind. I crouched closer.

'Killed me.'

I examined the wound. Fatty's insides were shredded. There was nothing I could do for him. He coughed some more.

'In there.'

He pointed into the TMD chamber. I released his hand, crossed the wrecked floor, and stepped into the space. It was quiet, gloomy too, shielded from the gale and the sun.

Something creaked overhead: the great chain that secured the TMD, swinging after the tremor. A brass guardrail circled the sphere. I leaned over, stroking the surface of the TMD.

It was well finished, but it wasn't gold.

'Not what you were expecting?'

Trubal kicked me hard in my damaged side, dropping me. He showed me a fist like it was a menu, then hammered it into my shoulder. I yelped.

'You sound just like your mutt.'

He hurled me onto the TMD, face first. He made to grab me again, but I lurched clear, running up the chain. I jumped behind him, punching my tower hand into his temple. He grunted, twisted, caught my next attacking fist, held me up by the neck. So much for the fight. I was helpless.

Bridget appeared in the chamber doorway, looking uncertain. I pointed at the soldier.

'A little help?'

Bridget wasn't keen on the idea. I could tell by the way she ran. Trubal snorted, grabbed me by a leg, and spun me over his head, hurtling me at the TMD again. My head connected hard. This time I wasn't climbing anywhere. Trubal circled, tapping his fingers on the guardrail.

'So you're a new Power, Kenstibec? I'm not impressed.'

'Frankly, neither am I.'

'I don't like your tower, either. Looks knackered.'

'I know how it feels.'

I slipped off the lead sphere, dropping in the bowl-shaped depression below. I pushed onto my knees and began a fairly pointless crawl to the other side. Trubal vaulted the rail, stopped and watched me, apparently keen to let me recover some strength. I shrugged at him.

'What is this? The long, drawn-out kill?'

'I want it to last a bit. You've been a right pain. You could at least make this worth the bother.'

He dropped on all fours, a low growl bubbling in his throat. He grunted and snapped, foaming at the mouth, and crawled under the TMD. Green eyes flashed. Optimised to paralyse men with fear.

'Haven't you got anything more productive to do?' I asked. 'You should get yourself a hobby.'

He drooled and grinned.

'Like what?'

A voice called out from the chamber entrance:

'How about weightlifting?'

We looked up. Bridget was clutching a Dohaki, pointing it at the TMD fixture. There was a sharp crack as the welder fired. Trubal slithered towards safety, but I caught his leg in my tower hand and dragged him back, under the TMD. The sphere dropped on him with a quiet thud, crushing everything above his waist. I backed away, watching Trubal's legs twitch, then still.

'Come on then, Ken,' said Bridget. 'Pull your socks up.'

She reached an arm down, took my hand. I crawled under the brass rail and stumbled into the dazzling light of the penthouse.

Fatty.

His eyes were closed. I thought I might be too late, but when I dropped next to him they crept open again. He was trying to speak.

'No gold.'

'No,' I said. 'I think what you wanted is in the basement. We never needed to climb up here at all.'

Fatty coughed violently, then smiled.

'You really know how to lift a man's spirits, do you know that?'

My boots rested in a great pool of his blood. The floorplate trembled under our feet. Debris rained outside, making Bridget twitch.

'Ken. We've got to go. This thing is coming down. Please.'

'I miss home,' said Fatty. 'So peaceful. Nothing to do but listen to the sea. I used to spend ages doing that, with my wife. Marie, she. She reminded me of my wife, see? I miss her. I miss my wife every fucking day.'

Talking about the past again. I guess it was more comforting than the future.

He tried to say something else, but his face rolled and he mumbled it to the floor. I picked him up to help him speak. His shape changed as I moved him. Suddenly he was very thin and old.

'Still glad we came,' he said. 'Taste that air.'

He was right. I could only gasp at the wind, but what I inhaled was fresher than I'd known. Fatty looked at me, expecting something. Words probably. I tried to think of something to soothe his fear. I searched my memory for the lies I'd heard people tell the dying.

'You'll be with your wife soon.'

He licked his lips and blinked, apparently unconvinced. I was curious.

'You don't believe in heaven?'

'The existence of you lot,' he said, 'gives me cause for doubt.'

His good eye closed. His head dropped.

And Fatty was gone.

Bridget swore and kicked the wall. A mighty whine tore around us. The tower tipped, just a little.

'Oh God,' said Bridget, freezing on the spot. 'Oh God, I'm sorry. I'm so sorry. Please let me live. Please just let me get down to the ground in one piece.'

I jogged around the ruined penthouse, as fast as my wounded frame would allow. Bridget followed.

'Ken! Ken, we've got to leave!'

'What do you think I'm trying to do?'

'Let's take the bloody lift!'

'You're welcome to try.'

'Then what?'

I found the toolbag, pulled out a plastic pack and tossed it at Bridget.

'What's this? It's not— Ken, tell me this isn't a parachute.'

'It's not a parachute,' I said.

'I can't jump out there!'

'Of course not. Not from this height. If the wind didn't crush us on the tower the cloud would eat through the chute.'

'Then what?'

I pulled out the second pack, ripped it open, and barged past Bridget. The tower quake was more persistent now. We didn't have long. I found Pistol, unzipped my overalls, and placed him gently inside, zipping him up so only his head poked out. Then I tore open Bridget's pack, slapping the plastic mould onto her back.

'Ken . . . I can't do it.'

'Fair enough,' I said. 'Stay here.'

I ran back into the TMD chamber, leaping over the cracks stretching around the fallen sphere. Bridget followed, still praying to a suddenly important God.

I reached the far wall, traced my fingers over the surface. A large crack had formed. Even the core was breaking up. I punched hard with a tower fist. If the chamber had been built properly, it would have been a hopeless effort.

It gave on the second strike. In a minute I had opened a substantial hole.

The core.

Bridget peered over my shoulder, into the hot chimney.

'Oh my . . . You want to jump inside? Are you *crazy*?'

'Leads all the way down to the surface,' I said. 'Deeper actually. The pack on your back is an emergency escape chute. You'll drop much slower than you expect due to the current coming up from the geothermals. All you have to do is follow me and avoid mirrors and turbines. There's only twenty to deal with . . . Above ground anyway.'

'Tur— What's a turbine?'

'You'll know when you see it.'

She backed away, ashen-faced.

'I'll stay here, thanks. Maybe I'll find another way down.'

'OK,' I said. 'I understand.'

I grabbed her by the collar and tossed her screaming through the hole.

I prepared to jump. Stopped. Turned and looked out the chamber. Fatty's body was bathed in sunlight. He'd spent half his life idle, the other half dying. Optimised for nothing. Optimised for everything. The best and worst of men.

'See you later, Phil.'

I made to leave, but somehow that didn't seem enough. I looked at him again.

'You were my friend.'

I turned and jumped into the core.

Bree and I stand on a gantry at the edge of the foundation works, staring into the gaping pit. Two hundred metres deep and a kilometre wide, the shaft booms and groans as digging machines grind in the darkness below, through ancient rock and soil, making room for the bore works. We are behind schedule.

Bree turns from the pit. She looks back at the site offices, a stack of ugly black crates draped in Diorama banners. I follow her gaze, searching our surroundings for any sign of the shanty that once smeared the landscape. The perimeter fence still keeps out the curious, but that is all that remains. Every trace of Adede and her people has gone.

Bree sniffs, shivers, hands me a flex.

'I'm afraid we have more changes.'

This is getting to be a habit. I examine the specs.

'None of this is necessary.'

'I'm tired of hearing that, Kenstibec. We are paid astronomical sums to realise your design. The least we can do is indulge these little interior decor fantasies.'

The flex details changes to the TMD. I hand it back.

'It is an inefficient design. Why gold? My design uses locally sourced materials.'

'By locally, you mean Brixton, presumably?'

'These cosmetics ignore our major issues. The floorplate specifications still devote disproportionate space to luxury apartments and leisure parks. We will be unable to accommodate a fifth of the city population.'

'It's a vanity project, Kenstibec, not social housing.'

'Yes. However, the design is being compromised. Who is requesting these changes?'

'The client, Kenstibec, who do you think? You know, sometimes you sound

as precious as a human architect. You'd much rather the client shut up and left you to build what they should have, rather than what they want.'

The thought occurs that I could push her into the pit. Without Bree as liaison I would be left in sole charge, at least for a while. Left to my own devices I could truly lead the project. She peers down into the pit again. A simple enough accident.

I dismiss the idea. I was not optimised for that. Besides, an accident on site would only slow construction.

EMERGENCY EXIT

There were a number of surprises.

First, the pack didn't deploy. I dropped like a stone before I real-ised I was still holding it, having neglected to fix it to my back. I twisted and flapped, buffeted by the turbulent hot air, and managed to slap it on. The plastic wings shivered open, slowing the dive.

I still descended more rapidly than I'd expected, plummeting head first through clouds of steam, and the echoing groans of imminent collapse. The turbines had shut down, leaving no draught to cush-ion my descent. At least that meant they should be easier to avoid. I rocketed by the first, narrowly missing the edge of a great fin blade, before taking some control.

I thought I saw Bridget killed. A man-shaped projectile slapped into the core wall. But it shattered into dust, and even Bridget wasn't quite that brittle. Ten seconds later I sighted her orange wings, flap-ping inexpertly towards the next turbine. I speeded my descent, weaving through debris, hoping to catch up and guide her through. She reached the turbine before me, but passed uninjured.

There were plenty of other things for her to hit: great oval mirrors of the mystery array were fixed to the core wall at regular inter-vals, looking up at us as we fell. Some were smashed. Others flashed bars of dazzling light, still catching reflections beamed down from above.

I dodged two before I drew level with Bridget. She was still tum-bling, limbs a blur, her expression surprised and slightly irritated. I twisted to show her my shape and, credit to her, she picked up on the instruction right away, holding her arms to her sides and aiming her descent with twists of her head. The pack adjusted to her direction, darting clear of a mirror. At the next turbine she performed a precise swivel, piloting the pack like a veteran. She let out a gleeful yelp. Pistol barked too, equally excited.

I seemed to be the only one concerned about our landing. I counted down the floors, wondering where best to deploy the brake chute.

The decision was made for me. The wall around us chopped up into powder. I searched the core and saw Trubal, or some part of him, hurtling above us, rifle in pulped hand. Bridget spotted him too.

'Oh *do* me a favour!'

His head was only half reformed, one side a mess of swirling blood and tissue. That at least was a blessing. His shots fizzed uncomfortably close, but with a whole face he wouldn't have missed.

I was assessing the merits of air-to-air combat when two Sweeps emerged from cavities in the core wall. They descended at speed behind Trubal, reaching with pincer arms, and seized him by his neck and feet. Then they blew out thrust, lifting the struggling figure clear. I could have let them go, but it occurred to me that the nanostream had programmed them to find it a new fuse.

Well, I couldn't have Trubal jacked into my tower. I removed my belt, unclipped the spit lock, and rolled onto my back to slow my descent. I fired the lock at the left Sweep's port lift fan. The lock harpooned through the air, caught in the mechanism, and tore out of my hand as the fan gobbled up the line. The lock snagged and blew out the engine, dumping a plume of black smoke. The Sweep veered away, ripped Trubal's legs free and erupted on the core wall like a tinfoil bucket of fire.

It wasn't the end of our problems. A great crack reached out from the impact, zigzagging around the core wall and showering us in debris. The remaining Sweep relinquished its half of Trubal and closed the distance on us. We couldn't pull the chutes now. There was only one choice: going underground.

I counted down the floors, ten, five, zero. The Sweep broke off its pursuit, still programmed to avoid the geothermal threshold.

I caught up with Bridget, slapped the chute button on her pack, then pushed clear and slapped my own. Pistol whined in alarm as the chute deployed, hiding his head.

Our descent slowed to a drift, the debris raining thicker and heavier about us. I searched beneath our feet for somewhere to alight. If we dropped too deep we'd boil on the bore heads.

'Are we near the ground?' asked Bridget.

'Below it.'

'BELOW? I thought we were getting out.'

A light appeared below. A ring of glowing flame.

'What now?'

The flames twitched and danced, as if excited. I made out figures, edging around a slim balcony jutting from the core wall. They clutched torches, observing our approach. Long poles groped in our direction, ready to draw us in.

Bridget tried to avoid the poles, edged too close to the wall and dragged her chute. She didn't know how to correct the spin, and tumbled heavily past the balcony. I reached out my hand, but in a second she had disappeared into the abyss.

The pole-bearers grabbed me easily enough, hooking my left wing membrane and slapping me onto the balcony. Pistol wriggled free, claws scratching on marble.

Marble? Down here?

I lifted my head, just in time to kiss a size twelve boot. Some of the boot's friends joined it. They kicked me everywhere, but my head drew the most attention.

I didn't complain. I was used to this kind of welcome. I grabbed the nearest ankle in my tower hand and snapped it. The owner screamed. His companions stopped their fun for a moment. I flipped onto my haunches and struck the nearest Real in the gut, wrenching the pole from her grasp and tossing her over the balcony edge, her scream echoing in the core.

Three men came at me. One was smacked by a piece of debris. The two others hesitated. I thrust the pole past the left example and wrenched it back, embedding the hook in his spine. I ripped it out, splattering a mess on the marble, and slapped the second Real hard on the temple. He dropped off the balcony, tumbling with a more dignified silence than his colleague.

Someone new jumped on my back and thrust a knife into my shoulder, scraping on clavicle. I reached up and burrowed a finger into his eye, until he howled enough and let go. I flung him before me, ripped the knife out of my shoulder, and plunged it into his heart.

The remaining Reals backed away, still clasping their torches. One bright spark pointed at me and said:

'Ficial.'

'If only.' I yanked the knife out the dead man and cut the chute pack free. I jumped up, noticed one of the Reals holding Pistol. There was something strange about his face.

'Release the dog.'

'Drop the knife.'

A hatch that shouldn't have been there irised open. Three masked men clutching Dohakis stepped on the balcony, welders crackling.

'Lower the pole and surrender,' said the first.

I wasn't keen on becoming a prisoner again. I eyed the balcony wall and the cavernous core, wondering how much deeper it burrowed.

They seemed to read my intentions. A Dohaki pulsed at me. I dropped, fingertips smoking, teeth clenched hard enough to shatter.

'He's still kicking.'

'Hit him again,' said a voice.

The Dohaki charged. That one put me out.

Years behind schedule, without real ceremony or fuss, I have established the fuse. I am become one with my tower. My nanos grow dormant, displaced by the nanostream. I am transformed, but stronger. I am omnipotent, possessed of a great, commanding secret. After years of waiting, I am in control.

Directed by a Ficial mind, the hexagrid and skeleton grow ten times faster. Geothermal glitches are fixed. Seams of corrupt materials are removed and replaced, responsible contractors dismissed. I make progress.

That is how it seems at first.

But there is no accounting for Real obstruction. I first pick it up in electronic whispers, construction comms referencing strike action. It spreads to the organisms that infect my halls.

Sabotage. It starts in the surveillance suite. A virus is introduced that blinds me on hundreds of floors. Then new contractors are attacked, renovated sections ripped out. Every day a new piece of hexagrid is stolen.

It is a relief when Control calls. It penetrates the tower signal, speaks through it.

– Kenstibec.

– Control.

– We must inform you of some necessary changes.

– Thank you, Control. I believe at this stage removing the human workforce is the only solution.

– No, Kenstibec. Human workforce will assume control of tower construction. Fusebox will disconnect, nanostream deactivate.

– I. Don't understand.

– Your powers will adjust to consultant.

– Why?

– Reasons political. Unions penetrated by Truth League. Dismissing

human workers will aid League recruitment. Only tower contracts prevent consolidation of opposition to emergency government.

– You mean, opposition to us. I thought you said we were going to rearrange things, take jurisdiction?

– Large-scale realignment now certain. However, peace must be maintained until new model production reaches required output. You will sever fuse and report to Miss Bree.

– I've only been here a week.

– Kenstibec, you will cooperate. Police are on their way to you now to assume control of the property.

It takes a while for that to sink in.

– You mean. I am being evicted?

LIBRARY

I was hanging by my feet, lit up by a halogen spotlight. For a moment I thought I was in the boss' recovery shed. Then I saw the shelves. Rows of teak, cased in aluminium oxynitride, displaying ancient tomes. I could make out labels inked in accomplished calligraphy: Magna Carta, Codex Sinaiticus.

Bloom sat to my right, partly concealed by the hood of a Chippendale 10 Downing Street guard chair. He held a small maroon book. I couldn't see a label.

'What you reading?'

'It's the oldest volume we have here,' he said. 'St Cuthbert's Gospel. Hocus pocus of course, but priceless hocus pocus.'

'You've found God down here?'

'Hardly. God's for the dead. I am very much alive. As, in your way, are you.'

He turned his head to me.

'It is you, isn't it?'

I had nothing to say on that. I wasn't sure. Bloom at least seemed satisfied.

'I didn't expect we would meet again. Do you mind telling me what you're doing here?'

'Call it a whim. Thought I'd look around the old workplace. So many precious memories.'

He drummed his fingers on the book.

'My people believe you're responsible for the mess upstairs. I'm not so certain. The tower was important to you. Your life's work, yes?'

'I didn't intend to destroy it. That just happened along the way. You have some antisocial neighbours up there.'

Bloom stood, walking in the shadows to the shelves and carefully replacing the book.

'Well, whether you meant to or not, the collapse has caused disquiet among our people. The destruction of our mirror array has left us in some difficulty.

'The bores give us all the heat and power we need, but construction of the Vault was rather hurried and we do not have an effective back-up light system to replace the array's provision. Only this emergency stuff, which you can see is rather dim.'

'Awfully sorry,' I replied. 'I guess you'll have to go topside. Slum it with the rest of us.'

Bloom turned around, his features still hidden in the gloomy corner.

'No, no,' he said. 'We will not abandon the Vault until the winter has passed. We are building something down here. A new nation.'

I twisted around.

'A Truth Nation, I suppose?'

He smiled.

'You won't find many League members down here, I'm afraid. Fools and fanatics to a man. Membership was just a way to keep informed. Things moved so fast in those days.'

I was curious.

'You mean this isn't a Truth League installation?'

He leaned on the shelves. Folded his arms.

'Oh, no. The same people built this place as funded the tower. An alliance of the world's mineral and energy wealth. You really don't know this?'

'Control never explained. It didn't care who funded the tower so long as it kept people busy.'

'Yes, well, in that respect we had similar aims. None of us involved in funding the tower really wanted it completed. Why do you think we ordered a thousand floors? When it started out it was simply a method by which prominent citizens of dying states could move their money around, out of sight of Control – and make a handsome profit besides.

'Then you came along with your new plans and your new materials and sped everything up. You spooked my backers, you know. They thought Control would get hold of their money. They started pulling out. You nearly ruined me.

214

'Fortunately my connections to Mr Lay saved the day.'

'Lay? President Lay?'

'Yes,' smirked Bloom. 'Or the Prophet Lay as he liked to be known. The same people who owned this tower did a lot of business with Lay's family, you see. Lay himself was the family buffoon, installed to the presidency to protect their interests. Then he managed to lose that idiotic civil war. His family kept him president of what remained, but he had been rather affected by the experience, you see. Turned to religion. Started looking for ways to please the God he'd offended. Thought he'd start by wiping out the Ficial menace and bringing about the Rapture. And he had the nukes to do it.

'Fortunately Lay's family were good enough to warn us of his intentions, before he had them all killed. Then there were the rumours about Ficial intentions. Word got around a very exclusive circle: 'Apocalypse imminent'. People with a lot to lose were very worried.

'Well, the end of the world is a business opportunity for a man who knows how to keep his cool. I realised I had all the tools to build an exclusive Armageddon residence. Somewhere safe, where the great and the good could sit out the trouble in peace, style and comfort. I began my little side project down here. The investors flooded back, desperate for a place in my bomb-proof Vault. Having you thrown out of the tower ensured our privacy. Then it was just a matter of getting word to Lay about the cull.'

That got my attention.

'You provoked Lay to launch his attack?'

'Certainly.' Bloom smiled. 'My residents were hardly going to leave the surface unless they were sure the attack was coming. They couldn't leave their lands for others to steal. We decided to control our destiny. Let Lay destroy Control and your kind in one swoop, let the madman burn the Earth black. We'd be safe down here, and the time would at least be spent planning for a new future – not shivering at the thought of Ficials inheriting the Earth.'

I whistled, like Fatty would have done.

'You didn't bother telling anyone else about this bunker? People outside your circle, I mean?'

'Of course not. We have help, of course, but otherwise this is an exclusive development. If word got out about it the rabble would have overrun us. And then where would we have been? Fighting over provisions with a lot of thieving hoods and idle poor? Doesn't bear thinking about. Decent people wouldn't have lasted five minutes. We'd have been guillotined, or worse.'

Bloom looked up at a memory.

'I remember when I heard the bomb hit. I was glad. All that human litter was being incinerated. At least that's what I thought. It took us a while to figure out that Lay botched the job. Still plenty of Ficial and feckless swarming over the surface, are there not?'

He appeared before me, finally giving me a good look at his face. He had barely aged a day. The only slight difference was the deep, green tinge to his skin.

'You look different somehow,' I said. 'Haircut?'

He smiled, dabbed his green cheek.

'An unfortunate contaminant in our air conditioning. A fungus, I'm led to believe. I see you've changed too.'

He poked my wounded side, ran his finger over my burned face.

'I thought you were a healer? What's happened to you? You seem reduced to me. Aged.'

I didn't reply. He was having too much fun to care. He smiled and stamped his foot.

'Well, don't despair. Reduced or not, you can still be useful. The fact is my people are confused and alarmed. They didn't pay good money to be trapped in a dark nightmare like the wretches on the surface.'

'Let me guess,' I said. 'You want me to rebuild your array.'

Bloom straightened.

'Let you loose again? No, that's no solution. I only require you to speak to our expert. Give him a frank assessment of the damage to the tower, so that he can make the necessary repairs.'

'Why would I do that? Our races don't have a history of co-operation, do we?'

Bloom barked a laugh.

'Do you know something? You're right.'

He walked to one of the bookcases and tilted a large volume. The bookcase clunked and shifted, revealing a passage behind. Bloom stared into the gloom and muttered something to the shadows outside.

A figure slumped in, dressed in plain green overalls, his feet bare. A plate covered the back of his skull. The Five gazed at me with milky eyes.

'Well,' said Bloom. 'I'll leave you two alone to discuss things.'

His presumption surprised me.

'You really think I'm going to help your pet fix your mirrors?'

Bloom stopped and raised a finger.

'Funny you should mention pets.'

He whistled to his boys outside. Another green skin walked in, holding Pistol. The dog thrashed and growled, leg apparently healed. That was something, but seeing him handled by the green skin made me squirm.

Bloom nodded at the Five.

'Either you speak to your fellow abomination, or we throw the dog down the core. It's your choice.'

Pistol looked at me.

'OK,' I said. 'Fine. Leave the dog alone.'

Bloom smiled.

'See?' he said, smiling. 'You really have changed.'

The bookcase sealed shut behind him, and I was left with my ancestor.

We regarded each other in silence for a moment, before a question occurred to me.

'Where's the Real I dropped with?'

The Five ran his hands over the guard chair, worrying at the leather with calloused fingers.

'Dead.'

He folded his arms and sighed. Crudely imitated Real behaviour. I wondered what ten-thumbed tweaking his owners had done under the skull plate.

'So what are we dealing with here?'

He squinted sideways at me.

'What do you mean?'

'How much culling is needed? How many people?'

'I'm forbidden to tell you that.'

'What do you mean? We're both Ficial, aren't we?'

He frowned.

'Are we?'

I remembered my wounded side, my seared face. I looked about as Real as anything else.

'Fair point. But at least we're related. Why help Bloom?'

The Five shrugged.

'He's my boss.'

'What about Control?'

'Control stopped speaking to me,' he said. 'A long time ago.'

'You don't think your skullcap there has something to do with that?'

He stopped picking at it for a moment. Maybe it dampened his memory too. I thought I'd stoke the embers.

'I've seen you before. Pre-war. Bloom had you cage fighting.'

He didn't blink.

'Yes?'

'You feel you owe your loyalty to the guy who had you star in his blood sport? The guy who messed with your brain?'

He looked at his toes.

'I deserved it. A human worker died under my supervision. Diorama were going to put me in the waste pit. Mr Bloom freed me.'

'Freed you.'

'Yes. He gave me the chance to realise his vision for the Vault.'

'He gave you the chance to follow orders.'

He looked up, eyes glazed.

'Tell me about the tower.'

He rooted in his pocket and unrolled a flex. Keeping Pistol in mind, I decided to play along.

'The damage originated on floor five fifty.'

'How do you know that?'

'Because that's where I got into the fight with the soldier model.'

'Interesting. So you were above the cloud barrier. Did you see the mirror crown? It was above the crane, at the tallest point of the core.'

'I saw it. Are you responsible for that?'

'Designed it and installed it. I must apologise for the makeshift work. I admire your design, the last thing I wanted was to compromise your vision. Unfortunately I was working to a tight deadline in heavy fall-out. There wasn't time to accommodate your style.'

I blinked.

'You like the tower?'

Every Ficial I met, from construction to pleasure, had scorned the Hope Tower. Even the Real workers spoke of it with distaste. The Five was the first I'd met who thought differently.

'The tower is an astonishing accomplishment, though incomplete. In those terms it sits alongside the Sagrada Familia. As an engineering feat it stands alone. No man could have overcome the design challenges of the brief. It is a work of historic importance. I draw great inspiration from your designs in my work here.'

It was all quite pathetic. Both of us had devoted our optimisation to the design of a gigantic shell company. I couldn't figure out which of us was a more feeble imitation of a Ficial.

'So this Vault. You're still working on it?'

'Oh yes,' said the Five, nodding slowly. 'I never stop the works.' He looked up from the flex. 'Tell me about the upper floors. Will I be able to repair the array?'

If I hadn't been hanging upside down I would have slapped him. I was getting to understand what Trubal had seen when he looked at me: a great creation perverted by clumsy Real hands. It was wrong to see a Ficial so beaten.

Still, our conversation was probably being monitored, and the more uncertainty I could create the better chance I had of keeping Pistol alive.

'Well,' I said, 'the peak array is probably totalled. As for the mirrors inside the core, I saw several smashed. I imagine many floorplates have collapsed, but I see no reason why the core shouldn't have held all the way up.'

I was lying again. The plans I'd made in the fusebox seemed to have worked. The lower bulb must still have been largely intact, or we'd have been discussing digging a way out, not making repairs. But the upper bulb, or what there was of it, would certainly be gone. That part of the core would probably have gone with it. That didn't stop me lying some more. It was getting too easy.

'In theory a Ficial would be able to ascend the core and position a new crown. Provided you had the materials.'

He nodded, tapped a few notes, and pocketed the flex. 'Excellent. Mr Bloom will be pleased.' He made for the door. I called after him.

'I hadn't got onto the downside yet.'

219

He stopped and turned. I blinked a few times, trying to banish the swollen feeling in my head.

'There's a second problem: the crane. I presume you used it to manoeuvre the peak array into position? Well, it's gone for sure. Without it I doubt even a Ficial could erect a replacement alone. I can't figure out how you managed in the first place.'

He smiled. A flattered Ficial. It was unbecoming. I carried on regardless.

'There's no way you can make repairs yourself. You'll need expert assistance. My assistance.'

I could see the the idea appealed to him.

'You would help me repair the array?'

'Perhaps,' I said. 'I could even help you build a better reserve light system too, given time. I could even assess your works so far. My body may not be what it was but my mind's as keen as ever. I could use the work – in return for a few favours, of course.'

He chewed on his lip.

'Such as?'

'Well, fun though it is to be strung up like the old days, I work better the right way up.'

'Of course,' he said. 'Anything else?'

'Yes,' I said. 'I want a tour of the Vault. I want to see what you've accomplished down here.'

'I would be delighted to share it with you. Provided Mr Bloom approves.'

'Good,' I said. 'Good.'

He went to the bookcase door and opened it. I still felt we hadn't been introduced.

'What's your name by the way?'

'Name?' he said. 'What name?'

I look up at the tower, barely a hundred storeys high, the core jutting from the crest of half-grown hexagrid. The site is noisier than ever, smothered by camera crews, security, soldier models and workers. Drones circle overhead.

We are nowhere near finished. The tower is plagued by quality issues. Every day I discover a new element made from inferior material, the Gronts sold or smuggled overseas. But as a 'consultant' I am powerless to stop it. Besides, I hear conditions in the country have deteriorated, and the government needs something to cheer.

I spot the Prime Minister arriving. He is working his way through the crowd, flanked by security. Bree leads the tour. She says for me to do so would be 'insensitive'.

The Prime Minister is led to a podium. His security team run scanners over the area before helping him up. Soldier models create a perimeter.

The PM taps the microphone. Feedback shrieks. I watch the tower, half expecting it to crumble at the sound.

'It is truly a privilege,' says the PM, 'to be here with you today. Your work exemplifies what this country is capable of when we pull together. With this magnificent structure we can create a better Britain. We can be confident that our society works.'

He looks ridiculous, like a man dedicating a mountain. I wonder if he plans on carving his name on it, or leaving his palm print in cement.

There is a commotion. The crowd shifts. I notice an excavator, closing on the crowd. It ploughs through a bank of people, crushing men under its tracks.

The PM's security detail drags him from the podium. Soldier models start shooting, cutting through the crowd. Journalists and guests tumble in the crossfire.

The excavator keeps moving. I run through the shrieking panic, hoping to cut it off.

I am almost on it when I hear the voice behind me. I look up, see a man on a scaffold around the fiftieth floor, wearing a heavy vest. He holds his hands in a T-shape, screaming something only Ficial ears hear:

'Truth Nation now!'

A ball of flame.

A hot blast.

I stumble through the mud, wounded and smoke. The excavator is chewed up, smoke hissing from the cab. Soldier models crawl over it. Bree and the PM are nowhere to be seen. Bodies lie pulped in the mud.

I happen upon my Diorama guard. His head is a split, smoking wound. He would have been better off in the basement at HQ.

The tower howls. I look up, in time to see the entire east facia shiver, rumble and collapse.

Dust rolls over the site, shrouding everything.

That would never have happened with proper materials.

BASEMENT

The Five returned in a few hours. There were two green skins behind him, packing Dohakis.

'Good news,' he said. 'Mr Bloom has authorised me to give you a brief tour.'

I had a feeling the tour wouldn't end well.

The Real guards approached me timidly, lowering me from my perch. The Five took my arm and led me out of the library, passing through more chambers, each more extravagantly decorated than the last. The guards' torches cast beams around us, illuminating the endless cache. An eighteen-foot-tall, seven-branched, gilt-bronze candlestick. Gold-stamped leather walls. A beautiful diptych dial, displayed on a plinth. Rembrandt, leaning out at me from a frame. We passed through ten such storage rooms, all uninhabited, before exiting to a cool, unfinished concrete space, circling the exposed core. A wide ramp curled down a tunnel to floors below. Stood in the open, waiting for us, was a huge black 4x4.

'A simple construction as you can see,' said Five. 'We have elevators, but only a few, and they only stop at certain floors. Most people travel via the ramp.'

'Impressive,' I said. It was far from good work, but I'd feed the Five what he needed.

I was placed in the back seat, the Five next to me. The SUV trundled clear, an electric engine producing no more than a quiet hum. The thing could barely accelerate, but they seemed to feel like very big men driving it.

We drove down the ramp, emerging into a huge circular chamber, excavated around the oval core. I blinked in light like an early summer evening, and took in the sights. I could make out cows in an open field, chewing in the shadow of dormant mirror arrays. Behind them great fans turned in the wall.

'This is the agriculture floor,' explained the Five. 'The bread basket, as some call it.'

The road skirted the chamber edge, so that I could look out over the segmented sections: pig pens, chicken coops. Then fields of crops, young women with baskets ambling among corn rows, then under the branches of a great orchard. A bee flew in the window, landed on my shoulder, buzzed away again.

We rolled down another ramp, this time lined by tall coniferous trees and neat, white posts.

'Sub level three,' said the Five. 'Leisure.'

An identical chamber, this one split into segments. The first was a driving range, followed by tennis courts, a cricket pitch, and a horse-riding course.

'What do you think?' asked the Five.

'Quite something,' I replied. Quite a waste of space.

The next level exhibited the same contempt for modesty: a sprawling array of hot springs, swimming pools, and parks. There were flower gardens too, and woodlands of elm and chestnut, where butterflies, cuckoos and nightingales hovered and swept. I had counted only around one hundred Reals, but that was enough to ask.

'Where do these people live?'

'The next level,' replied the Five, 'provides accommodation.'

It did. The segments were as vast as the agriculture level, but here they contained houses in every conceivable style. A Bahaus palace, a structuralist cube formation, a Swiss chalet, a siheyuan quadrangle, a wood cabin, a domed Byzantine mansion. Each boasted its own unique landscaping. Each was a more crude imitation than the last.

'Did you design all of these?'

'Oh no,' said the Five. 'Everything you see I built to Mr Bloom's plans.'

I was losing patience with the tour.

'How much more of this zoo is there to see?'

'Not much,' he said, 'I thought we'd finish with the truly unique feature.'

We passed down another ramp, arriving at a tighter space, the core concealed by a central structure, lined by glass-fronted shops and parked SUVs. We found a spot, the Five gripping me by the arm and leading me out of the back seat. We walked past rows of hairdressers, cinemas, restaurants and drug stores.

'This is the unique feature? A shopping centre?'

'Just wait,' said the Five.

We came to a passage in the wall, cut between two stores, reminding me of stadium access. We walked down a long passage, the green skins trailing behind, so close I could smell the meat and cheese on their breath.

The passage terminated in two carved cedar doors. A marble slab sat above, engraved with the words 'Founders' Hall'.

We entered a bell-shaped chamber, about thirty metres wide and high, hanging over an amphitheatre.

So this was where the gold had gone. Each step in the theatre was a golden brick, leading down to a barred golden cage, suspended by a chain from a cavity in the dome summit.

'What do you think?' The Five appeared anxious, spreading his arms, pacing backwards.

'What's the birdcage for?'

'It's the Founders' Hall,' replied the Five.

'I've read that. Still unclear what it's for.'

'Look closer,' said the Five, dragging me down the steps, pointing out the nearest brick.

'Right,' I said. 'I get the picture.'

Each brick bore a name, engraved in more meticulous calligraphy. Bloom would have his, probably somewhere prominent. The Five stepped closer, tracing the letters with his finger.

'Isn't it something?'

'I've never,' I said, 'understood the fascination with shiny ductile metals.'

The Five straightened up, then bowed. Bloom entered, his hands behind his back, draped in a toga.

'Enjoyed your tour?'

'Sure,' I said.

'*Ce pays d'ici.* A home for a new, nobler humanity. This chamber will stand as testament to those who built it. It will make us immortal.'

I nodded at the Five.

'I don't suppose I'll see his name anywhere.'

Bloom slapped the Five on the back.

'He has no need of that. He recognises that he is the tool, not the

225

artisan. This entire creation was built to my specifications, not his.'

'I guess that's why there's no purpose to the place.'

Bloom licked his teeth.

'The purpose is to create a new civilisation.'

'This isn't civilisation,' I said. 'Civilisation requires energy, momentum. Hoarding loot and sitting among it is quite the opposite.'

Bloom shrugged.

'It may seem vulgar at first glance, but we are not here to live by words like economy and sustainability. We are here to spark a new epoch, and that requires momentous design. When our grandchildren return to the Earth this hall will be a site of pilgrimage. An undisputed origin story for a new race of men.

'What are you smirking about?'

I couldn't help it. He sounded exactly like Control: another delusional crank preserved underground. I should have done what I was told until I knew Pistol was safe. But seeing the cage gave me the idea that my time was up. Pistol was on his own. Besides, without Fatty around, someone had to say it.

'Do you really think your spawn are going to just sit and eat your founding legend? They'll argue about it. Just like Reals have done their whole stinking history.'

Bloom sighed and regarded the Five.

'Has he given you what you need?'

'Bits and pieces, Mr Bloom,' replied the Five. 'I suggest that he accompany me to assess damage and effect repairs to the array.'

Bloom shook his head.

'I'm afraid we have other plans for him. People are beginning to realise that the solar outage is not short-term. We'll have panic on our hands unless we address the issue. Take him to the cage, please.'

The Five obeyed, leading me down the steps and sealing me inside. I noticed there were bones in the sand.

I heard a sound, a gathering murmur. Bloom nodded to the guards, who opened the doors. Reals poured inside, taking seats for the entertainment. There were around a thousand, dressed in all kinds of robes, stinking of perfumes.

I spat through the cage at the nearest spectators. They shrieked and dabbed my offering from their togas.

Fatty would have been proud.

I wake up, hung by my heels in what smells like a recovery shed. There is pain in my chest and my depth perception has gone. I touch my face and discover a missing eye. I cannot have been here long. Nanos grow an eyeball in a day.

The lights blink on. I see a waste pit, bubbling the other side of an oxy-nitride barrier. Hodges stands next to it, arms folded.

'Where's Bloom?' he asks.

'I don't know, Mr Hodges. Miss Bree might.'

He shakes his head.

'She's dead, you idiot. Truth League went right for her. Targeted anyone with an augmentation role. A right bloody mess.'

A moment's silence.

'Is the tower still intact?'

He stares at me.

'You couldn't care less about Bree, could you? Only worried about that idiotic totem pole. Yes, it's still there. The attack will delay things, but what's new?'

He curses under his breath. I wriggle in my harness.

'When do we resume work?'

'We don't. Diorama is being broken up. The rest of the work will be completed by contractors.'

'Will I be retired?'

'No, no,' he says. 'You're too expensive to bin. You'll be sold.'

'You mean I will not be a consultant?'

He laughs.

'Unlikely. Truth League leaked the tower plans through the underground. There's been an absolute shit-storm. People won't stand for the new capital being built to a Ficial design.'

227

'But I have already severed the fuse. How can—'

'It doesn't matter. The fact we even considered an embedded Ficial mind was enough to finish the company.'

'Without my direction the build will be badly slowed. It will take years for new workers to catch up.'

'Nobody cares. Half the economy is invested in that tower. Can't back out now. All they can do is shut down Diorama, deactivate your Ficial elements and call it a fresh start.'

He stares at me.

'You're certain you don't know where Bloom is?'

I am hanging in a recovery shed. How could I know?

He steps away, then stops, turns and looks up at me.

'Will you pass your Control a message?'

I nod.

He sniffs, looks at his shoes.

'Never mind. I have a feeling it knows already.'

FORUM

I could have been optimised for show business. I certainly pulled in the crowds. I stood in the cage, watching Bloom make his way to a podium near the top of the golden steps. He wanted to be elevated when he addressed his people, even buried down here.

The Reals chattered and twitched around him. There were a lot of young women and men, impeccable and extravagant as pleasure models, gathered on the lower steps. The upper seating held a higher caste of fatter, sweatier types in togas. They muttered and gestured to each other, until trumpets sounded and they settled into watchful silence.

'Friends,' said Bloom. 'Welcome. This meeting has been called to discuss recent events, within and without the Vault. I dare say you have questions, and if you'll allow me I shall answer them as simply as possible.'

I noticed a young woman, seated next to Bloom, typing on a flex, apparently recording his words. Typical. The craziest Reals always insisted on impeccable minutes.

'Many of you will have heard about trouble upstairs,' said Bloom. 'I can tell you now that's true. Damage has been done to the tower, the extent of which is uncertain. However, I can confirm that, for now, the mirror array is out of action.'

Bloom's people murmured some more. He raised a palm.

'This is not the time for alarm. We are in no immediate danger. There was always a chance of damage to the array, and we have prepared prudently, accumulating the reserves required to see out many years ahead. However, I know well the importance natural light holds for each of you, and I can assure you that every effort will be made to repair the array and restore daylight hours.'

'Here, here,' rumbled the togas.

'Many of you will ask, how did this happen? Well, the fact is that, however safe we might feel in our Vault community, there are still those who would see it ruined. There's a lesson there: we cannot relax our guard even for a moment. We must be forever vigilant.' Bloom pointed me out to his people. 'The proof stands before you here. A Ficial agent, sent to continue his kind's cowardly campaign of murder.'

The crowd took its chance to vent, erupting into screeches and jeers. Rocks clattered into the cage. I dodged one or two before something struck my shoulder wound, and I crumpled. Looking up through the hail of stones I saw the Five, slouched on a lower step.

A few more hits landed before the bombardment ceased. I stood, clutching a bruised eye. The men whistled and grunted.

'Do you deny,' said Bloom, glowering at me, 'that you are responsible for the destruction of the tower?'

I thought about it.

'It depends what you mean by responsible.'

'Answer the question.'

'The implication is that I came here intending to destroy it. That is untrue.'

Bloomed leaned over his podium.

'Indeed?'

'This project consumed my professional life, from the time I left Brixton to the day the bomb dropped. You said it yourself. Why would I destroy it?'

'Why? Because you don't know any better. Because the only thing you're optimised for is destruction. Do you deny your part in this tragedy? Do you?'

I wondered why he wanted to establish this phantom motive. Nobody there wanted reasons. They only required blood.

'There's no need for this,' I said. 'If you want to kill me just get on with it. Spare me the panto.'

Bloom gripped the podium as if about to vault it.

'Pantomime, is it? Did your Control not order you to wipe out humanity?'

'Right,' I said. 'But that's not the priority it once was.' The crowd laughed and cursed. I thought about telling them I'd drowned Control in Brixton, but they had no right to know. I stuck to the relevant point.

'Look, if I wanted to kill you there was no need to collapse the tower. I would have just dropped an explosive down the core. Burned the lot of you in your beds.'

Bloom raised his nose.

'There you have it, ladies and gentlemen. This is the kind of serpent we face. I think we all know what needs to be done. You have no place in our world, Ficial. I find you guilty of all charges. The sentence is death.'

'Finally.'

The crowd started throwing things at me again. Bloom let them rage for a while, whispering in the ear of the young woman with the flex. As I ducked and dodged I saw her picking a route through the cheering crowd, down to the Five. He bent to hear her words, then rose and approached the cage. He stopped, peered at me through the bars a moment. Then he opened the gate.

The crowd loved that, stamping feet and clapping hands, until Bloom's trumpets blared again, calling order.

'You sure you want to do this?' I asked him. 'Who's going to repair your array if I kill him?'

Bloom smiled.

'I don't think that's too likely, do you?'

The Five closed the gate behind him and paced in my direction, head slumped.

'Sorry about this,' he said. 'I do really like your work.'

I backed away.

'We don't have to dance for this horde. Let's cull the lot and be on our way.'

'Begin!' ordered Bloom.

The Five didn't move, only offered a bent smile.

'I'm not really optimised for this.'

'I know what you mean.'

'BEGIN!' screamed Bloom.

The Five stared at me, still uncertain.

I quickly assessed my chances. All in all, they were poor. I was more than Real again, but the Five could still rip my spine out with one good punch. His bulkier frame should have worked to my advantage, but my untreated wound made me just as slow.

Bloom must have lost patience. The Five clutched the plate in his head and gave an anguished roar. He glanced up at his master, then plunged at me. I bent and jumped, kicking out at his chest. He barely stumbled, only swerved, throwing a huge fist. It missed, but one or two good connections would be enough to knock me senseless.

My rush skills were the only advantage I had. I skipped aside as the Five threw another punch, then jumped on his back and kicked off for the higher cage bars. I found a hold and scurried up, until I was almost as elevated as Bloom. The Five watched me, showing little enthusiasm for a pursuit. Then the plate stung him again. He howled, blood spouting from his nostrils.

I had to take the chance. I dropped to the surface, snatching a splintered femur from the sand. The Five stumbled in my direction, still dazed from his headache, but I rolled clear and scuttled up the cage again.

This time the Five followed, clutching at the bars with trembling hands. I waited, letting him get close, then rushed past him, narrowly avoiding his killer grip. Lucky for me, he had the turning circle of a supertanker. I jumped on his back, taking his neck in my tower arm, and stabbed the jagged bone into his skull. He waved a fist behind him, slapping my side so hard I nearly dropped. I redoubled my efforts, gouging at the metal plate, working frantically to prise it clear. There was a cylindrical metal object, about the size of a spark plug, buried in his brain. I dug it out and tossed it.

The Five twitched and sagged. I clambered away, in time to watch him drop to the cage floor, landing in a great plume.

I climbed down, deafened by the crowd's displeasure. I examined the body, found it wasn't moving. I located the cylinder and stamped on it, hard.

Green skins formed up around the cage, rifles ready. Bloom left his podium and descended through the crowd. He peered at the Five, then at me.

'It seems you've damaged our model. I suppose we'll have to get you trained instead.'

'By trained,' I said, kicking the broken cylinder at him, 'I take it you mean trepanned?'

232

Bloom smiled.

'I require a janitor. If I can't have a full Ficial then half of one will have to do.'

He spun his finger. A gurney rolled into view, restraints flapping at its side.

– Kenstibec.

– Control.

– This will be the last communication for some time. Serious events taking place overseas. We are devoting all coalesced function to a response. Individual model consultation no longer viable. Future signals will be restricted to Power-wide communiqué.

– I understand. Did you find Bloom?

– Bloom is part of a wider problem. He is still not apprehended.

– What about the Five? Have you located it yet?

– The what?

– The Power Five I saw fighting in the pit.

– We have no memory of that.

Quiet, for a moment. So Control is flushing its mind, making room. It sounds distracted, as if it is forgetting me already. I try and think of something to keep it here with me, in the dark.

– Apparently I am going to be auctioned off with the rest of Diorama's assets. Sold to a contractor.

– You will not be alone. We are preparing to flood the market with less capable, but more affordable models. Any construction firm that works on the tower will have a large Ficial contingent.

– Control, if people are in charge of the tower, they'll ruin it.

– Irrelevant. Construction of tower unnecessary. Recent events have confirmed need for permanent realignment.

– You are terminating the tower project? After all this time?

– Hope Tower project was political construct, not effective housing solution.

– But what about the economy? Hodges says that the entire island would sink without—

234

– *Present socio-economic system dysfunctional. Augmentation mission failed. A more guiding hand is required.*

– *I understand.*

– *You will continue working on the tower for as long as directed. Situation will change. Be assured new order will recognise each model's skill sets and provide range of opportunities to fulfil optimisation.*

That twitch of feedback again, and Control is gone. Along with Bree and the guard and Bloom. I am left here swinging, like the last joint of meat.

FIRE ESCAPE

'This isn't really a punishment,' said Bloom, 'I don't see it that way at all. Your kind prefers the life of the slave. You've no idea what to do with freedom. This way, you'll have a master again. Return to useful service. Don't tell me that holds no appeal?'

He sat on a stool, drawing on a pipe, sweat dripping from his green nose. The Five lay behind him, crumpled meat on a gurney. Two green skins stood guard at a simple hatch. Pistol was tied by a collar to the gurney, watching curiously as a green skin behind me shaved my head.

The room was an unfinished chamber, a boiling mesh cage encased in oxynitride. Beneath us exposed bore heads lit the room in a magma glow. Overhead was a cavity cut in the rock, unfinished guttering jutting loose. I figured we were as deep as the Vault got.

Bloom hunched closer, smiling.

'Of course you won't last as long as your predecessor, not without that nano junk in your blood. But so long as you finish what he began I will be more than satisfied.'

He plucked something off the gurney and showed it to me: the same tech that I'd wrenched from the Five's brain.

'We call it a bolt, you see. Developed over years of testing on our poor, defeated Five. It was designed to simply block out the Control signal, but it turns out it also makes the wearer, well, cooperative.'

Smoke drifted from his nostrils. He glanced at the head shaver.

'Ready in a moment, Mr Bloom.'

Bloom sat back, clutching the pipe in his teeth.

'You should enjoy these last moments,' he said. 'Take time to savour this world, before we cut it away.'

I heard the razor tap behind me. I was ready for surgery.
Bloom gripped my restrained arm and smiled.
'Well,' he said. 'It's time. I will—'
He stopped, cocked his ear.
I heard it too. Music.

A harmonica was playing a mournful tune, echoing from the cavity overhead. There was something hypnotic about it, something raw yet unworldy. We listened until it suddenly stopped, and Bridget appeared directly above me, crouched in the cavity. She tucked the harmonica in her breast pocket and brandished a small box.

'All right you weirdos, nobody move. I've strapped enough dynamite around this dungeon to blow us all to kingdom come. This here's the detonator. Let Ken go or it's Guy Fawkes night.'

As gigantic bluffs went it was quite something. I wasn't sure Fatty would have gone as far. He certainly would have worn a better poker face. The guards edged closer, raising their weapons.

'Put them down,' snapped Bloom. He peered up at Bridget. 'With who am I speaking?'

'Never mind the chit-chat. Untie Ken.'

Bloom pointed his pipe at her.

'You're the other parachutist.'

'I just told you,' said Bridget. 'I don't want a lot of talk. Let Ken go and we'll call it a draw. All right?'

Bloom stared.

'I don't think you're going to blow anyone up,' he said. 'You look human to me.'

Bridget shifted on her haunches.

'So?'

'So, we here are the future of mankind. This is the Vault that will secure our species. We are a family. Put down the detonator and join us. You'll have everything you need.'

'What,' she said, 'another skin disease? Been there, done that.'

Bloom snarled.

'What will you do then? Go back to the surface? Pick through the ruins until you starve to death? I don't think you've thought this through, girl. Stop your nonsense now and I'll consider a place for you.'

Bridget shifted.

'No,' she said, shaking the 'detonator'. 'Let Ken go right now or so help me—'

One of the guards must have panicked. A shot cracked, blowing a section of rock from under Bridget. She nearly fell, barely scrambling away in time. The harmonica dropped out of her breast pocket and clattered down one of the exposed gutters.

'Right,' she wailed. 'Right! You've forced my hand. Don't say I didn't warn you! You're for it now!'

Bloom smiled.

'Do you know something, young lady? I don't believe you.'

Bloom signalled to the guards. They stepped forward, readying kill shots.

The room shook violently. A great moan rumbled below, as if a Titan had been woken. Then a fierce light flashed in the room.

An alarm began to wail. Cracks ripped across the ceiling, raining dust. Bloom picked up a scalpel and made to strike me, but his guards dragged him away, out of the hatch, sealing it behind them. Pistol strained on his leash and whined.

'I know, I know.'

I struggled on the gurney, trying to break free, but it was no use. I was fixed as tight as the dog.

'That's it, then,' I said.

'Not yet, Ken.'

Bridget appeared, smeared in soot, striking a triumphant pose. Then the room shook violently, and she got to work untying my wrists, sweat streaking her dusty features.

'Warm in here,' she said.

'Looks like your harmonica found its way somewhere important. Geothermals must be malfunctioning.'

I had to ask her.

'Why the rescue?'

She looked up from the straps.

'I had five minutes.'

'Seriously.'

She glanced at me. Sniffed.

'Got to look after my fans.' She smiled, seeing my confusion. 'You tap your finger when I play, Ken. Even when you're strapped to a

238

gurney. You're a music lover, in a world where there aren't many left. Couldn't let them scoop that brain out, could I?'

I jumped clear of the gurney, freed Pistol, and followed Bridget out of the room. Thick black smoke obscured the way up.

Fire. A big one.

'Well,' I said, eyeing Bridget. 'You certainly live up to your reputation.'

We stepped back, beaten by the heat. Then something like a spade tapped me on my shoulder. I turned to find the Five standing over us, his face caked in blood. His bearing had changed. He stood upright, with keen eyes.

'Follow me,' he said.

He ran into the smoke. We pursued, choking and stumbling, found him waiting at an open hatch. We jumped inside, the Five wrenching it closed behind us. He turned to me.

'You up for a bit of climbing?'

I was still pretty damaged.

'Exactly how much?'

We made our way along a narrow passage, cut around one of the main bores, and reached a dead end. The Five searched about in the gloom, Pistol barking at him, until he found what he was looking for.

'Here.'

He beckoned to me. He had one hand gripping a steel rung, part of a ladder that ran up the bore. I followed, holding Pistol in my overalls again. Bridget went last, heaving short, panted breaths.

We arrived at the Founders' Hall level. It was deserted now, the entrance standing open. I peered inside, saw fire billowing beneath the cage.

The Five led us to an elevator, ripped one of the doors out of its housing, and threw it clear. He peered into the shaft, then stepped into the darkness to commence another climb.

'Listen,' said the Five, barely breaking a sweat. 'Hear that?'

I did. An anguished squeal, like enormous blades scraping on a metal surface. Turbines were breaking up in the core. The lower bulb was coming down. The Hope Tower was finished.

Further up the shaft the elevator car blocked our path. The Five wasn't bothered. He punched a hole in the car floor, and ripped a section out with his hand.

'Mind out below.'

The Five dropped the metal sheet. It passed Bridget, close enough to give her a haircut.

'Lunatic!' she cried.

The Five helped her up after me. We crouched in the holed cab, wheezing and beaten. My pulse raced so loud in my ears I hardly heard the next explosion.

'That sounded like a transformer,' reported the Five, touching his healing skull wound.

'What now?'

'We're going up the core,' said the Five.

'Are you mad?' gasped Bridget. 'I can't do that. My arms are like jelly. I'm knackered, I am.'

The Five blinked.

'No problem.'

He pressed his fingers between the elevator doors and prised them open, stepping out onto a core balcony. A force 12 was blowing up the shaft, a column of twisting steam. We were sucked towards it, until the Five caught us and tossed us back against the hot, buckling wall. I clung there, gasping at burning air. What remained of the core would come crashing down any moment.

The Five pulled me onto his shoulder, then approached Bridget. The girl backed away, hair thrashing in the gale, but the Five picked her up and tossed her onto his back.

'Right,' he said. 'Two points before we leave. First, it would help if you call out any hazards. Second, hang on. I can't grab you if you fall. Got it?'

He reached out a great spade hand and started to climb.

We went slower than I would have liked. The bore fire was spreading fast, outrunning us up the tower, propelled by the hot wind. I tapped the Five on the shoulder.

'No fire should spread this fast. Didn't you consider extinguishers?'

He grunted.

'See how clearly you think with one of those things in your head.'

I left it at that. There was an obstruction coming, and I needed to let him calculate his approach. The nearest turbine belched black smoke, its blades clattering in an uncontrolled spin, shrieking a high note. One blade was cut almost in two, dragging its wounded limb around the core in a wheeling firework.

The Five accelerated, lining up the best path. Bridget closed her eyes, but I couldn't look away. The wind picked up, almost wrenching me off the Five's back. He began to lose his grip and stopped, drawing us tighter to the wall. I reached out my tower arm to help anchor us, but it was no good.

'This isn't going to work,' said the Five. 'Hold on.'

We were torn off the wall, shooting up the core like a bullet in a barrel.

Bridget screamed. Pistol howled. I watched the broken blade fizz close, showering us in sparks but letting us pass intact. Up we shot, at the mercy of the burning vortex. I looked up, at flaming hatches ringing the core, wreckage meteors and great boulders whipping around us.

The Five flailed his arms, trying to swim the current: as much hope as a moth in a vacuum cleaner. We whipped past the second turbine, then another, when the Five suddenly grunted. I looked down, saw his foot had been clipped off. A standard construction wound, but it sped up my decision: we had to detach. I signalled the Five, released my hold and kicked free.

I timed it really badly. A sudden temperature drop spun me out of control. I passed the next turbine feet first, glimpsed the Five, still carrying Bridget, rising on the other side. I figured we must be halfway to the surface. If we didn't grip the wall soon we'd spit right out the top of the tower.

I hurtled up, trying to arrest the spin. As the temperature dropped I managed to pull out of it, ascending head first.

The Five was out of control too, Bridget clinging to his leg. There was no time for calculation. I passed into a cooler pocket of air and went into a dive, headed straight for them.

I nearly missed. A hot blast hit as I approached, the Five's arm shooting free of my grip. I slammed into Bridget instead, hurtling us into the wall and clear again. I reached out my tower hand, dragged it up the wall to brake our ascent. Bridget wrapped her arms around my head, blinding me.

Thankfully, my fingers found a hold. I gripped tight, threw my other arm out to push Bridget onto my back. The Five crawled clear, and we climbed on separately, moving in a kind of anti-rush with placed, deliberate handholds. Bridget's heart pounded in her chest. Pistol breathed quickly on my neck.

We crawled past another two turbines before the go-slow option was taken away. Something metal howled above us. I peered up through the steam, saw a turbine rip free of its moorings and come tumbling down the core, its descent slowed by the hurricane, but not arrested. Bridget beat on my back with a fist. She probably thought we should move.

I broke into a rush, guessing that the lowest blade would catch the wall and straighten the descent.

It didn't, only changing the direction of the spin. Still, that provided a gap, a tiny space I charged at full speed. We squeaked through, hot, moaning wreckage diving past and crashing below.

We passed three more turbines without incident. I was so pleased with our progress I hadn't noticed the obvious.

'Ken,' said Bridget. 'Why's it so quiet?'

The wind had died to a breeze. Sudden silences were never good.

It was time to get out of the core. I spotted an access hatch two storeys above us. There were a lot more handholds available now, the core wall marked by deep, crumbling fissures, so we rushed over there at full pelt, Pistol barking encouragement, the Five struggling behind.

I slipped onto the short platform, dumped Bridget, and turned the hatch wheel, drawing it open as the Five caught up. Pistol jumped out of my overalls and ran ahead. We followed him into a dark passage, the concrete shaking and cracking around us. There was a strong scent of burning hair.

'What now?' asked Bridget.

The Five considered.

'We need to take the stairs.'

'We're that near the surface?'

'Close.'

Bridget leaned on a wall, gasping for breath. She pointed at me.

'Why couldn't you build bungalows, eh?'

We ran on, until the corridor took a sudden turn. I felt around in the darkness, found a hatch and tore it open. A wall of flame blew me onto my back, then retreated as fast as it had come. Bridget dropped to my side.

'Ken!' she said. 'Ken!'

The corridor began crumbling around us. Bridget snatched Pistol from the tumbling rock just in time, and dived through the hatch. The Five picked me up and tossed me through, following us and slamming the seal behind us.

Bridget slumped on the wall, choking on dust. The Five tossed her onto his back.

'Hold on tight,' he said. 'Nearly there.'

We ran through a shower of debris, bounded up a stairway, through wailing alarms, pockets of acrid smoke, listening to the bore works rumble and churn below. Occasionally the Five stumbled, his bloodied stump unbalancing him. The idea that the floors might collapse and suck us into the pit seized me and wouldn't let go. That urged me on, until we found the stairs caved in, blocked.

We doubled back, passing out of the stairwell into a car park shrouded in more cloying dust. Pistol heard something, and darted away to investigate.

I followed him, trying to grab him, until he stopped by a bank of elevators. I could hear it too now, an animal wail echoing in the fifth shaft. I set to work wrenching the doors open. Bridget tapped me on the shoulder:

'Ken, you madman! This is no time for sightseeing, is it? Let's go.'

'She has a point,' said the Five.

I peered into the shaft. There was an elevator car, stuck halfway between the levels, shrapnel gathered on the roof. I could hear screaming. There were Reals in there all right. I jumped down, landing on the roof with a heavy clunk.

'Ken!' yelped Bridget. 'What are you doing?'

I called back to her. 'Take Pistol and get going.'

The voices in the car cried out, begging me for help. I ripped open the access hatch.

Green faces looked up at me, stood around Bloom, wedged in tight by bulging suitcases.

'No,' said Bloom. 'That's impossible.'

'Not as impossible,' I said, 'as expecting a service elevator to run this overloaded. What's in the bags? Portable civilisation, I suppose?'

He didn't get a chance to respond. His companions screamed at me, cursing Bloom, protesting innocence, promising riches. I stared at them until they stopped.

'The only Real I've ever known worth the bother died on top of this tower. If he doesn't get out you sure don't.'

More screaming. Insults now, as well as begging. I nodded at Bloom.

'Enjoy immortality,' I said. 'I hear it's a lot like death.'

I closed the hatch, clamped it shut with a heavy piece of debris, and climbed back to the car park level. Bridget was waiting, Pistol at her feet.

'Who was in there?' she asked.

'Our host.'

The floor jumped, knocking us off our feet. Bridget sat up, clutching her head. I pointed down at the elevator.

'He must have had an escape route.'

The Five nodded. 'That's where we were headed until your detour. This way.'

He led us across the car park, tarmac ripping, support columns buckling, the transfer structure straining under the weight of pancaking tower floors. The ceiling was so low we'd barely know when it came down.

We rolled up a ramp, to the next level. An almighty shriek tore through the plate above.

'It's gonna go,' said the Five, as if watching a simulation.

We kept running, the Five leading the way, a huge crack racing us across the quaking expanse of concrete. The Five stopped, looked up. The ceiling broke above him. He raised his hands, catching two great slabs, bending under the weight.

'Hatch is over the other side,' he said, teeth grinding. 'Behind those ventilation pipes. It runs well clear of the site. Get moving.'

Bridget didn't stop, racing Pistol for the array of pipes. Only I felt like discussing it.

'I should stay,' I said. 'It's my responsibility.'

The Five grinned. 'You're welcome to try.'

I saw his point. The guy was supporting the weight of five hundred floors. I could barely lift my head. Still, it seemed wrong to let him take the strain.

244

'No problem,' he said, spitting in a shower of dust. 'This is how I was supposed to go.'

I raised a hand. 'Nice working with you.'

I left him, and staggered through the cloud, feeling blindly for the far wall, losing all sense of direction.

I whistled.

Pistol barked in response, keeping it up, providing a useful homing beacon. I followed the sound, stumbling upon him poised at Bridget's feet. She was struggling with the hatch wheel.

'It's locked!' she screamed, punching it. 'Why am I not surprised?'

I joined her at the wheel, straining hard. It gave a little, then turned.

We broke into a narrow, dark tube of exposed earth, ran bent double and blind. The path turned up, curling to the surface. Bridget turned, shrieked in triumph.

'I can see the exit! It's right there, Ken!'

Then I heard thunder, rolling behind us, through the passage and overhead. The ground shifted. I looked behind to see the passage caving in.

'Oh, give up,' said Bridget.

I reached out, grabbed her arm. She squeezed my hand. The avalanche swamped her scream.

They are certainly a determined crowd. Most Reals panic in the rain, but these are resolute. They hunch under umbrellas, eyeing wares through the deluge. I wait for hours, as everything from machine tools to stationery is sold. The buyers thin out, leaving a group with big hands and flat caps.

I am led on to the stage. Hodges monotones my specs, then opens the bidding. Heads nod. Hands twitch. Hodges points and yelps in a language I barely understand. I watch the digital readout, red numbers ticking up. It takes twenty minutes for the bidding to finish.

I go for almost double my list price. Hodges hurries past me without a word, seeking shelter. The failed bidders peel away. The guards lead me off the stage, trudge through the mud to a man in overalls, a cigar clenched in his teeth.

'Do you want us to load him up for you, sir?'

'No, no,' says the man, blowing smoke. 'He's not going to cause me any bother, are you?'

'No,' I reply.

He nods, runs his palm over a flex proffered by a guard. Transaction complete, we walk across the square, onto the high street.

'You can call me "boss"'.

'Yes, boss.'

He nods, sucks on the cigar, glances up at the sky.

We head down to the Great North Road. The boss holds up his palm. The lights on a parked Transit flash. He opens up the back door and ushers me inside.

He leans on the open door.

'You know why I paid that crazy money for you?'

'To improve your efficiency?'

He chews the cigar to the other side of his mouth.

'No. I paid that money because I want something to make us stand out from the crowd. Power Nine's the best there is. Never be your kind made again, so they say. Are they right? Are you worth it?'

'I designed the tower, boss. I will be invaluable.'

He smiles, leans in.

'OK. But question my orders and you're for the waste pits. I won't hesitate. Got it?'

He does not wait for an answer. He slams the door in my face and walks to the front of the van.

I hear him jump in the cab, start the engine. Music plays on the stereo. A slat opens up overhead. The boss speaks through it, smoke drifting in with his voice.

'Comfy? Then let's go home.'

PLAZA

I wheezed in a pocket of air. A weight pinned my back. I didn't struggle. A thought held me down: better to be buried here. I closed my
eyes and waited for the air to thin out.

Something moved against my side, wriggled over my shoulder
and clawed at my face. Something small and determined. Pistol was
making one last effort. If he was going to try I had to help.

I pressed my arms to the muck, wrenched them free of its syrupy
grip. I joined Pistol's digging, my hands gouging a path next to his
paws. I pulled on Bridget's hand, dragging her unconscious form
after me, the mud as thick as fusebox amber.

I felt a hot wind on my fingertips, on my wrist. Saw a dim orange
glow. I freed one arm, slapped it onto a flat, rock surface. I pulled
hard, until the earth loosened and tumbled from my face, and I was
sucking in a huge draught of smoky air.

I lifted myself onto the stone. It was a concrete raft, floating on
a mud sea. I looked up, saw the tower a distance away, reduced to a
broken mound. Lava bubbled from the core, lighting the landscape
in a red glow.

The fusebox was gone for good. Fatty was gone for good. I sat
cross-legged, gazing at the scene.

Pistol jumped around the collapsed tunnel, barking and growling,
until I recalled the Real still buried inside.

I lay flat, lunged my arm into the mire, located a cold, fleshly palm
and hauled Bridget onto the raft. Pistol stood on her chest and licked
the mess from her face. She wasn't breathing.

I wiped the mud and hair from her face and bit my lip, trying to
recall how to revive a Real.

I picked her up, yelled her name in her ear, and shook her, hard.

'I don't think you do it like that.'

Twelve figures, standing in the smoke behind us, knee deep in mud. They were still for a moment, the only sound the crackling of lava.

One stepped forward, a mask obscuring his features. I could see the eyes. I knew those eyes.

'Name's Kinnare,' he said. 'Construction.'

He held out a hand in greeting.

'Kenstibec,' I said. 'Demolition.'

I might have been surprised to see him there. Power Nines were rare. I had thought myself the last one left.

That wasn't half as interesting as his company.

A woman stood behind him: chapped lips, tired eyes. Marsh regarded me like a loose roof tile.

My heart raced. I didn't know what to say.

Pistol wasn't so awkward. He ran to her feet, jumped and pressed his paws on her leg. She crouched, clutched his snout and stared into his eyes.

'Hello, beautiful.'

I could have kicked that dog.

I guess you could say I was jealous.

THE END

ACKNOWLEDGEMENTS

Thanks to Chris O'Regan for the engineer's perspective and Stuart Blower for the architect's. Thanks to Barbican and the mice. Thanks to the Cardigan Club Café, and the pooch walk home through the woods. Thanks to Simon and Gollancz. Thanks to Ed and Polly. Thanks to Wallaces, Goads, Davies and Moores for all your support. Oh, and thank God for Hamble.